All For Victory: A Romantic Comedy

The Dartmouth Diaries Book Three

Beverley Watts

BaR Publishing

Cover design by Karen Ronan: www.coversbykaren.com

Contents

Chapter One

It's not often that a fledgling career in Event Management kicks off with the wedding of a Hollywood superstar. Of course the fact that this particular Hollywood star is marrying my best friend might have had something to do with the fact that little old me landed the job.

It's amazing just how things can change in the blink of an eye. Two months ago I was the owner of a small but very successful gallery here in Dartmouth. However, unfortunately the word *owner* didn't actually include the property the gallery was housed in, which was (and still is – just) owned by my self-absorbed and largely absent parents.

Until a month ago, I hadn't actually seen them for five years, and before that only sporadically.

Just after my fourteenth birthday they left me in the care of my dad's sister Florence while they *travelled.* Mum had inherited a substantial amount of property in Dartmouth – even back then, it fetched a premium - and over the years, they sold each one until there was only the property on Fore Street left. My gallery.

Dad said they needed to sell it so he and mum could do true justice to South America – after all, travelling on a budget is no fun at all. He made it clear that he thought they were doing me a favour – giving me the push I needed to get proper job.

I have to say it feels more like a kick in the nuts (or I'm sure it would if I had any).

I'm trying very hard not to be bitter, telling myself that everything happens for a reason.

By the time my parents finally arrived back in Dartmouth after dropping their little bombshell, I'd managed to sell most of my stock, so when they visited me at the gallery, I suppose their image of a daughter playing at being an entrepreneur seemed justified. But then, they really don't know anything about me.

Don't get me wrong, life as a teenager with Aunt Flo was the best part of my childhood; for one thing, it was never, ever dull.

My Aunt Flo is a well known author of romantic bodice rippers, which she thankfully writes under a pen name, as her books generally abound with heaving bosoms and throbbing members.

By the time I left school I knew at least twenty different words for penis in three different languages…

She was, and still is the most wonderful loving person, and I know she adores me. Plus I have Victory, my best friend since forever, and the soon to be wife of multimillionaire Hollywood golden boy Noah Westbrook.

Which of course is why, when it looked as though I was about to become homeless and penniless, she announced that she wanted me to plan her wedding.

There is one other teensy weensy reason that I've landed the job that wedding planners everywhere can only dream of – one that only Noah and I know about.

Tory is pregnant.

Apparently it happened on the night of their big reconciliation just over six weeks ago…

Now, delighted they both are, but here's the kicker. Noah is refusing to wait until after the birth to make an honest woman of her. (To be fair I can't blame him. Tory is my dearest and oldest friend and I love her to pieces, but it has to be said she has a disturbing tendency to make life difficult for herself, and consequently everyone around her.)

So Noah is determined that the wedding will go ahead before he begins filming his next movie in the spring– even if he has to drag her to the altar.

Tory has absolutely refused to be a bride with a bump – citing the fact that her father would have a coronary. We are of course talking about the Admiral here, who's a stickler for protocol when it comes to anyone other than himself.

So the wedding has to be pre-bump and is tentatively planned for the twentieth of December.

Seven weeks away...

Of course the Admiral is insisting on full pomp and ceremony for his only daughter, which means he wants the whole shebang held up at Britannia Royal Naval College which he presided over as Commodore for a brief, though apparently memorable, period.

So, just to recap and make sure you're in the loop so to speak. I am being asked to organize a wedding in seven weeks time with approximately one hundred and fifty guests - including several Hollywood A listers, as well as anyone who's anyone in *Hello* magazine – all to be held in a naval establishment requiring full details of every single guest down to what they had for breakfast, as well as the names and addresses of all their ancestors going back to the middle ages.

And I've never done it before.

Still, never let it be said that I don't like a challenge and at least it's stopping me thinking about my woes.

Who knows, it could well lead to an exciting new career. If I don't balls it up in the meantime as the Admiral would say.

~*~

It had just started to rain as Admiral Charles Shackleford (retired) finally opened the door of his favourite watering hole. Before striding into the bar at The Ship Inn, he glanced down to see exactly where his dog Pickles was. The elderly Springer Spaniel had recently developed an irritating habit of getting under the Admiral's feet which had caused him to go embarrassingly arse over tit a few times in polite company. Anyone would think the bloody dog was worried about being left behind.

Pickles however, was way ahead of him, happily fussing round the small man already seated at the bar. Jimmy Noon looked up as his oldest friend made his way noisily to his usual seat. Huffing and puffing, Charles Shackleford hoisted himself up onto the stool. It had to be said, this ritual was getting a trifle difficult – the Admiral admitted privately to himself that he might have put on a smidgeon of weight. Mabel had been threatening to put him on a diet. Bit of a bloody cheek since it was her cooking that had caused the sorry state of affairs in the first place. Never any problem with putting on weight when Victory was cooking.

'How are you Sir?' Jimmy interrupted his maudlin reverie, and the Admiral sighed before taking a long draft of his pint, ready and waiting for him.

'Would you believe the damn wedding's been brought forward to December,' he responded finally after putting his glass back onto the bar. 'December, I ask you. What's wrong with having a decent length of time to plan the bloody thing properly?'

Jimmy frowned, a little perplexed at the Admiral's attitude. 'What's wrong with that?' he asked with a bewildered shrug. 'I know it's a bit quick, but it's not like you've got to organize it, and come on Sir, it's good news really. Now you and Mabel won't have to wait so long to do the necessaries.'

The Admiral glared down at his friend before sighing again. It wasn't Jimmy's fault that he'd gone and got himself in a bit of a tight spot. Of course the problem was, as usual, that he was too charitable for his own good.

The Admiral took another drink of his pint while he debated whether to just come out with it. He wasn't sure exactly what Jimmy would be able to muster up to salvage the situation, especially given the fact that his best friend would be inclined to lose a debate with a doorknob. Still, it had to be said that Jimmy was probably the only person he *could* speak to about the slight issue. Well, either him or Pickles.

After a couple of minutes meditating into his pint, the Admiral plonked his now empty glass onto the bar decisively before turning determinedly towards the smaller man. 'The thing is Jimmy lad, you know me. Sometimes I'm just too bloody giving for my own good.'

Jimmy stared silently back at him with his glass poised half way to his mouth. The Admiral waited a second for his friend's agreement, but after a few seconds it appeared Jimmy had lost the use of his tongue. Not the first time it had happened.

Sometimes he privately thought that his former master at arms might not actually have both oars in the water. So, frowning slightly, he continued.

'Well, a couple of weeks ago, I had a phone call from that amen wallah – you know, the one who used to be chaplain up at the College when I first signed up?'

Jimmy frowned. 'You mean Bible Basher Boris? The one with the terrible flatulence problem? I thought he died years ago.'

'Well, it has to be said, so did I,' responded the Admiral glumly. 'Then he just popped out of the woodwork a few months ago. He must be ninety if he's a day. Thing is, he's heard about Noah and Victory and put two and two together…'

'Well, that's nice of him,' Jimmy mused taking a sip of his pint. There was a certain measure of relief in his response, but he couldn't help wondering what on earth his meddling friend was getting so worked up about. 'Perhaps he wanted to buy them a present. Did you tell him about the wedding? I thought we were all supposed to keep schtum about it.'

'No he didn't want to buy them a bloody present,' the Admiral replied irritably. 'Thing is, old Boris did me a bit of a favour a few years ago – got me out of a spot of bother so to speak.'

Jimmy's heart started its familiar thumping, and he held his breath, sensing that Charles Shackleford was about to deliver the punch line. He closed his eyes, waiting to see what disaster the Admiral had got himself into this time.

'Well, of course when he got me out of this tight spot, I was suitably grateful, and, well… come on Jimmy lad, you know how sentimental I am.' He paused for a reaction, but for some reason Jimmy was sitting with his eyes shut, so, shaking his head slightly, he ploughed on.

'Well, our Victory was only a few weeks old at the time, and in the heat of the moment I sort of promised him he could do the business when she got married.'

'Do the business, what business?' Jimmy opened his eyes up again with a frown.

'I promised him he could marry her.'

'You said he could marry her? Oh Sir, why on earth did you say that? She's marrying Noah.'

'What the bloody hell are you talking about Jimmy? Have you finally lost your marbles? The Admiral was now waving his hands about in agitation. 'I didn't say he could be her bollocking husband, I said he could take the ceremony. He's a God walloper isn't he?'

'But Sir, he's got that awful wind problem.' Jimmy response was a disbelieving whisper. 'You know he once cleared out the Old Naval Chapel at Greenwich.' Then he paused slightly before going on to hammer the final nail in the coffin, 'Have you told Tory?'

The Admiral opened his mouth to speak, then sighed and shook his head mournfully before taking another swallow of his pint. Then, despondently staring into its amber depths, he said finally, 'No, I thought there was no sense in sticking a bloody spanner in the works when we had months to go 'til the damn nuptials, and chances were old Boris would've had the decency to pop his clogs in the meantime.

'But now, well, now we've got seven bloody weeks. And he's unlikely to cash in his chips before then.'

'Well, why don't you just tell him he can't do the ceremony?' Jimmy responded reasonably. 'I'm sure he'll understand. After all, he's pretty ancient. Probably be too much for him anyway.'

'If only it was that simple Jimmy lad,' the Admiral replied sorrowfully. 'The problem is, he says he's got his heart set on seeing my daughter wed properly. When he spoke to me, he said that doing this wedding would be his life's pinnacle, and once he'd done it, he could die happy.

'And I promised him Jimmy, on my mother's grave. And you know what a sensitive soul I am, so how the bloody hell do I break it to him that he can't live out his lifelong dream because of his anal acoustics...'

~*~

So, here I am, brand spanking new filofax in hand battling my way up through the gates at BRNC with what feels like a ten force gale trying its best to bring me to my knees. So much for the up to now glorious autumn weather.

I have an appointment with the Captain of the Naval College to talk about my best friend's upcoming nuptials and to discuss the detailed plan I have to avoid the whole thing turning into a media circus.

The problem is, I don't have one. Not yet. But as I've already postponed this meeting twice, I can't do it again.

So I spent all last night (and I mean *all*) trying to work out just how we're going to manage it. By three o'clock I hadn't even come up with a preliminary strategy. The sad fact is that I'm so far out of my depth the fishes have lights on their noses.

The trouble is Tory thinks it's all in hand. She *trusts* me. Oh God...

I've dressed extra carefully this morning – might as well look the part at least. I've exchanged my customary jeans and t-shirt for a business like skirt and blouse.

Before leaving my flat, I stared critically at myself in the mirror. I had my hair cut a couple of weeks ago into a short pixie crop with some funky gold highlights. I thought it looked pretty cool, and Tory said she loved it. However, Freddy - our local guru of all things fashionable, insisted that the look was more reminiscent of an extra out of *The Hobbit*.

At the time I thought he was being bitchy, but looking at myself before leaving for a hugely important meeting, I could actually see his point.

I'm suddenly very glad my outfit isn't green.

I'm given a pass at the College Gate by a guard, who after having a few minutes of every word being swallowed by the howling gale, resorts to pointing at the visitor's book and handing me a pen to fill in my details.

As I hang my temporary ID card around my neck, I shout to confirm that Captain Taylor is expecting me. Unfortunately his reply is pretty much lost in the storm, so I simply wave my thanks and pass through the gate, tucking my head into the collar of my jacket, in an effort to lessen the impact of the gale and concentrate on putting one foot in front of the other.

I've been inside the College grounds several times, and normally I enjoy the walk up the hill, with the beautiful Edwardian red brick building of the Naval College towering above me on one side and the breathtaking view of the River Dart below me on other. Today however, the part of me not quaking in my shoes at the thought of the upcoming meeting is doing its best to keep said shoes on my feet.

Up to now the weather has been lovely, carrying on from the fabulously hot summer we enjoyed. This year's autumn colours have been amazing with the leaves drifting down from the trees in a gradual cascade of red, yellow and orange.

As I fight my way up the path, I can't help but reflect that today's blustery weather might have seen off the last of autumn, and plunged us kicking and screaming into winter.

By the time I finally reach the turn off to the Captain's house at the top of the hill, I feel as though I've done a marathon, and pause in the drive for a quick breather, and a chance to restore some semblance of order to my hair, which I suspect now bears more resemblance to a gonk than an elf.

Standing in the shade of a large azalea bush protecting me from the worst of the wind, I notice a white Audi TT in the drive next to the house. Somehow it looks familiar, as though I've seen it somewhere before. I frown, racking my brains for a second before dismissing the notion. It's not as though Audis are a rarity.

Taking a deep breath, I tuck my filofax under my arm and march determinedly towards the large front door before I have the chance to lose my nerve and run back down the hill.

I can hear the bell ringing somewhere deep in the house and mentally I rehearse my excuses – mainly focusing on the idea that I'm currently working on several different approaches to the problem (which is true really – I'm definitely working on them, it's just that none of them make any sense as of yet).

A couple of minutes later, the door is opened by what appears to be a butler. Bloody hell, it's like stepping into Downton Abbey. After leading me into a large central hallway, obviously serving as the main avenue of traffic and entrance area to the adjacent rooms, the butler (if that's who he is) politely asks me to take a seat, then promptly disappears. Sitting gingerly on one of the formal chairs up against the wall, my nerves lessen slightly as I look around me with interest.

The hallway flows into a large wide staircase and everywhere are paintings and memorabilia depicting our glorious naval history. It's all very queen and country – in fact it all looks very similar to Tory's house. I can so picture the Admiral ensconced in this building and can't help but smother a grin at the mayhem he probably caused while he was here.

'The Captain will see you now.' I jump at the quiet voice abruptly coming from the entrance to what I assume is the drawing room. I've no idea how he got there, he left through a door in the other direction.

Heart suddenly pounding, I hurriedly get to my feet feeling as though I'm heading towards my execution. 'For pities sake get a grip girl,' I tell myself sternly as I cross the hall, 'He's not bloody royalty.' Mentally I go over his name – Captain John Taylor. With a nod I step past the butler, my hand already held out in preparation. 'Captain Tay...' I start with an artificial smile plastered on my face, only to sputter to a halt as the man facing the window turns towards me and my eyes meet the icy silver gaze of Jason Buchannan.

Chapter Two

'Good morning Ms Davies, would you like some tea?'

'What are you doing here?' My rude response comes out before I have time to bite it back and Jason Buchannan's raised eyebrows at my bad manners makes matters worse.

'I was expecting to be meeting with Captain Taylor this morning,' I continue, trying for a much softer tone on the off chance that the Captain in question is lurking somewhere behind the sofas dotted around the room – at the end of the day I don't want to get off on the wrong foot with the man responsible for allowing us access to the College on the big day.

'Captain Taylor has moved on. I am now responsible for BRNC.' His voice is cool and distant, giving no indication that imparting this little gem has given him any satisfaction at all. Even though my face must be a complete picture.

I continue to stare at him wordlessly. I just can't believe it. The knob is responsible for consenting to Victory and Noah's wedding being held here.

'Would you like some tea?' he asks again politely as the ongoing silence starts to become oppressive.

I make a concerted effort to gather my scattered wits. 'Err, yes that would be pleasant.' *Pleasant.* Oh my God, from rudeness to a bloody extra from *Pride and Prejudice*. Just kill me now.

'Tea for both of us PO Steward,' he speaks over my shoulder giving me the uncomfortable realization that the damn butler, steward, or whatever the hell he is, also witnessed my boorish behaviour.

'Please, take a seat Ms Davies.' He waves towards one of two sofas facing each other over a large coffee table. As I gingerly sit on the edge, I can feel my cheeks bloom and my forehead begin to get clammy. Add to that sweaty armpits and I've got myself a full blown panic attack about to descend at any moment. Trying hard not to hyperventilate as he sits opposite, I lean forward to place my completely empty filofax on the coffee table between us, before coughing and surreptitiously trying to wipe my sticky forehead with the back of my hand.

'Are you hot Ms Davies?' His question is mild, but something in his tone makes me glance quickly at his face. Yep, the bastard's enjoying this.

Unexpectedly this knowledge has the effect of calming my nerves, and taking a deep breath, I lean back against the comfortable sofa.

'I'm fine thank you.' My voice is now a study in politeness. Two can play at this game. 'How are your father and grandmother?'

'My father's well thank you, I think all the, err, excitement over the summer actually agreed with him. Not so my grandmother I'm afraid.'

'She's not ill is she?' My efforts at polite nonchalance disappear as I lean forward anxiously. Tory will never forgive herself if something had happened to the old lady as a result of our brief but memorable visit to the Buchannan family pile (or should I say ruin) in Scotland.

'No, nothing like that. She's simply become more reclusive than ever. I think she's a little afraid of our resident ghost.'

I shake my head in dismay, but stay guiltily silent (mainly because I have no idea what to say - the whole ghost episode was more my fault than Tory's).

Luckily the PO Steward chooses this moment to reappear with our tea, and any response I might have made is overtaken by the time honoured English ritual of pouring the perfect cuppa.

There's a large plate of chocolate biscuits, and as the plate comes towards me, I realize I'm actually starving, having eaten nothing up to now due to my almost hysterical anxiety. I'm just about to refuse (in the interests of politeness of course, and the fact that for some reason I don't want the knob to think I'm greedy – sad I know), when my stomach growls loudly enough for everyone to hear. The steward says nothing but keeps tactfully still, holding the plate out in front of my nose. Primly, I take a single biscuit off the top of the pile. 'Thank you David,' I murmur, staring fixedly at his name badge.

'Please help yourself to more Ms Davies, it sounds as though you're hungry.'

'One is fine, thank you,' I respond through gritted teeth, fighting the urge to tell him exactly what he can do with his biscuits. After a quick look at my face, Dave the steward diplomatically withdraws, leaving us to our little *tête à tête*. Oh joy.

For a few seconds I preoccupy myself by nibbling on the edge of the biscuit, trying to eke it out as long as possible. I really could have done with half a dozen. Unfortunately long before I'm ready, Jason decisively places his cup back onto the coffee table and looks at me expectantly.

I cough self consciously and reluctantly pop the last of the biscuit into my mouth, following it quickly with a gulp of tea. To my horror, as the tea goes down, I feel the biscuit lodge itself in my throat.

Closing my eyes, I attempt to swallow, frantically trying to dislodge the lump without alerting the knob. Time seems to stop completely as my life slowly flashes before my eyes, and it's only as I start metaphorically writing my own epitaph that my fear of death finally overcomes my fear of embarrassment, and I manage to cough and splutter back into my cup. Luckily Jason has a tissue and hastily stands up to hand it to me before I begin decorating the sofa and coffee table.

As the coughing subsides however, death definitely begins to feel like the better option. My face is now the colour of a ripe tomato and my eyes are watering profusely, completing my humiliation. The obnoxious bastard in front of me is only making a token effort to hide his amusement.

Swallowing an insane urge to burst into tears, I blow my nose, then try to find an unused bit of tissue in an effort to wipe underneath my eye without getting strings of snot or gobbed up biscuit in it.

Finally, staring down into my lap, I take a deep shuddering, and thankfully crumbless breath. 'Would you like some water?' he asks softly after a moment – incredibly I can hear sympathy in his voice.

'No, I'm fine, really,' I wheeze without looking up, 'Just give me a couple of seconds.'

He doesn't appear to believe me however and I hear him stand up and head towards the door, reappearing a couple of minutes later with a large glass of water which he places on the coffee table without speaking. After taking a long gasping drink, I return the glass to the table and finally look up.

He's seated back on the sofa and is staring at me silently. His silver eyes are hooded and completely unreadable. The light from the large French doors is turning his chestnut hair to a burnished copper, and I realize it's shorter since the last time I saw him.

The way he's sitting is plastering his shirt to his chest, barely concealing the play of muscles beneath. Idly I reflect that this is the first time I've seen him in naval uniform, and I can't deny that he looks good enough to eat. The whiteness of the short sleeves contrasts almost shockingly with the deep tan of his arms and I suddenly find it difficult to catch my breath again, even though this time there's nothing blocking my airways.

'Are you okay to continue?' His voice when he finally speaks is polite but clipped, immediately breaking the spell.

'Yes, yes, of course,' I answer nervously, hating myself for feeling so intimidated. I have no idea how to get back on an even footing with this enigmatic man. If anything, the conversation to come is likely to end with me being tossed out on my ear. Hurriedly I lean forward to pick up the hated filofax and fumble around inside my bag for a pen.

'So.' He leans forward with his arms crossed and resting on his knees, waiting.

'Aren't you a little young to be a Captain?' I ask, stalling, and causing him to blink a little at the abrupt change of subject. His eyes narrow as he recognizes my delaying tactic, and my heart hammers in response.

'I'm very good at my job,' is his curt response. Then sighing, he looks pointedly at my still tightly closed filofax. 'Let's cut to the chase Ms Davies. It's my understanding that Ms Shackleford and Mr Westbrook would like to hold their wedding here in the Naval College on the twentieth of December. Is that correct?'

I nod my head wordlessly and simply wait for him to continue. Frowning at my continued silence, he carries on. 'Of course we both know that this whole affair is going to be very difficult to manage, especially given the fact that the groom is so, err, well known and there are only actually seven weeks to the date suggested.' He waits for my comment, so I dutifully nod my head again. I'm seriously hoping that if he continues talking, he might end up organizing the whole thing for me...

'Ms Davies,' he barks finally, making me jump and quickly quashing any vague hope I might have of handing over the reins. 'I would like to know how you intend to organize this wedding without it turning into a complete cake and arse party as Admiral Shackleford would no doubt say.'

I clear my throat. 'Please call me Kit,' I finally reply faintly.

~*~

It was five pm, which in Florence Davies' book meant the sun was definitely over the yard arm, and as the blustery weather of yesterday had unexpectedly reverted to back to the more clement Indian summer, a glass of chilled white wine on the patio was definitely called for.

Seating herself with a sigh at the small round table on the terrace, Florence sipped her wine appreciatively and admired the beautiful vista before her. The sea looked almost turquoise today and lapped gently against the pebble shore of the beach below. Her cottage sat high on a bluff with panoramic views over the privately owned beach of Blackpool Sands one way, and the whole of Start Bay on the other. She never tired of this view and often mused that the only way she would ever leave her beloved home would be in a box.

Which actually might not be that far away. Grimacing, she thought back to her recent hospital appointment. The shadow on her lung may or may not have been caused by her forty a day habit when she was (much) younger. Nowadays she limited herself to the occasional spliff – when Kit wasn't around of course. To be fair, the consultant hadn't yet given her a final prognosis, and her own doctor had ordered her not to go planning her funeral yet.

Her thoughts moved quickly on to a much pleasanter subject - her much-loved niece. Kit would never have to worry about money when she was gone. Florence vowed to herself that she'd make sure her niece was well provided for when she finally exited this mortal coil. Which is more than her bloody good for nothing brother and his wife were likely to do. The only thing they were good at was actually spending money.

Florence's blood boiled when she thought of the last conversation she'd had with her sibling. His complete lack of appreciation for anything that Kit had achieved was mind boggling. Florence took another large sip of wine in an effort to calm the frustrated anger inside her. Kit's hurt and confusion over her parents' actions during the last couple of months had been so very hard to watch. Luckily her friend Victory had stepped in and things were finally looking up now that Kit had got the job of Tory's wedding planner.

Suddenly her dog Pepé appeared from goodness knows where. His muzzle was completely covered in soil. Florence sighed. He'd obviously been digging again. Leaning down, she picked the little Yorkshire terrier cross, and placed him gently on her knee. He promptly busied himself turning in little circles in an effort to achieve the optimum position, completely ignoring the dirt which was now liberally spread all over his mistress's skirt. Patiently, Florence waited until he was settled to his satisfaction, then planted a small kiss on his head. At least the earth now decorating her skirt wasn't muddy.

She loved this time of day. The peace and quiet was so soothing, just the bird song and Pepé's gentle snoring.

Abruptly the tranquility was shattered as her mobile phone shrilled loudly. Glancing down, to see who the caller was, she was disappointed to find it wasn't Kit. Her niece had gone yesterday for a preliminary meeting with the Captain of the Naval College and she'd yet to call to say how it had gone.

Instead the caller was her agent. Grimacing slightly, Florence let it go to answer phone. Her publishers were champing at the bit for the initial draft of her latest book. It was pretty much done, but she didn't want to get into a wrangling match with her agent over deadlines late on a Friday afternoon. It was the start of the weekend, and she'd always made it a rule that her writing stopped at wine o'clock. It didn't stop her agent harassing her though. They'd been working together for nearly twenty years, and Neil was more than just her agent. He was her friend. With benefits…

The phone pinged to say a message had been left. Neil knew better than to think she'd call back and Florence smiled. He never changed, but then neither did she. They had the perfect relationship. Thinking about that of course caused her to think about the relationship that finished long before she met Neil. The one that had ended so disastrously that her life had spiralled out of control, and she'd felt there was no reason to live anymore, except for one thing.

Perhaps it was finally time to tell Kit the truth.

Chapter Three

'Bloody hell Kitty Kat, that's a disaster.' Victory's face is suitably horrified at my announcement that our old friend Jason Buchannan is now the Captain at BRNC.

'Tell me about it,' is my glum response. I am still battered and bruised over yesterday's encounter with Captain Buchannan.

Victory and I are sitting in my flat with a bottle of wine. Unfortunately for me I'm the only one drinking it. Tory is sitting with a glass of sparkling water, along with a bucket next to her chair. To say she's suffering from morning sickness would be to completely ignore the throwing up she's doing during the afternoon, evening and night time. I think it's safe to say that she's not exactly enjoying her pregnancy. I sincerely hope she doesn't have to carry a bucket up the aisle in lieu of a bouquet...

'What are we going to do?' she continues, picking up her dog Dotty who is still shivering at her feet after witnessing the last bout. It's a good job I'm her best friend or I'd be down there too.

'There's nothing we can do,' I respond gloomily. 'We're just going to have to work with him. At least he didn't throw me out on my ear.' Victory takes to biting her nails, which just goes to show her level of agitation given the fact that she trying to grow them for the wedding.

'So what did he say?' she whispers finally after disgustingly spitting out the piece of nail she's torn off with her teeth. I resist the urge to tell her to put it into a bin – with the hormones and the anxiety about the wedding, I'm seriously beginning to wonder whether we'll all make it in one piece. Come back Noah, all is forgiven.

'Is Noah still coming back from Ireland next Wednesday?' I ask, trying hard not to show how desperate I am for his calming influence.

Tory frowns as if she can't understand my reason for asking. 'What does that matter?' she snaps. 'You think we can't deal with the knob without male backup?'

'Of course we can,' I sigh. God knows what Tory would say if she knew the real truth. That her best friend is likely to completely screw up her big fat Hollywood wedding. I take a large sip of my wine while Victory looks on longingly.

'So what happened yesterday?' she continues with a huge effort to speak more calmly.

I heave another sigh. 'It would be so much easier if you're weren't holding the wedding in a military establishment.' I wait for the inevitable snappy retort, but to my surprise it doesn't come. Instead she nods her head.

'I know Kitty Kat, but it's so important to my dad. It would break his heart if I did it anywhere else.'

'I know, I know,' I respond with a small scowl. And I do. A royal pain in the arse the Admiral might be. But his beloved College means everything to him.

'Anyway, back to business. Captain Buchannan wants a detailed list of absolutely everyone who will have access on the big day, including guests, caterers, florists, hairdressers, photographers, cake makers and uncle Tom Cobley and all. And he wants it by next weekend.

'Shit,' breathes Tory. She might not be aware of just how far I am from coming up with such a list, but she can recognize a tall order when she hears one.

'He would also like to have an informal chat with you and Noah at the earliest opportunity.'

Tory screws up her nose and is about to respond when I deliver the punch line.

'So I invited him up for dinner at the Admiralty next Saturday.'

~*~

Jason Buchannan came out of the shower and looked at his watch, registering the time – eighteen hundred - still an hour before dinner. Wrapping a towel around his waist he walked to the window overlooking the River Dart. The wind had died down from yesterday and the sun was casting a late afternoon shadow on Dartmouth situated on this side of the river mouth, bathing Kingswear on the opposite side in bright sunshine. The view was breathtaking. He shook his head. How could a place so beautiful hold such bitter memories?

His arrival at BRNC just over a week ago was almost the first time he'd set foot in the College since his passing out here nearly twenty years ago. Now at thirty eight, he was pretty much the youngest captain in the Royal Navy and being groomed for bigger things. The politics surrounding BRNC were an excellent training ground for someone who had the legs to get to First Sea Lord. It didn't matter to those doing the grooming that he absolutely hated this place.

As he stared over the parade ground, completely unchanged since he was here as a cadet, Jason felt his thoughts pull back to the last time he'd stood on the hallowed ground in front of him. The last time he'd seen Laura.

Closing his eyes, he turned away from the window in an effort to banish the memories, and thought instead of the woman he'd entertained in the drawing room yesterday.

Kit Davies. He wondered idly whether Kit was short for Catherine, and even now he couldn't help but chuckle at the priceless expression on her face when he'd turned to face her for the first time. Her green eyes had been wide with alarm; her full lips caught half open in the act of greeting.

He found himself wondering what those lips would feel like trapped under his, and without warning he felt an unwelcome stirring. Irritated, he pulled on his shirt. He wasn't an adolescent for God's sake, and while pretty in an elfin way, she certainly wasn't fantasy material. He thought back to their conversation and frowned. It was pretty clear that she hadn't got a clue what she was doing.

He'd been so tempted to call her up on it – it's what he would have done to any of his junior officers, but somehow, looking at her pale determined face, trying so hard to look as if she had everything under control, pen poised above her empty filofax, he just hadn't got the heart to reduce her to a shivering wreck. Not yet anyway.

Nevertheless, everything he'd said to her was true. She certainly needed to get it together pretty quickly if this wedding was going to happen in the College at all. He may not be a complete bastard, whatever she and her friends privately believed, but that didn't mean he wouldn't hesitate to pull the plug on the whole thing at the last minute if he deemed it necessary to do so.

~*~

'Hey Peps, who's a good boy then? No sweetie, please don't hump my foot.'

It's Sunday afternoon and I've just arrived at Aunt Flo's for lunch. Her dog Pepé has launched himself at my right leg like some kind of limpet - his idea of showing affection is to mate furiously with whatever appendage he can access. I frequently thank God that he's less than a foot tall. It may be he developed this habit living with an owner who writes porn for a living – makes total sense when you think about it.

'Come in sweetheart.' Aunt Flo's voice is coming from the kitchen, so after gently shaking my leg from Pepé's fervent embrace, I head into the room that's always felt to me like the heart of my aunt's cottage.

Not that she's the world's best cook per se – her culinary skills tend to border on the eccentric – but so much of my teenage years were spent seated at the old pine table discussing philosophy, the state of the world and whether to include the use of a *Rampant Rabbit* in her latest bonk buster.

As I enter the kitchen, Aunt Flo has her back to me and I sniff to see if I can guess what we're having for lunch. Mmm, decidedly fishy.

'Sit down my lovely and help yourself to a glass.' There's a bottle of white wine in a cooler on the table with more than two thirds already gone. Aunt Flo likes to cook with her wine...

'I'm driving Flo, so I'll save my one glass for dinner. What are we having?'

'Scallops with black pudding and spaghetti,' she responds without turning round. I frown a little at the idea of a north country delicacy in my pasta, but I know better than to say anything. Telling my Aunt Flo that you don't like anything usually makes her cook it for you all the more. She's always believed that having a varied palate is the sign of good breeding.

'Grab the garlic bread out of the oven for me will you sweetheart, it's just about ready.' As I open the oven door, the delicious smell of roasted garlic wafts into the warm kitchen air, and putting the large loaf onto the table, I snatch a piece from the end, juggling the hot bread and nibbling bits off the edge.

'Here we are,' she says, turning finally with a large pan full of enough pasta to feed the five thousand.

'Is someone else coming for lunch?' I can't help but ask, popping the last bit of garlic bread into my mouth and greedily licking the butter off my fingers.

'You need to put on some weight my girl,' she responds, ladling a large helping into my bowl. 'If you had Victory's curves, you might bag yourself a hot actor like hers.'

'That wasn't what you were saying when you served Tory that cabbage soup the last time we were here,' I mumble round a mouth full of pasta.

'That was then,' she responded with a wave of her hand before digging in to her own lunch. 'Big beautiful women are now all the rage. My latest book is a BBW mystery romance.'

I look up with interest. 'Is it finished yet?' I ask, eager to get first dibs. I've always been the first to read my aunt's books. I suspect when I was fifteen, it was her way of giving me sex education without all the boring stuff. Mind you, it did set the bar a bit high – probably why I'm still single.

'I'll email you the mobi file so you can read it on your Kindle,' she replies nodding. 'Neil's not even seen it yet, but my publishers want it out in time for Christmas.' She sighs as she helps herself to garlic bread. 'I think this might be my last one Kit. I'm getting too old for deadlines.'

I look up in surprise. Aunt Flo's always lived for her writing. The sun is shining through the French doors leading out onto the flower strewn patio so I can't see her face clearly, but her voice sounds frighteningly weary.

'Are you ok Aunt Flo?' I ask, suddenly concerned. There's a short pause, causing my heart to bump uncomfortably, then she responds with a smile. 'I'm fine my lovely, don't you worry about me. You know how I am when I've come to the end of a story. I get a bit maudlin and soppy. Anyway, enough about me. Let's talk about the wedding. How did it go on Friday?'

I knit my brow slightly at the abrupt change of subject, a little uneasy and unwilling to let the matter go so easily. My aunt's face however shows clearly that the topic of her writing is now closed – and if she doesn't want to talk about something, she won't. Apparently I get that trait from her...

'It could have gone better,' I admit eventually, causing her to raise her eyebrows and stare at me, clearly waiting for me to continue.

'Did you know that Captain Taylor is no longer at the College? He was replaced last week.'

'I had no idea. It must have been a quick decision. There was no mention of it at the Ladies Afloat meeting last week.'

'Yeah, well, as much as they like to think they're a font of knowledge regarding all things naval, your middle aged dinghy sailing cronies are not always the first port of call when it comes to College appointments.'

'Very obviously,' is her quick response, 'But it's not often I'm the first with the gossip. So spill.'

'It's not good Aunt Flo,' mumble finally, after making her wait while I finish the last of my spaghetti. 'You remember when we went up to Scotland and I told you all about Jason Buchannan?

'You mean, the complete moron whose father owned the place you were staying in?'

'Yep, that's the one. Well, he's the new Captain.'

'Oh,' is her answer.

After that, we put off the rest of the discussion until after lunch, Aunt Flo citing that talking about rude obnoxious people while eating can bring on indigestion. So we kept the conversation light, and two more helpings of pasta, followed by a generous piece of apple pie and cream later, I waddle out onto the patio while Aunt Flo makes coffee.

I sink into one of the old comfortable garden chairs with a sigh of satiated contentment and Pepé wastes no time in giving my leg a quick token hump before jumping up to settle himself on my lap. Although situated high up overlooking the sea, the terrace is nevertheless sheltered on three sides and the weak October sun is hitting all the right spots. Slowly I feel myself relax and begin to drift.

I recall the first time I met Jason Buchannan in Bloodstone Tower. It was clear from the onset that he didn't like either Tory or her father – or any of us for that matter.

I still don't know all the ins and outs of the story about the Admiral and the Thai prostitute (pardon the pun). Tory's been very cagey – says her father would disown her if she told me everything. I think the real reason she's not spilled the beans is probably because she doesn't know what really happened either. But like or not, there's still such a thing as manners, and Jason Buchannan most definitely didn't have any - even though he'd taken my breath away when I first clapped eyes on the bloody man.

Damn it, why do the good looking ones always have to be either gay or complete idiots?

I'm brought back to the present by Aunt Flo's arrival with coffee and cream and a side shot of Cointreau. 'Bloody hell, I can't drink that, I'm driving,' I protest weakly as she places the tray on the table.

'Well, you're not leaving any time soon are you?' Aunt Flo responds with a shrug, 'And anyway, you can always stop over. There are advantages to not being tied to a bricks and mortar business you know.'

It's actually quite embarrassing just how quickly I give in. I decide there and then that I will stay overnight. Aunt Flo and I haven't spent much time together over the last few weeks with the whole gallery thing, and I'm still feeling a little bit of disquiet over our earlier discussion. Settling back, I take a small sip of my liqueur followed by the hot aromatic coffee and freshly whipped cream. No one makes coffee like Aunt Flo.

We sit for a few moments, enjoying the peace and quiet, content for the moment to let the silence run. Idly I watch the dappled sunlight flicker on the deep water swell far out to sea, until abruptly the stillness is broken by Pepé's loud snore.

'So, tell me.' Aunt Flo further disrupts the tranquility in her usual brusque no nonsense manner.

Sighing, I sit forward, dislodging a disgruntled Pepé from his comfortable position. 'There's not really much to tell,' I answer vaguely at first, earning me a rude snort – the only indication that she doesn't believe me for one second. I try again.

'We just don't get on Aunt Flo. He's... well, he's the very worst kind of naval officer. You know the sort - thinks he can just wave his hand and his subordinates will scuttle around to obey his every whim. And he's just so bloody rude.'

'What does he look like?' she asks, completely ignoring my scathing assessment of Jason Buchannan's character.

I slump back in defeat. 'Drop dead gorgeous,' I mumble, causing my know it all aunt to nod her head shrewdly.

'So was he rude to you on Friday?'

Silence. I so want to say that he was a complete jerk, but my sense of fairness would get in the way. In the end I content myself with a sullen, 'Not exactly.'

Still no response. Aunt Flo has a way of dragging things out of you like she's pulling teeth. The problem is, I can't really explain my feelings about Jason Buchannan. Just thinking about his near perfect face and body gets my heart racing, but he just has to open his mouth and it starts racing for completely different reasons.

'I don't think he believes I'm capable of organizing such a large affair,' I say quietly after a while. 'The thing is Aunt Flo, I think he might be right. I so want to do the right thing for Tory, but I'm frightened I'm going to mess up. There's just so much to do. This is so not like me. When did I ever turn down a challenge? Then I spend half an hour in Captain Buchannan's company and I feel like a pathetic little girl. And what's more, I act like one.'

There's a small silence while my aunt processes what I've said. 'I think you need to take a step back my lovely,' she says after a moment. 'You're getting completely overwhelmed, which is understandable given the importance of the occasion. But you've organized tons of events for your gallery in the past. This is no different – just bigger, that's all.

'For starters you need to make a list of tasks, then put them in order of importance. Then we'll get everything onto a spreadsheet and look at the critical path timeline.' I look over at her, for the first time feeling something approaching, not confidence exactly, but less of a desire to throw myself off the edge of her patio.

'Come on sweetheart, we might as well get stuck in now if you're staying. Go into the fridge and grab us another bottle of wine.'

Chapter Four

It's Wednesday evening and the four of us - that is me, Tory, Noah and Freddy - are sitting round the kitchen table in my flat. It's a bit of a squeeze, especially seeing as the open pizza boxes are competing with the ever increasing guest list and various brochures depicting everything from flowers to favours. And that's without the mound of ideas I've printed off the internet.

Noah has just arrived, and after kissing his bride to be as though he's never going to let her out of his sight again, he throws himself into a chair, sighing with pleasure as Freddy hands him a beer.

'Tell me again why we're planning the biggest event of the year in your pokey flat as opposed to Noah's sumptuous six bedroom house?' We completely ignore Freddy's sarcasm as he removes Dotty from his seat. The little dog wastes no time in jumping back up onto his knee without taking her eyes off the half eaten pizza slices.

'You know why Freddy,' I remind him impatiently. 'We want to keep the details of the wedding under wraps for as long as possible. As long as it's simply a rumour, we're unlikely to see the world and his dog descend on the town in a tail back that's likely to turn the M Five into a car park.'

'I think most of the shops and hotels would leak the information themselves given half the chance. They've never had such a busy twelve months. Any one of them would worship at the altar of Noah in a heartbeat.'

'You're such a cynic Freddy.' Victory's observation is shrugged off nonchalantly. 'I'm just a realist sweetie. So how are you getting everyone to keep quiet? You forcing them to sign the official secrets act?'

'Everything will be on a need to know basis and I can't imagine anyone wanting to risk such a potentially lucrative contract - not to mention the publicity they'd generate after the wedding – just to get five minutes of fame now.'

'You'd be surprised just what people will do to their picture on TV,' Noah butts in drily.

I nod my head in agreement, before continuing, 'So the fewer people involved in the early stages, the better.'

'Do you think Jason Buchannan will keep it under his hat?' Tory's voice is a little anxious.

'I don't think you have any worries there honey,' Noah reassures her. 'Captain Buchannan has issues about security as it is, so he's unlikely to want to make things more difficult for himself. Anyway, he sounds like a pretty straight kind of guy.'

'Yep, as a poker,' Freddy interjects caustically, and I grin despite myself – poker straight sums up the knob exactly. Still, time to get back to business.

'Right, has everyone finished eating?' I clap my hands to get attention and even Dotty takes her eyes off the leftovers for all of two seconds.

Standing up, I pick up the mostly empty cartons and take them into the kitchen, leaving the little dog sitting faithfully guarding them for the rest of the evening. I don't think an earthquake would get her to move right now. That's what I call dedication.

Despite Tory's assertion that pizza really is not good for dogs, I sneak her a little piece of pepperoni to reward her for her staying power. Then seating myself back at the table, I proudly pick up my beautiful new spreadsheet before handing everyone a copy.

'Wow someone's been busy,' comments Freddy, then subsides into silence as I frown over at him.

'I'd just like to say thank you Tory and Noah for giving me the honour of organizing your special day. I know you're doing it for me…' I hold my hand up with a small smile as Tory opens her mouth to interrupt.

'You don't have to deny it, we all know it's true. I just want you to know how much I appreciate it. You could have used the best, but instead you chose to use me. I really hope I don't let you down.'

Unaccountably the stress of the last couple of weeks chooses this moment to make itself known, and my bottom lip begins to wobble as I say, 'down.'

'Oh Kitty Kat, please don't be upset.' Tory jumps up and rushes round the table to enfold me in her arms. 'You could never let me down. I really don't care if it turns out a complete and utter disaster. You're my best friend and I love you. Whatever happens, I know the day will be memorable.'

Prophetic words…

By the end of the evening, we've whittled down preferred caterers; florists; photographer, wedding cake, chair covers; table decorations and a choice of Champagne. Apparently Noah's going to be in charge of organizing the band for the evening, which causes a brief flurry of excitement. He refuses to elaborate however, saying it's a surprise.

We have a guest list of just over one hundred and fifty people – two thirds of them connected to Noah, who's promised to get me all their dirty secrets going back to the Norman Conquest, before the deadline on Saturday.

The locals on the guest list shouldn't prove too much of a problem since most of them have been in Dartmouth since the year dot and any dirty secrets they have are probably already in the College archives. That only leaves the Admiral's personal guests. Let's hope he doesn't know any Russian spies…

Thank God we haven't got *Hello* magazine to contend with.

~*~

Admiral Shackleford was sitting in his study, ostensibly to put together a list of friends he'd like to personally invite to Victory's wedding, but the sad fact was, there weren't any. Not really. Jimmy was pretty much it.

Oh there were all his retired cronies, but although he was a bit thick skinned, he was well aware that they only tolerated him. He'd always been too outspoken to fit in with most of the lily livered landlubbers.

They'd had no hesitation in hanging him out to dry when they thought he'd be ending his days in the Bangkok Hilton, but now look at them all. One sniff of a celebrity wedding and he's suddenly the best bloody thing since sliced bread.

The only one of the buggers who'd kept in touch over the years had been Bible Basher Boris. When the shit had well and truly hit the fan over the summer, old Boris had been firmly on his side, loyally defending him to all the damn scuttlebutts queuing up to point the finger.

The Admiral sighed, suddenly and uncharacteristically wishing things had turned out differently. Picking up a photo from his desk, he gazed at the picture of his dead wife, Victory's mother.

Celia would have loved all this shenanigans. If she'd been here, she would have been in the thick of it. It was at times like this he missed her the most. She was the one person in the whole world who truly understood him – in fact she knew him better than he knew himself. What would she have done in this situation?

But he didn't really need to ask the question, because he knew the answer. Loyalty was something else Celia understood. But he had yet to broach the subject to Victory and Noah. At the end of the day, it was up to them whether they went along with the notion of having a doddering old priest officiate at their big day.

One with a flatulence issue so bad that it could well result in none of the guests actually surviving the ceremony - all with the whole world looking on, and of course providing old Boris didn't actually keel over during the service.

He heaved another sigh, wondering why life had to be so complicated and whether it was it was too early for a glass of Port…

~*~

By Saturday I'm finally beginning to feel as though I'm on top of everything. My filofax is no longer empty, in fact it's satisfyingly bulging at the seams, and I'm no longer looking forward to tonight's dinner with the same enthusiasm that I'd be approaching my own execution, so all in all, things are looking up.

We're supposed to be assembling for pre dinner drinks at seven. I glance down at my watch. Five o'clock. I need to allow an hour to get over the river to the Admiralty if I want to avoid arriving as though I've just taken part in a marathon, so that gives me an hour to get ready. Plenty of time...

...Or not. It's nearly six fifteen by the time I'm finally ready. To be fair it never usually takes me this long, and I don't normally go through my entire wardrobe before picking an outfit. I glance over at the mound of clothes still piled high on my bed. Still, it's my duty to look my best as the person managing such a large and glamorous affair, and as I stare critically at myself in the mirror, I almost believe it. I've finally plumped for a pair of wide leg chiffon trousers in a dove grey, together with a slightly loose black silk top, which slides with a certain amount of sexy sophistication just off one shoulder. I don't have to worry about wearing a bra as my top half in no way compares to Tory's impressive rack. Nevertheless I stick my chest out slightly, wondering if I could be actually mistaken for a boy. The first time he saw my boobs on holiday, Freddy had peered closely at them before asking me if I'd tried Clearasil.

Nope, despite being the butt of Freddy's ongoing itty bitty titty jokes, I think I actually look quite feminine and desirable. Not that I care what anyone at dinner is likely to think...

Sticking my tongue out defiantly at my reflection, I fluff up what's left of my hair and head out of my bedroom to grab the satchel holding the nuts and bolts of my best friend's wedding. Then I hunt around for my car keys.

I've left it too late to do my mountain goat impression up the steep hill that masquerades as The Admiralty's front garden and looking like a Sweaty Betty is not how I want Jason Buchannan to see me. Although, of course, I don't care really…

Naturally I'm late. I love living in Dartmouth but it has to be said that whenever there's a ferry involved it's always a bit hit and miss. Unfortunately, the only way over the river is via one of two car ferries, a single passenger ferry, or, as a last resort, by rowing - so I don't really have much choice.

However, it does mean I'm the last to arrive, just when I so didn't want to look unprofessional in front of Mr Poker Pants. I creep in through the back door, hoping to make an unobtrusive entrance, but with two of the world's noisiest dogs in residence, there's practically no chance of that.

Dotty, who can hear a biscuit wrapper at one hundred yards, is first, and comes tearing into the kitchen to launch herself delightedly at my lovely silk top, followed by Pickles who contents himself with jumping up at my chiffon trousers. Unable to help myself, I shriek, trying to pull Dotty away before the off the shoulder turns into off the arm, dangerously exposing my right breast. (Why oh why didn't I wear a bra…?)

'What the bollocking hell's going on?' Oh joy, first on the scene is of course the Admiral, whose idea of low-key is to keep his voice down to a level of less than a hundred decibels.

Pickles takes one look at his master, and very obviously deciding that discretion is the better part of valour, gives me a last hurried lick before doing a runner to parts of the house unknown. As the spaniel dashes through the kitchen door, he's replaced by Noah, who luckily wastes no time striding into the kitchen to take the enthusiastic little dog from my arms before the slippery black silk drops off my top half completely.

'Sweetie, the just been laid look is so you…' The next arrival is Freddy, leaning nonchalantly against the kitchen door, and I glare murderously at him while trying to readjust my clothing. However, just as I'm about to deliver a scathing retort, Jason Buchannan appears next to him.

'Kit what on earth are you doing?' Tory's astonished face appears behind Freddy, completing the line up. Yep, I think that's everyone. My humiliation is complete.

'Oh Kit, I love your top. Is it hot culture? I once had a top just like that - it was Channel.'

No, not quite everyone. I forgot about Mabel...

Fortunately, the combined efforts to interpret Mabel's cryptic announcement, aside from being a potential bonding experience, also takes the attention away from me, and by the time everyone's worked out that she actually meant haute couture and Chanel, I've managed to put myself back together and escape into the living room, where I'm firmly ensconced with a large fortifying glass of wine and an even larger bowl of peanuts.

Tory sits down next to me. 'Sorry,' she mouths, helping herself to a handful of nuts. 'I really think I'm going to have to take Dotty to dog training classes.' I look down at the object of our discussion, now shamelessly sitting on my feet in an effort to get closer to the nuts.

'I think she needs to go on a diet,' I murmur, leaning down to give her a quick fuss, just on the off chance that my comment might hurt her feelings. Good grief, I'm getting as bad as Tory. Goodness knows how little miss centre of the known universe is going to take to playing second fiddle to a baby...

Slowly the others filter in and I'm relieved to see Noah talking animatedly with Jason. 'How are we going to do this?' I ask Tory, noting with concern that she's now looking a little pale, which might actually be a result of all the nuts she's scoffed, rather than her usual morning sickness.

She takes a deep breath before responding. 'Thought we'd have dinner first then get on to the nitty gritty. You know, give everyone a chance to relax a bit.' My best friend looks anything but relaxed and as I watch, her face slowly goes an interesting shade of green.

'What's for dinner?' I ask, hoping to take her mind off her roiling stomach. Unfortunately, it appears to have the opposite effect, and after abruptly shouting, 'Chicken,' she jumps to her feet and dashes towards the door, leaving a sudden silence in her wake.

'What the bloody hell's wrong with her?' the Admiral mutters gruffly in her wake, 'Just lately she's been behaving like a damn fart in a colander. Why only yester...'

'I'm sure she's fine,' Noah butts in quickly, before the Admiral has chance to get into his stride, 'I'll just go check on her.'

'I'll go if you like,' I volunteer hastily. Even holding Tory's hair while she vomits into a toilet is preferable than making small talk with Jason Buchannan and the Admiral - not to mention Freddy who's nearly as bad as Tory's father at making polite conversation without giving offence.

Noah grins at me, totally understanding my reasons for offering to go to Tory's aid (to be fair, I am slightly concerned about my friend as well...)

'It's okay Kit, I've got this. Why don't you go check if Mabel needs any help in the kitchen?'

I grasp his suggestion like the lifeline it is, and grabbing my glass of wine, I thankfully escape, with Dotty close on my heels (I think she heard the word kitchen). As the door shuts behind me, the last thing I hear is Freddy saying serenely, 'So Jason, any good looking sailors up at the College this term?' I wince and grin in equal measure, wishing I could be a fly on the wall during the three way conversation that's sure to follow.

Which unfortunately is likely to be sooner than I'd hoped. The merry widow appears to have everything in hand, and after lingering, making small talk and generally getting under Mabel's feet for five minutes, I'm unceremoniously sent packing with instructions to tell everyone that dinner will be ten minutes. Once back in the hall, I hover outside the living room door for a second, reluctant to go back in. Idly I glance round the large square hall with its oak panelling and sweeping galleried staircase. I can totally understand why they wanted to use this house to film *The Bridegroom.*

Then, knowing I can't put it off any longer, I lift my glass to take a quick sip of my wine, just as the door to the living room is thrown open and I find myself face to face with Jason Buchannan. The shock ensures that I miss my mouth completely and I now have a large trail of red wine decorating my sadly crumpled best silk top.

We stare at each other for what seems like hours but can only be a couple of seconds, before the Admiral appears behind him. 'I'm just showing Jason where the heads are,' he booms at his usual level of decibels. Then glancing at my top, continues, 'What the bloody hell have you done to yourself now girl? Is that wine you've poured down your front? You'll be needing a bib soon. You're not drunk already are you?'

Surprisingly the dinner didn't turn out to be the disaster I was dreading. Once we were called to the table, Mabel (who has inexplicably morphed into Delia Smith) prepared an amazing meal, and Tory was able to keep it down without rushing off to the bathroom. I could see that Jason and Freddy clearly had their suspicions, both eyeing her carefully during the meal, but as usual, the Admiral was as observant as one of the three blind mice, so luckily it went over his head.

Now it's my turn to take the chair, and given that I've managed to get through the meal without spilling anything else over myself, or getting completely trollied - although it was tempting - I'm now reasonably confident that I have everything under control. I cough to get everyone's attention and risk a glance at Jason seated opposite.

To my surprise, he's already staring at me. Or more accurately, at my mouth. Self consciously I run my tongue experimentally over my lips, wondering if my certainty about not dribbling anything may have been a little premature. I glance up again and this time my heart slams hard into my ribs as I experience the full heat of his gaze, until he turns away, leaving me feeling strangely bereft and disorientated.

Face flaming, I look down at the paperwork in front of me, willing my pulse to slow down. It was only a look for goodness sake. But my heart knows differently. For a few brief seconds, Jason Buchannan had looked as though he wanted to devour me, and my whole body had undeniably tightened in response.

Self consciously I begin passing round the wedding details I've collated so far, before risking a quick glance back up to see Jason scrutinizing the wedding list spreadsheet. What is it about the man that makes me act as though I have nothing in between my ears but fresh air? He's sitting in between Noah and Mabel, and contrary to earlier, he looks relaxed and at ease, as though he's actually enjoying himself.

I continue to throw covert glances at him as I finish handing out the spreadsheets. The white shirt and black dinner jacket he's wearing accentuates his dark maleness, and right now his beautiful silver eyes are for once dancing with mischief and delight as he laughs at an anecdote about a previously attended Hollywood wedding being related by Noah. No poker in sight.

I cough self consciously, bringing everyone back to the matter at hand. 'Well, that's everything I've got. Jason, I think you'll find that the guest details are pretty comprehensive, and as soon as we've made the final decision about flowers etc, I'll make sure that you have full details of all the suppliers immediately.' My heart sinks as the smile slowly leaves his eyes and he turns his attention back towards the reason he's here.

Picking up the guest list again, he nods acquiescence. 'I'll keep you informed if there are any security issues with any of these names. Have you worked out the timings yet?'

'Not yet. Tory and I are getting together this week to finalize. I think we've got everything under control – apart from the evening entertainment, but you'll have to speak to Noah about that.' I smile over at the actor who winks and gives me a lazy grin in return.

'There is one slight problem we might have to contend with,' comments Jason, causing all eyes to turn towards him. 'I'm assuming that you're expecting the College Chaplain to conduct the ceremony?' Tory and Noah glance at each other, then at me. 'Well, yes I think so,' Tory responds at Noah's shrug. 'Why, is that an issue?'

'It could be I'm afraid,' Jason answers, hands busy stacking his sheets in some semblance of order. 'We're actually between padres at the moment - the new one was due to arrive at the end of November. However, it appears he's broken his leg rather badly and I think it unlikely he'll be joining the College until the New Year. Do you know of anyone else who could officiate at the ceremony at such short notice?'

There's a silence as we all rack our brains for possible chaplains we might have hidden away in a spare closet somewhere. Just when it looks as though the small problem could be a much larger one, the Admiral, who it has to be said has been uncharacteristically silent during the meal, coughs, and with a smile big enough to strike terror into the heart of everyone who knows him, says happily, 'Well, it just so happens, I might be able to help you out there...'

Chapter Five

Jason tossed and turned in the big four poster bed that had been the resting place for first commodores and now captains since BRNC was first built. Despite the long walk back to the College, he wasn't tired.

He was anxious about the celebrity wedding to come and heartily wished that it wasn't taking place on his watch. But that wasn't the real reason he knew. Images of soft green eyes and streaky blond hair were preventing him from sleeping.

Without even looking, Jason had been overwhelmingly aware of Kit throughout the evening. The look her eyes when she'd caught him staring and the smell of her perfume as she leant forward to lay the spreadsheets on the table in front of him had incredibly left him hard and aching, something that hadn't happened since he'd been a naïve cadet.

He'd allowed himself to glance at her once, and nearly lost himself in her clear gaze, wanting nothing more than to drag her up in to a bedroom, any bedroom, and bury himself in her soft willing flesh. He hadn't dared to look again.

He groaned. What the hell was the matter with him? She'd intrigued him when they first met in Scotland. But now?

Turning over yet again, the only certainty Jason knew, as he abandoned the possibility of sleep any time soon, was that attraction had somehow turned into almost uncontrollable desire. He hadn't craved a specific woman's touch in years, and since Laura, he'd never let a woman get under his skin.

Until now.

~*~

'It couldn't have worked better if I'd planned it.' The Admiral's self satisfied smirk caused Jimmy to look at his friend carefully.

'You didn't, did you?' He wouldn't have put it past the Admiral to have engineered something dodgy, but he'd be very concerned if Charles Shackleford had stooped to grievous bodily harm.

The Admiral looked over at the small man irritably. 'Don't be so bloody ridiculous Jimmy. It was just a lucky coincidence that's all.'

'I don't think the God walloper who's lying in hospital with his leg up in a brace is likely to see it quite that way Sir,' Jimmy responded mildly. 'Anyway, I assume you warned everyone about Bible Basher Boris's err, *issues*?'

'Come on Jimmy, your turn to get the drinks in, I'm dryer than a popcorn fart.' The Admiral's abrupt change of the subject told Jimmy all he needed to know.

'You haven't told them have you?' Ignoring the question, Charles Shackleford waved the barmaid over, and looked pointedly at his friend. Heart sinking, Jimmy ordered their drinks. He was sick and tired of keeping the Admiral's bloody secrets, but this was one skeleton he was determined would see the light of day long before it resulted in a nasty surprise on Tory's wedding day.

'I've been in touch with old Boris,' the Admiral continued once his pint was placed in front of him, and he's coming down in a couple of weeks to stay in a flat until after the wedding.'

'What about his *problems*?' Jimmy put his pint onto the bar and leaned towards his friend, emphasizing the word problems. 'Come on Sir, what if he starts letting fluffy off the chain right in the middle of the service? There are going to be important people at Tory's wedding, and she'll never live it down. YOU CAN'T JUST IGNORE THIS SIR.'

The Admiral looked at Jimmy in astonishment as the small man's outburst got the attention of the whole pub. He opened and closed his mouth a few times. Then, finally, sulkily, 'I thought I'd mention it on the day.'

Jimmy sighed. 'That's like rearranging the deckchairs on the bloody Titanic Sir. You just can't do it.'

To Jimmy's amazement, the Admiral simply blinked a little before resting his head in his hands. 'I've got to Jimmy lad, I can't get out of it. I just can't let the old bugger down. It means so much to him. I promised him Jimmy, I *promised* him.

'What am I going to do?' he whispered finally, actually wringing his hands in anguish.

Jimmy stared at his former commanding officer with something akin to horror. In all the time they'd known each other, he'd never seen the Admiral this worried. Not even when he'd gone to London to confront Noah. And since when had it ever bothered the old reprobate about breaking a promise? Jimmy smelled a big bloody rodent.

Oh God, not more bollocking secrets.

~*~

Tory and I are sitting in the Cherub for a celebration. Which for me consists of a bowl of chips washed down with Prosecco, and for Tory, ditto bowl of chips washed down with her usual sparkling water. It's just after six and Freddy's going to join us as soon as the preliminary rehearsals for the Flavel Centre's Christmas panto are finished. They're doing Cinderella this year which I whimsically thought was very appropriate in light of the fact that we have our very own Cinderella set to marry her prince.

Taking a sip of my sparkling wine, I glance over at our Cinders who might be about to tie the knot with her Prince Charming, but right now is looking very much as though she's not been invited to the ball. She's picking at the chips listlessly, handing most of them to Dotty who thinks it's her birthday.

We're supposed to be celebrating having organized the flowers, photographer, and - massive achievement if I say so myself - the catering. Not only that, but we've managed to use all local suppliers which Tory insisted on. All of them have had to sign a secrecy document (which Freddy thought they should sign in blood, but I thought was a bit excessive), although the rumours are inevitably beginning to circulate. And with the band being sorted out by Noah, which let's be honest is pretty exciting, Tory should be over the moon.

'What's wrong sweet?' I ask her, wondering if she's pining after said prince who's had to go back to Ireland again for a few days filming.

Tory glances over at me and smiles wanly. My heart goes out to her. I know she doesn't feel well. The morning sickness is really beginning to take its toll. She's actually started carrying extra large doggy poo bags in case she needs to put her head in one (obviously unused of course). There's no way she's going to be able to keep the happy event secret for much longer.

I put my arm around her and she rests her head on my shoulders. 'What am I going to do if I'm still like this on the day?' she whispers eventually.

For a second I don't answer. The truth is I have no idea. It's going to look pretty bloody strange if she carries a sick bucket down the aisle – even if we decorate it with ribbons and flowers. I know that the thought of throwing up in front of Hollywood's glitterati is really worrying her.

'Have you spoken to Noah about your fears?' I ask, stroking her slightly damp forehead with concern. Tory shakes her head.

'I know he'll postpone the ceremony if I say I can't go through with it, but I don't want to disappoint him.' She pauses, then continues with a sigh. 'And I don't want him to think I'm getting cold feet. I did a lot of damage with my stupidity in the summer Kitty Kat.'

'Look, we've got six weeks yet – ages to go. You'll be much better by then Tory, I'm sure. And look on the bright side. You've not put on any weight – in fact I think you might have lost some.'

'That's six weeks and I haven't even got my wedding dress yet,' she snaps and I'm actually relieved to hear her grouchy response. But still, I have no answer for her. We've not been able to go dress shopping at all. The prospect of vomiting all over a designer wedding gown is just too awful for words. Even if it is only a sample...

'OH NO I DIDN'T!' signals the arrival of Freddy, still very obviously in pantomime mode, posing at the pub door.

'I'm pretty bloody sure you did actually – pervert,' counters Tory with the first smile I've seen her give since we got here.

Chuckling, Freddy allows the door to shut behind him and, grabbing another glass from the barman, heads over to our table.

'Hello you greedy, dirty little madam. If only they were all like you sweetie.' He's obviously not talking to either me or Tory as he bends down to stroke an ecstatic Dotty who wastes no time rolling excitedly onto her back.

'So, bring it on my lovelies.' He sits down and holds out his glass before glancing over at Tory's sparkling water and sighing. 'So when are you going drop the charade and come clean Victory Shackleford, soon to become Westbrook, not to mention mother to be of the first of the Westbrook dynasty?'

We stare at him in surprised silence. 'Oh come on peeps, surely you didn't expect to keep something so momentous from little old me did you?' His response is scornful, but underneath I can see he's actually quite hurt, although he covers it up well with a small cough and a large gulp of sparkling wine.

I share a quick look with Tory. We both know it's useless to deny it and anyway, who'd have guessed that our mocking sarcastic friend has a sensitive side. I can only say he's always kept it well hidden...

'I'm sorry Freddy,' responds Tory, putting her hand on his arm. 'We haven't told anybody. Only Noah outside of this room knows about it. I just didn't want my father to find out. You know what a stickler he is for doing things in the right order.'

'Unless he's the one doing the doing,' is Freddy's wounded retort, not yet ready to forgive.

'Oh come on,' I can't help but interrupt. I can see where this is going. Any minute now, he'll be applying for sainthood. 'You can't keep a secret if your life depends on it. The last time you were told to keep something hush-hush, we had a call from the Daily Mail within forty eight hours.

Freddy sniffs before sighing in acceptance. 'I'm just not made to keep things in the closet sweetie. In the words of Andy Warhol, 'I'm a deeply superficial person.'

'You will try to keep this to yourself though won't you?' Tory stares at him earnestly. 'This is so important to me Freddy. I don't want my father to find out from anyone other than me.'

'I'm afraid it's pretty bloody obvious to anyone capable of looking further than the end of their nose with you rushing to the bog every two minutes. It's a good job your old man's nose generally never gets any further than his feet.' Freddy's response is typically caustic, but I can see that Tory's entreaty has hit home. 'Mind you, I think old Jason what's his face might have twigged during dinner.'

'Shit, do you think so?'

'Pretty bloody difficult to miss. It's where I would have cottoned on – if I hadn't realized long before then of course.'

'Look it's no good worrying about things we can't control Tory. Nobody will tell the Admiral, and it's not like your social calendar is full to bursting is it?'

'And that's another thing. With Noah in toe, our Victory has become the numero uno in Dartmouth. Everyone and his dog wants her to be at their shindigs. She can't keep turning everyone down.'

'I do have some personality of my own you know,' Tory retorts indignantly, her sudden huffiness doing wonders in taking her mind off her stomach.

'Of course you do sweetheart, and we love you. But it has to be said that before *The Bridegroom* circus arrived and Noah decided that you were the one key to fit his lock, your average invitation was to speak about soft furnishings at the Women's Institute.'

I can't help it, I snort into my drink as Tory turns to look over at me crossly. 'Some friends you two are,' she grumbles, although I notice she doesn't argue.

'Have you been to the docs sweetie?'

'Of course, but he just said that feeling like shit is normal for the first trimester. Actually said it far too cheerfully if you ask me. Naturally he has no idea I'm walking up the bloody aisle on the twentieth of December.'

'What's a trimester?' We both look at him in astonishment.

'Don't look at me as though I'm a complete plank. It's not like babies have ever been my thing is it?'

'Clue's in the tri,' Tory responds sarcastically. Yep she's back to nasty. Yippee. 'It's the first three months of pregnancy, which for me ends just before the big day...'

'Well there you go then. That's good isn't it?'

'Absolutely,' I respond quickly before Tory manages to slip in more doom and gloom. I'm definitely going for an extended holiday when she announces the conception of baby number two.

'All we need is to catch you on a day you're feeling pretty good and go find your dress. Easy peasy.'

Freddy looks at me in horror. 'You haven't bought the dress yet?'

I glare at him, mouthing, 'You're not helping,' as Tory puts her head in her hands. Freddy gives a sigh of one long suffering, and puts his arm around the bride to be.

'Come on sweetie, buck up. Have you seen anything you like on the internet?' I wince as Tory looks up, her face stricken. Way to go dumbbell.

'Lots. But everything has to be ordered months in advance.'

'Oh come on, get with the programme people. You're marrying the world's most famous actor. Any designer worth their salt would knock you up a dress overnight to bag a commission like that. Have you mentioned this little problem to your husband to be perchance?' Tory's face lights up as she grasps what he's saying.

I want to kiss him and kill him at the same time. Why the hell didn't I think of that?

'It'll be easy,' he continues, on a roll now. 'Once you've chosen the dress you want, we'll measure your bits. Then you can tell

Noah – without giving him the details of course – and he'll make sure you get it. I mean, come on, you could order half a dozen while you're at it and choose the best one.' Excitedly, he shares the remainder of the Prosecco and downs his in one.

'Come on ladies, finish your chips so we can go and shop.'

~*~

Florence put down the phone with a feeling of satisfaction. Although it hadn't yet been confirmed that the shadow on her lung was cancer, she wanted to make sure she had all her ducks in a row regarding her will.

Of course, everything was to go to Kit and she needed to make sure there were no loopholes that might allow her money grabbing brother to get his greedy hands on her money. But now she'd been assured that there was no chance of that, she could relax. Leaning back, she looked out onto the terrace feeling melancholy. What she'd told Kit was true. She did always get over-emotional and weepy when she'd completed a book, because she inevitably followed it with a trip down memory lane. Of course, waiting for her hospital appointment wasn't helping either.

What she needed was a distraction. Idly leaning forward to pluck Pepé off her leg, she snuggled him on her lap and kissed the top of his head. The rain was beating against the window making it all but impossible to see anything past the edge of the terrace. She hoped the weather didn't stay like this. It would be nice if Tory had a dry day at least, and all this rain wasn't very Christmassy at all. Certainly wouldn't help people get into the spirit of the season.

Then she had a sudden idea. That's it, something to get everyone into the Christmas spirit

A murder mystery night to celebrate the release of her latest book. It would be perfect, as her latest was a suspense, and a bit of a departure from her usual hot romance. She'd hold it at the end of November, far enough away from the wedding that it wouldn't interfere with any plans, but close enough to the holiday season to get everyone into the right spirit. Maybe she could do it the weekend before Thanksgiving in honour of Noah.

Full of excitement now, she mentally counted off guests she'd invite. She'd even send an invitation to Charlie Shackleford, even though they hadn't seen or spoken to one another for years. Perhaps it really was time to stop harking back to the past.

Hopefully by the end of November, her brother and his wife would be too far away to come.

Just let the bastard attempt to find a loophole in her will. She didn't doubt for a second that he'd try, and the knowledge that Kit was to inherit everything would in no way deter him. After all said and done, she wasn't really his daughter.

Chapter Six

It has to be said that Tory's been significantly happier since the dress problem has been sorted out. I had no idea that it was bothering her so much. Some friend I am...

In the end it took us two days to come up with three designs we could all agree on. We measured every available inch of Tory's body - even her squidgy bits (Freddy's words – I used cuddly, but then I'm her BFF, and even if I don't cotton on to her innermost feelings, it's got to be good for something). Of course in the next few weeks the cuddly bits will start to disappear, along hopefully with her morning sickness and bad temper...

Anyway, Noah simply instructed his new agent to get in touch, and hey presto, we've got three gorgeous choices, plus a couple of (stretchy) "going away" outfits winging their way to us by the end of next week. God I love what money and influence can do.

We're now down to five weeks before the big day, and this afternoon we've been invited up to BRNC to have a look round the Chapel for the ceremony, and the Senior Gunroom where the wedding breakfast will be held. We've got to be a bit circumspect obviously as the College population are still very much in residence. Mind you, it is a Sunday which means that most of the cadets and a large number of the officers will be away doing the weekend thing, and if we do bump into anyone, I can do cloak and dagger – I love a good whodunit. And we mustn't forget after all that the queen of crime, Agatha Christie was born in this neck of the woods, so it's got to have rubbed off somewhere.

Of course the only fly in the ointment is the Admiral who's also coming along, and obviously doesn't do circumspect – or if he does, I've never seen it.

So, after we've had a good old snoop, we're having a late lunch with Captain Buchannan at his house. See, I've graduated to calling him Captain instead of knob. I daren't let myself use Jason. It's far too intimate and, although I haven't admitted it to anyone, I'm actually having a lot of intimacy issues with regard to the gorgeous Captain. Well, my body is – especially those bits that haven't seen the light of day in far too long.

Unfortunately our efforts at incognito are not as polished as they could be as our cavalcade arrives up at the Captain's House. We might as well have had a fanfare and ceremonial fly past by the Red Arrows to announce our arrival. By the time we've all managed to extract ourselves from Noah's Mercedes, the guys on the Main Gate have obviously sent a signal to the rest of the College that we're here.

I sigh as I glance up at the main façade, spying the curtains twitching and faces pressed to the windows. So much for keeping a low profile. There might only be a fraction of the College population in residence, but that won't stop the pictures appearing on Facebook. Maybe I was a little naïve thinking we could do this without anyone knowing. Still, they might think we're just having lunch with the Captain.

I slam the car door a little more loudly than I intended, my irritation getting the better of me. Noah glances over at me, eyebrows raised. 'Sorry,' I mumble, watching as he helps Tory out of the passenger side.

'Something wrong Kit?' he asks calmly, and I sigh in response.

'Just a bit frustrated. I thought we'd managed to arrange this visit without anyone finding out, but, well, look?' I give an exasperated wave towards the windows high above the Parade Ground.

To my amazement, Noah chuckles. 'In my line of work, nothing is ever done without someone finding out honey. You get used to it. Sometimes it's actually better to give the gossipmongers something to talk about - kinda like a false trail – while you get on with the real job.'

'Mmm, a red herring,' I respond – obviously still got my sleuthing head on. Giving one last speculative glance up to the faces pressed against the windows, I follow the other three towards Captain Buchannan's front door, already open and waiting with good old Dave, the PO Steward, at the door.

As we go through into the large reception hall, I see Tory take hold of her father's arm with a smile. I'd forgotten that she'd spent three years of her childhood within these walls. The Admiral is strangely silent as he pauses, glancing around, no doubt looking for possible changes. Then he exhales noisily and pats Tory's hand before laboriously making his way towards the drawing room where Dave is waiting respectfully in the doorway.

'Good to see you again Sir,' the tall man murmurs with a slight dip of his head. The Admiral shrugs off his sombre mood and somehow seems all of a sudden taller and more imposing. Letting go of Tory's arm, he nods back, and holds out his hand. 'Good to see you again David, it's been too long.' His voice is crisp and authoritative and I have to do a double take to check it's actually our Admiral speaking. I feel like everyone is holding their breath, wondering if some alien has somehow inhabited Charles Shackleford's body.

Fortunately, before we get chance to insist on a full body scan, he reverts back to his usual tone of voice, saying 'Well, I have to say you're definitely smelling a bit sweeter nowadays. Last time we were together, I remember your armpits being about as sweet smelling as the inside of a sumo wrestler's jock strap.'

We all gasp at the Admiral's rudeness while being somehow reassured that, yes, this is definitely Tory's father, and his unique charm is still very much evident.

There's a small silence as everyone wracks their brains for something polite to say about Dave's obviously new found personal hygiene habits, but, to the surprise of all and sundry, the tall man throws back his head and laughs. Then, without enlightening the rest of us, he shakes his head, and still chuckling, indicates we should follow him in to the drawing room. As we step forward, Noah and I glance over at Tory, and she shrugs, obviously as much in the dark as we are. I can tell Noah is definitely filing this one away for later – probably over a glass of Port, with no delicate females present...

Tea and stickies are already laid out on the table. After instructing us to help ourselves, Dave announces that the Captain will be with us shortly, before withdrawing discreetly.

In the end, it's another twenty minutes before said Captain shows and I really hope he's not hungry. The forlorn looking Jaffa cake left in the middle of the plate is not likely to appease all but the slightest hunger pangs. As he strides into the room, I can't help but draw in my breath. Still in uniform, although it's technically his day off, Jason Buchannan oozes authority and sex appeal in equal measure. I don't think I've ever felt quite so intimidated by anybody.

I glance over at Noah rising from his chair with a genuine smile of welcome on his face. He doesn't appear to feel threatened at all, but then he's a Hollywood A lister and pretty hard to intimidate. Mind you, Tory gives no indication of being overawed either, remaining in her seat with slightly pursed lips, indicating that the verdict on the good Captain is still out as far as she's concerned.

And the Admiral? Well I don't think he's ever been intimidated by anyone in his life. His only comment when asked his opinion of Jason Buchannan was to huff and say, 'He's got more bollocks than his old man, but I don't think I could warm to the chap if we were cremated together.'

So it's just me then.

I become aware that the object of my night-time fantasies and daytime anxiety has finished speaking and is now looking at me enquiringly. I have no idea what he's just said and feel myself colouring up. Tory looks over at my face and gets it in one. With a frown that promises an in depth conversation for later, she jumps to my rescue. 'I'm sure Kit is more than happy to go over the initial VTM with you before catching up with us.'

I look from her back to Jason Buchannan before whispering sheepishly, 'Err, what's a VTM?'

The Captain sighs loudly before saying in impatient, clipped tones, 'Visitors Temporary Memorandum. At this stage it's basically an initial outline of the events of the day.'

The look on his face is doing nothing for my self-confidence, and suddenly, for no earthly reason I can fathom, my backbone chooses this precise moment to stiffen.

'Captain Buchannan, it really isn't necessary to talk to me in quite that tone. You're beginning to sound like a possible descendent of Attila The Hun. You're not are you?' I finish sweetly.

There's a small silence while everyone looks at me as though I've grown another head, and I wonder if I've taken it a tad too far. That's what comes with being the confrontation avoiding type. When I snap, it usually involves bad manners. He's actually lucky I didn't use a few more choice words.

I can see Tory mouthing, 'WTF?' at me in the corner of my eye, but just as it looks as though she intends to jump in with some kind of damage limitation exercise, Jason nods his head and gives a slight smile.

'Touché,' he murmurs softly before continuing in a much milder voice, 'I apologize Ms Davies. You're absolutely correct. I don't suffer fools gladly, but sometimes I forget that not every person I speak to is one. Would you mind stopping behind to go through the initial VTM with me?'

We stare at one another, and for a few heart stopping seconds everyone disappears except for the two of us. His eyes are intent, unfathomable and I feel the breath hitch in my throat.

Then a discreet cough brings me back to my surroundings, and glancing over at Noah's amused face, I clear my throat and stare down at my lap before saying gruffly, 'Of course I'll stay behind, and please, call me Kit.'

The other three have left in the company of a young officer

who was so obviously excited to meet a Hollywood idol, he was like a large puppy. The awesome red herring we've come up with is that the Admiral has a great nephew who is interested in joining the Royal Navy and Noah simply wanted to come along for the tour. Okay, so maybe it's not so amazing, but it was spur of the moment and it might actually keep the masses from putting two and two together – at least for a little while.

Jason (see I'm using Jason now we're best buds...) has popped out to do whatever it is Captains do when they pop out, and left me with a ten page VTM to have a look at. God knows how long the final version's going to be.

Apparently, his Personal Assistant put it together, but when I queried her discretion, he drily responded that if she could keep a private visit by the Queen under her hat, then she should have no problem doing the same for a simple wedding.

In the spirit of our new found camaraderie I gamely resisted the urge to point out that while a visit by Her Majesty might well cause a stir with the locals, the marriage ceremony of global superstar Noah Westbrook is more likely to cause a complete uproar. And not just with those living in the vicinity. Oh well, it's his call...

I'm sitting with my back to the door but know the instant he walks through it. Not by sound - his footsteps are silent - but by the something inside me that tingles every time he's near me. I know, ridiculous, but there we are. My heart starts beating faster as he approaches, and the words in front of me smudge and blur. He places a hand on the back of the sofa to the right of my shoulder and leans forward. I can smell his cologne – the subtle spicy scent that's uniquely Jason Buchannan. Heart hammering, I sit completely still and wait for him to speak.

He doesn't say anything, just bends his head towards me so I can feel his breath, warm on my neck. Unable to help myself I lean my body to the left and look up, over my shoulder. He's closer than I thought, and as I turn my head, his eyes lock on mine. I can feel the pull of attraction, so sharp it almost hurts.

He watches me unsmiling and it suddenly dawns on me that

he doesn't like whatever it is that's between us. Doesn't like it one bit. I wait for him to make some kind of scathing comment – anything to put an end to this weird draw.

'Would you like some more tea?' When he finally speaks, his voice is low and distracted, as though the words that came out of his mouth were not what he really wanted to say.

I blink and shake my head, no. Then, still trapped in the strange otherworld where only the two of us exist, I bite my bottom lip, succumbing to a question that I've wanted, needed to ask since our first meeting.

'Why do you dislike me so much?'

Without answering, he frowns and straightens up sharply, pushing himself away from the sofa. For a few seconds, I think he's not actually going to respond to my question. I watch him walk around the coffee table and seat himself opposite me. Then, with a sigh, he leans back and raises his eyes to look at me.

'I don't dislike you Kit.' His voice when he speaks is mild and impersonal. 'I must apologize if I gave you that impression.' He pauses, and thinking that's as much as he's going to say, I can't help but sag back in disappointment. Until this second, I had no idea how important his answer was to me.

However, to my surprise, he continues, his tone no longer cold and aloof, but filled with an almost dark humour. 'I'm not a patient man Kit. I take my duties and responsibilities seriously and I hate things I can't control...'

He stops abruptly, leaving the impression in the air that I am one of those things, then his voice deepens, all humour gone from it. 'You are not...'

But I have no idea what he thinks I'm not, because we're interrupted by a discreet cough, causing him to look up, sudden surprise etched on his face, giving me the fleeting impression that Jason Buchannan is not a man used to being caught unawares.

'Yes?' he says over my head. His voice has changed back to politely distant and I swallow my disappointment.

'I'm sorry to bother you Sir, but you asked me to give you a half an hour warning for lunch. Would you like me to serve the predinner drinks in here?'

'Thanks David, I'm sure the others will be back shortly. We'll give them ten minutes, then yes, aperitifs in here will be good.' He turns back to me, asking in the same bland tone, 'Are you happy to wait for ten minutes Kit, or would you like a glass of wine now?'

I'm torn between concern that he thinks I've got a drink problem, and frustration that I might never get to know what he thinks I'm not. Any intimacy has vanished. I could actually do with a drink, but not wanting to further any belief that I'm a closet alcoholic, I laugh lightly and say that of course I'm happy to wait.

After David withdraws, equally discreetly, I say nothing, hoping that Jason will continue where he left off. But his next words quickly make it obvious that that particular ship has well and truly sailed.

'So what are your initial thoughts about the VTM?'

I glance back down at the forgotten document in my hand. 'I think you've pretty much covered everything but the kitchen sink,' I say drily. 'I take it you've been briefed fully by Noah about the, err, entertainment for the evening?' To my surprise he grins slightly, making him look much younger. 'Absolutely. I only hope I get an invitation.'

'Well then, as I see it, the only question still outstanding is the name of the padre who the Admiral intends to ask to conduct the ceremony, and I'm afraid I have no idea what...' We're interrupted again, this time by the loud voice of the subject of our conversation.

'...Speak of the devil, we can ask him.'

'Well it's all looking ship-shape and Bristol fashion.' The Admiral's booming voice precedes him into the room. 'Good to see you're looking after the place Captain Buchannan.'

'Thank you Admiral Shackleford, I'm very glad you approve.' Jason's tone is completely free of sarcasm, but nevertheless manages to convey just the right amount of irony to leave the Admiral frowning slightly and the rest of us looking at him admiringly. I glance over at Tory who's trying hard not to grin. I can tell she's thinking that maybe our good Captain is not such a stuck up, unapproachable knob after all…

'How come you didn't get to catch us up?' Tory asks, her voice deceptively nonchalant as she seats herself next to me.

'I wanted to make sure that both Kit and I are singing from the same hymn sheet,' Jason cuts in smoothly. 'I'll be more than happy to show her around the areas to be used for the wedding if she feels it's necessary.' Somehow his voice manages to convey both willingness and reluctance, all in the same sentence.

Tory raises her eyebrows at me as I answer stiffly, 'I don't think that will be necessary at the moment. I've been to the College before.' I turn back to my best friend who's now smirking at my awkward tone. 'What about flowers, decorations etc Tory?'

'I think I'd like flowers in the chapel and in the Senior Gunroom if that's where we're holding the wedding breakfast. Also, perhaps along the main corridor?' She says the last bit as a question, turning towards Jason as she speaks.

'It's all very spectacular Captain Buchannan, but could possibly be a little, err, dark on a winter's day.'

Jason waves off her apologetic tone. 'The place is a bloody mausoleum, no need to beat around the bush. There will be lots of Christmas decorations around the place though, which should cheer it up a bit if the day's overcast.'

'*Hogwarts*,' I announce suddenly, only to be interrupted by David bringing in the aperitifs. My mind starts racing as the predinner drinks are distributed, and I absently note Tory frowning at her glass before reluctantly taking a small sip. I know she doesn't want to add any more fuel to the fire while her father's sitting there, but personally I think she's over thinking things. The Admiral is so thick skinned, she could be nine months pregnant and he'd probably just comment that she's put on a bit of weight…

After informing us that lunch will be in fifteen minutes, David withdraws and everyone turns back to me.

'We should deck the whole place out like Christmas at *Hog-*

warts in the *Harry Potter* movies,' I continue excitedly, 'You know, lots of Christmas trees, festoons of lights and holly and mistletoe. It will look amazing.' Tory is nodding her head in enthusiasm.

'Can we do that?' she asks Jason eagerly.

The Captain frowns in response, and for a second I think he's going to refuse, but in the end he just nods his head slightly.

'I don't see why not, providing you can get a security approved company to do the decorating. It will have to wait until the College is closed and the staff and cadets have left for the holidays. That will only give you a couple of days, but if you think it can be done…'

He allows his voice to peter out, looking towards Noah who simply grins back, saying, 'Kit and I are on to it. We'll keep you in the loop.'

Lunch is a very animated, light-hearted affair with everyone putting in their two pennies worth. I make copious notes in between the roast beef and apple crumble, and suddenly trepidation is replaced by excitement. I can't wait to tell Freddy. My best friend's wedding is going to be simply amazing, I just know it is. This day will be talked about for years to come.

It's only as we're leaving that I remember we haven't asked the Admiral about his choice of padre. Too weary to tackle the question in the car, I make a mental note to give Tory's father a call over the next couple of days. I mean, the guy's a naval chaplain after all, so it's not like it's going to be a problem is it?

Chapter Seven

Admiral Shackleford squeezed himself at the small table right at the very back of the coffee shop he'd deliberately picked for his first meeting with Bible Basher Boris. Directly on the tourist trail in the middle of Dartmouth, it was less likely to be frequented by anyone who knew him. Obviously he'd have preferred this meeting to have taken place well away from Dartmouth – The Outer Hebrides actually sprang to mind. However, at this stage he didn't want to give old Boris the idea that he was keeping their meeting under wraps.

Once seated, he looked furtively round at the coffee shop's other customers to see if he recognized anybody. After a second, he relaxed. His was definitely the only cup of tea in a sea of bloody lattes, and no doubt after Boris had finished doing his party piece, neither of them were likely to be invited back.

Taking a large bite out of his cheese scone, the Admiral reflected that this would be the first time he'd seen his old friend since Celia's funeral, and God knows the old padre had looked as though he'd just been dug up even back then.

'Charles, how are you, you old rascal?' The Admiral winced as he turned in horrified disbelief towards the doddering bag of bones heading his way.

~*~

It's been three days since we had lunch up at the College, and for some reason Tory's father seems reluctant to give out the details of the chaplain he's got stashed away. I'm sitting at the balcony window idly people watching while eating toast and marmite – my go to breakfast when I'm pondering a problem. The problem here is, while I'm not sure there *is* an actual problem, I have enough experience with the Admiral to know when there's *something* fishy going on. And therein lies the problem…

I can't call him up on it. He's had decades of experience in the art of being slippery and evasive – I'm a mere babe in arms when it comes to the kind of cloak and dagger stuff the Admiral thrives on.

I don't want to worry Tory, for obvious reasons, and Noah's up in London meeting with his agent. Anyway, what if I'm completely wrong?

Sighing, I pop the last piece of crust in my mouth. Everything else is going so well. We have a special effects company coming down the day after tomorrow to do a recce up at the College, and I just know that the whole place really is going to look completely amazing when they've done their stuff.

Glancing down at street below, I spy the postman dropping something into my letter box, so deciding to let the whole chaplain thing go for now, I pop down to grab my mail instead.

Most of it's the usual junk, but as I walk slowly back upstairs, I spy an envelope with Aunt Flo's writing. Frowning slightly, I prize open the seal and pull out the contents.

It's an invitation to a murder mystery evening at her cottage. Surprise stops me in my tracks. This is so not like her. While my aunt loves informal gatherings, staged parties – especially in her private sanctuary – are something she's never really indulged in. I glance down at the date and notice it's scheduled for the end of November. Curiouser and curiouser…

Putting aside my concerns about Tory's scheming old man, I run up the rest of the stairs, determined to give her a call.

Five minutes later, I'm juggling a cup of coffee, another slice of toast and the phone.

'Okay, you scheming old witch, what's all this about? You planning to murder somebody for real while trying to cover your tracks, or is this a publicity stunt for your latest literary masterpiece?' I question without preamble. The ribald chuckle at the other end of the line does a lot to alleviate my disquiet.

'Why, you think I'm too old to host a party?' is her caustic comeback.

I snort inelegantly into the phone before responding, 'Of course not, it's just that your usual idea of having a good time is to let someone else do all the hard work. Who have you invited?'

'Well, there's you of course, and Neil. Then there's Tory, Noah, and Freddy. I've even invited Charles and Mabel.' I suck my breath in surprise. There's never been any love lost between Tory's dad and my aunt – I have no idea why. I've always assumed they've just never seen eye to eye. 'Blimey, that's a turn up for the books. What's it all in aid of?'

'It's to celebrate the release of my new book of course. This one has much more mystery in it than my usual offering.'

'Ah, lots of bonking in cupboards then.'

She chuckles again, before going on to say, 'My editor's coming too. As you know, he came out of the wardrobe recently, so I thought it was about time he met Freddy.'

'You mean he came out of the closet,' I say with a grin. For all that my aunt writes pretty racy stuff, she's actually not very clued up with a lot of modern slang.

'I've arranged it specifically for the weekend before Thanksgiving in case Noah's missing his family.'

'Well, as to that, he might not actually be missing them,' I say, remembering the recent conversation with the actor. 'I think Noah's sister's family are coming over early to get into the spirit of things so to speak, so you might have a few more guests than you bargained for.'

'The more the merrier,' Aunt Flo replies breezily, 'It'll make the whole murder thing more interesting, and get everyone in the mood for the wedding'

I'm about to ask how solving a murder is likely to help everyone get in the right kind of mood for a wedding, when all of a sudden my attention is diverted as I spot the Admiral skulking in the street below my window. Only half listening to my aunt's plans, I open the balcony door and lean out to see what the old bugger's up to. I can't hear his words, but he's definitely talking to someone and as he steps into the road, that someone comes into view. He's wearing a dog collar and I wonder if this is the elusive chaplain. As he turns round, I draw in my breath. The man seems ancient. He's thin, stooped, and looks as though a gust of wind would blow him over.

And I feel as though I've seen him somewhere before.

~*~

Jason Buchannan was on his way to a meeting at The Ministry of Defence's main building in the heart of London. He should have been spending his time on the train reading up on the forthcoming brief and making the necessary notes.

Instead, the documents lay unopened in front of him while he doodled on a blank piece of paper, his mind completely elsewhere. He was well aware that Kit Davies was dominating far more of his thoughts than was sensible, but he couldn't seem to help himself.

It had been so long since he'd had a proper relationship, spending years avoiding any kind of emotional contact. There had been plenty of women more than happy to share his bed, and he made sure to stay well away from any woman who was likely to be more than a passing fling.

After Laura, his life had been completely dominated by work, and up until now, he'd been content to leave it that way.

But since Kit had unexpectedly appeared on his doorstep at Bloodstone Tower, nothing had been the same. The emptiness he'd closeted away so carefully, now threatened to rise up and choke him. The stupid thing was she didn't even like him.

The mechanical tones of the train's speaker system signalled their imminent arrival at Paddington Station. Sighing, he gathered together the unread papers and put them back into his briefcase, then shrugging on his greatcoat, made his way to the nearest door. He was completely unaware of the impressive figure he cut in his naval uniform as he strode up towards the concourse at Paddington.

Maybe he should offer to take Kit out for dinner. The upcoming media circus would provide a good excuse. Once the whole thing was over, he knew he'd stand no chance of getting her to see his good side. He chuckled mirthlessly at that thought. Most people would declare categorically that Jason Buchannan didn't have a good side – he'd been described as a hard ruthless bastard on more than one occasion.

As he handed over his ticket to the guard, and headed out towards the taxi rank, he made an effort to drag his thoughts back to the upcoming meeting. Joining the queue, he checked his mobile phone to see if there were any messages from his PA, and settled down to wait. He knew from experience that getting frustrated with London cab drivers was a futile exercise – the only thing that ever came out of it was high blood pressure.

As the queue crept forward agonizingly slowly, he filled in the time by scrolling down his messages. Suddenly, to his left, he heard his name being called in a breathless but familiar voice. Lifting his head with a slight frown, he looked directly into the eyes of the woman he hadn't seen in over eighteen years, the woman who had broken his heart.

~*~

We're cosily ensconced in the drawing room of Noah and Tory's house watching the rain beating a tattoo on the large bi-fold doors, which under more clement conditions provide the most stunning view of the River Dart and the open sea. Now, the downpour is obscuring all but the edge of the patio, creating the impression that we're adrift in a timeless dimension. I share my whimsical notion with Freddy as we wait for Tory to bring in our picnic lunch, but I should have known better. All I receive in return is a loud snort.

'You have no romance in your soul,' I mutter sourly in answer, 'God knows how you got involved in the creative arts.'

'I'm a bloody good shag darling, surely you knew that?'

I look up, interested despite myself. I never did know how Freddy got his current job. I open my mouth to ask the question but the irritating man drags his index finger across his closed lips before saying dramatically, 'My lips are forever sealed.'

'FREDDY.' The demanding voice of our hostess puts an end to the conversation before I can use my womanly guile to get him to spill the beans. To be fair, Freddy's not really susceptible to womanly anything, but as I may have previously mentioned, keeping secrets is not really his strong point.

'Coming sweetie.' I can't help but notice his eagerness to put an end to the conversation, and I make a mental note to bring it up later when we haven't got bridesmaid stuff to sort out.

A minute or so later, Freddy emerges from the kitchen with a tray nearly as big as he is. 'Bloody hell,' he puffs, staggering towards the coffee table, 'How long are you expecting this to take?' Hard at his heels is Dotty, as always on the trail of her next snack.

'We could be here sometime,' our hostess retorts, following him in with plates, napkins and cutlery, and anyway, I wanted to do something nice for you both. I'm well aware that I.. err...' She pauses, grimacing as she tries to find the right words.

'Well,' she finally continues quietly, 'It has to be said that I've err been a trifle difficult of late.'

Of course Freddy who's about as tactful as a sledgehammer, deposits his load, and, collapsing onto the sofa, declares that dealing with her over the last few weeks has been akin to working with a bomb disposal unit – we're never quite sure when she's likely to go off.

Tory opens her mouth to respond, then closes it firmly with a wounded sigh, refusing to rise to the bait. I look at her admiringly. She does martyrdom very well, but to be fair it doesn't usually last. Deciding a change of subject is in order before she gives in and they start bickering in earnest, I lean forward and help myself to a warm slice of salmon en croute – God I love Marks and Spencer.

'So okay, long overdue, but what is the bridesmaid - aka me –

going to wear?'

'I'm hoping there are going to be two of you,' Tory murmurs, helping herself to some pie. 'Noah's niece Madison is coming up to eight. His sister Kim says she thinks her daughter would love to be a bridesmaid.

'Of course, you'll be my maid of honour Kit,' she adds hastily, and I wonder when she decided I'm so sensitive that I might actually be jealous of an eight year old. Hormones...

'Excellent,' I respond enthusiastically to head that particular worry off at the pass. 'So what colour are we going for? I'm happy to wear any colour except mauve. I really don't look good in mauve.'

'Well as we're pulling the big guns out with the Christmassy theme, I thought we'd go for red velvet – sort of like Vera Ellen in *White Christmas,* you know the one? Do you think that would be a bit tacky?' Her voice is tentatively excited and I know she's hoping I'll agree with her. And you know what, I don't care if it is a bit tacky – this is Hollywood baby.

'I love it,' I reply warmly, 'You think we're going to be able to get something like that made before the deadline?'

'We'll just ask Noah,' the three of us shout together before falling about giggling.

'Of course we're going to need Madison's measurements pretty sharpish,' I say when we're back to serious.

'Kim's emailing them to me as we speak.' Tory's face is flushed and her eyes are shining. I grin at her. It's so good to see her looking like her old self.

'Okay, so what about me peeps?' Freddy says leaning forward excitedly, 'I'm sure I could do a mean Bing Crosby.' We both look over at him, wordlessly. The thought of Freddy in red velvet and a white fur hat rendering both of us speechless. 'What?' he asks crossly when we start giggling again...

Two hours later I think we've nailed it. Red velvet, fitted to the waist with a white faux fur trim. Mine will be slightly off the shoulder and Madison's will have a collar. Of course Dotty will be there too - an additional doggy bridesmaid, complete with her very own red satin bow. I predict it will last half an hour before she manages to get it off...

We've managed to persuade Freddy that red velvet for him is not the way forward, at which point Tory moans that she hasn't even thought about what the groom and the best man are going to wear.

'Who is Noah's best man anyway?' I ask while we're on the subject. I can honestly say, it's never occurred to me to ask before. Some wedding planner I am.

'A chap called Ethan Sullivan, he's a singer.' Tory murmurs absently, frantically googling morning suits. She's staring down at her iPad so doesn't realize for a few seconds that we've gone completely silent. 'What?' she asks finally, looking up at our identical stupefied expressions.

'I can't believe you never thought to mention this before,' Freddy eventually manages to splutter. 'Are you serious? Ethan Sullivan – *the* Ethan Sullivan is Noah's best man?'

'Yes he is. He and Noah have been friends for donkey's years apparently. I thought I'd told you.'

We both shake our heads simultaneously, still seriously lost for words. Ethan Sullivan is the lead singer of *Chemistry,* one of the most famous bands in the world. Tall, blond, with a body to die for, and a reputation of being a notorious womanizer, his exploits off the stage make as many appearances in the gossip columns as his antics on stage.

Suddenly it all clicks in to place. OMG, Tory is going to have *Chemistry* playing at her wedding. I feel quite faint and put it down to the central heating Tory's got cranked right up.

In a frenzy of excitement, Freddy jumps up and grabs the remnants of the French stick to use as an impromptu microphone before launching into *I Want You Now*, the band's most recent hit.

Now Freddy has all the components to be a fabulous singer - except the voice. He actually sounds like he's being strangled to death. Dotty enthusiastically adds to the mayhem by dancing around his legs barking. After an excruciating thirty seconds, I can't stand it any longer, and jumping up, I rugby tackle him to the sofa armed with a pillow to smother the awful racket.

'Don't give up the day job,' I laugh when he finally waves his hand in surrender from under the cushion.

'I think you might have broken my nose,' Freddy groans when he eventually manages to sit up.

'Good,' I answer bluntly, throwing the pillow back into the corner of the sofa. 'You're much too pretty anyway. And if it isn't broken, I swear to God I'll definitely do the deed properly if you so much as even hint at the idea of a duet with Ethan Sullivan during the wedding.'

'You never know, it might go viral, make me famous,' answers Freddy, tentatively pushing at the fleshy part of his nose

'Yep, and for all the wrong reasons. Tory's drunken rendition of *How Can I Live Without You* during this year's Dartmouth Regatta is still doing the rounds on YouTube. Last I looked, it was up to five million hits.'

'That's probably because Noah keeps sharing it with everyone,' Tory butts in indignantly, 'He says he's never laughed so much in his life. I really don't know why I'm marrying the insensitive bastard.'

'Because you love me sweetheart.' Noah's deep voice comes unexpectedly from the doorway causing Dotty to jump up with a fresh round of barking, before dashing over to her second favourite person.

After bending down to give her a fuss, Noah continues into the room. 'What was that god-awful noise I heard as I came in?' he asks sitting next to Tory and pulling her to him in a hug.

Tory snuggles into him with a sigh and I look over at them enviously. It's so obvious that Noah absolutely adores my best friend, and she's just as besotted. I wish I could find someone to love me as much.

Without warning, Jason Buchannan's face pops into my head. What would it be like to be loved passionately by a man like the Captain? Instinctively I know he's an all or nothing kind of guy, and I give an involuntary shiver as I remember the look in his eyes as he stared at me over the dinner table.

Fortunately, before I descend too far into the realms of fantasy, Freddy interrupts my reverie by deciding to take the stage. Jumping up, he poses dramatically, and points accusingly in Noah's direction.

'Aha, Noah Westbrook, Dartmouth's most beloved son, you dare flounce in here as though you have not most vilely withheld from us your closest - nay your bosom - companions, information of such import that it is uncertain as to whether we will be able to find it in our brave though wounded hearts to ever forgive you? Forsooth, you are indeed a cruel and pitiless ally. How could you not tell us your best man is the world famous bard Ethan Sullivan?'

Noah looks at him, eyebrows raised for a second, then grins, playing along. 'How could I dare to entrust such a secret with someone who's as loose lipped as a brothel keeper's morals?'

There's a silence as Freddy tries to think of a suitable comeback, then he collapses in defeat, saying, 'Not fair, you got that from the Admiral.'

Noah laughs saying, 'Are you kidding? I write them all down – you should try it yourself sometime.'

'We've been sorting out bridesmaids,' I cut in, putting an end to the banter after looking at Tory's anxious face, 'But we've just realized that we haven't given a thought to what you or your best man are going to wear.'

'Or the usher,' Freddy pipes up helpfully.

'Well I was thinking that as your old man's gonna be in his uniform, how about if me, Ethan and Freddy do the whole black tie thing? In fact we could extend it to all the male guests.' He grins enthusiastically. 'I've always wanted to play James Bond.'

Tory smiles in relief. 'That's a great idea, I love it,' she enthuses, throwing her arms around his neck.

'Can we leave all that to you and Freddy then?' I ask, equally relieved to pass over that particular problem.

'Yep, we'll get on to it. How about it Freddy, you up to making me look like the next double o seven?'

Freddy's face lights up, but before he can frame a suitable reply, I lean forward to warn him, 'No red velvet.' Freddy frowns in disappointment before giving in with a sigh.

'Have you spoken to Kim?' Tory asks Noah, deciding that a change of subject is in order. 'Are they coming for Thanksgiving?'

'I don't think so honey. Ben's folks can't make it over for the wedding, and as they're not gonna see their grandchildren over Christmas, Kim said it's only fair they get to spend Thanksgiving with the kids.'

Tory glances up at Noah as he's speaking. I know she's trying to gauge whether or not he's upset at the thought of not spending such a traditional American holiday with his family. Last year he was away filming. When she questions him softly, he responds by touching her face gently, murmuring, 'You're my family Tory – you and our baby. My home is wherever you are.'

As he speaks, I feel tears unexpectedly gather in the corners of my eyes. I feel like I'm intruding on a very private moment. I glance over at Freddy, expecting some caustic remark, but instead his face is serious, almost wistful, and it occurs to me that I'm not the only one who longs for the kind of relationship that Tory has.

I suddenly remember my last conversation with Aunt Flo, and her intention of inviting her editor to the murder mystery night so that he can meet Freddy. There and then, I decide that I'm going to do my damndest to get my second best friend fixed up. I ignore the small voice in the back of my head asking, 'What about me?' Instead, I ask my friends if they've received their invitations.

Both Tory and Freddy got theirs in the post yesterday, but as he's only just returned, Noah doesn't know anything about it. Enthusiastically we all fill him in on what's expected.

I explain that we'll be given our parts once Aunt Flo has received all the RSVPs. 'I know it's a bit of a busman's holiday for you Noah,' I grimace slightly, 'But I promise it's good fun. And, just in case you're too good, the rest of us amateurs will do our best to beat the thespian out of you.'

'Sounds great,' Noah laughs, 'Kim will be gutted to miss it.'

We finish the rest of the indoor picnic as the rain continues to beat on the windows, and Noah does his best to give us all some impromptu acting lessons. Eventually, however, after deciding the awful weather is probably in for the night, I reluctantly make a move to go.

'Come on Freddy, time to brave the elements before it gets too dark to see and we end up in the river.' Grumbling, Freddy follows me through to the hall and five minutes later I'm driving carefully down the winding lane towards the Lower Ferry.

'You okay?' I murmur eventually as Freddy' sits uncharacteristically silent. The brief glimpse of his face earlier has opened up a whole new side to my gay friend and I feel humbled and chastened, determined to amend my former opinion of him. 'What are you thinking about?' I continue softly.

There's a short pause and my heart goes out to him. I know he's trying to find the words to say how he feels. 'It's okay,' I murmur, patting his knee with my free hand. 'I understand. Sometimes it's difficult to put things into words.'

He looks over at me gratefully before letting out the loudest, longest fart I have ever heard. As I scramble to unwind the windows, he mutters, 'Thank God for that, I've been holding that in since the scotch eggs.

Chapter Eight

Although the wind and rain continued to rage into the small hours, the only signs of the night's stormy weather this morning are the multitude of damp leaves littering the pavement. The sun is casting a welcome watery light overhead as I hurry through the College gates to meet with our special effects experts.

Although Tory wanted to come with me this morning, I persuaded her not to with the excuse that she needs to badger Noah to order the bridesmaids dresses. But that's not the main reason. This, out of everything in the whole day, is my idea. I really want to make it spectacular for her, and of course, that includes giving her a wonderful surprise. I hope…

Keeping a low profile, I follow the two guys from Planet Gold as they wander from the Chapel, along the Main Corridor, onto the Quarterdeck and down to the Senior Gunroom. They are making copious notes and exude restrained excitement which is most definitely rubbing off on me. After about an hour, we retreat back to the Captain's house for coffee and planning.

I was told when we first arrived that Jason Buchannan was in London. I stifled the disappointment, telling myself that his absence was good. Much, much better to keep everything on a professional footing.

Of course, he's going to want to see exactly what kind of special effects we're intending to use in his College – obviously gold snitches, real live fairies, and fire breathing dragons are unfortunately out of the question.

The two men from Planet Gold are called Richard and Rupert – I know, sounds like a comedy duo. They've not actually been told about the wedding, just that a large private party is going to be held while the College is closed for the Christmas leave. I've gaily informed them that money is no object (haven't you always wanted to do that?) and by the time we've finished, I know that *Hogwarts* is going to have nothing on Britannia Royal Naval College on the twentieth of December.

They propose that the evening be finished off with a spectacular firework display – suggesting some fire breathing dragons might be possible after all. I nod my head excitedly, completely forgetting that permission has to be obtained for large scale displays of fireworks. I think the "money is no object" bit is going to my head. I'm not sure Noah had bribing local officials in mind when he said it.

After about an hour and a half, they depart, leaving me with a stack of sketches and leaflets, promising to come back with a firm price tomorrow.

Obviously there's no time to lose seeing as we've only got just over four weeks to go, so I stay behind in Jason Buchannan's drawing room to make some notes. I've asked Dave if he can get the sketches photocopied while I wait, so I can leave copies for the Captain. All in all, I'm feeling pretty good about myself.

Five minutes later he comes back into the room with a tray. 'Oh don't worry about more coffee,' I say looking up, 'I'm leaving as soon as the sketches have been copied.'

'Captain Buchannan has just returned from London ma'am,' the steward responds, putting down the tray. 'He's requested that you give him a few moments of your time before you depart.'

My heart thumps uncomfortably at the thought of meeting Jason so soon. I'm torn by wanting to see him again and hoping to avoid any possibility of him putting a kibosh on things – at least until he's had some time to actually go over Planet Gold's proposals.

I look down at my clothes – jeans, sweater and trainers. Not exactly hotty material, but then again, in the interests of keeping things purely professional, I'm spot on.

Nevertheless, I hurriedly I run my fingers through my hair and purse my lips together in an effort to get a bit of colour in them. I'm just in the process of adjusting my Wonderbra to try and give anyone looking at least the illusion of a cleavage, when the object of my thoughts strides in. He has the original sketches as well as the copies in his hand, but I don't know if that's a good or a bad thing.

'Kit,' he says in his usual clipped tones, and I have to fight the urge to stand up and salute. 'Would you like some coffee?'

I shake my head, murmuring, 'No thank you,' and nervously watch as he sits down and helps himself to a cup. Without speaking, he hands the original sketches over to me, then leans back to look at the copies.

In the ensuing minutes you could have heard a pin drop, and I mentally began to put together counter arguments for when he dismisses the whole idea. However, when he finally puts the drawings down beside him, all he says is, 'It's certainly going to look… spectacular.'

'Does that mean you'll allow it?' I ask the question quickly, wondering if I should have brought a tape recorder.

'I don't see that the decorations will be a problem,' he answers, shaking his head, 'Although I'm not so sure about the fireworks'

'I'll contact the local council and see what they have to say,' I respond eagerly. He frowns slightly, taking a sip of his coffee, and I try very hard not to focus on his oh so kissable mouth.

'Let me deal with the council,' he says eventually, to my complete surprise. 'I think you've probably got enough on your plate.' The last is spoken drily, but I don't detect any hint of sarcasm. In fact, if anything, he seems a little distracted, and I can't help feeling ridiculously peeved that I'm not the sole object of his attention. How silly is that?

'Thank you, that would be very much appreciated.' I resort to distant politeness, wishing, not for the first time, that I could read his mind. Then, briskly gathering up the drawings, I stand, murmuring, 'I'll be off then. I'll keep you informed of any further developments.'

He simply nods his head in answer, and with an inward sigh, I take that as my cue to leave. I'm almost at the door when he speaks my name, this time hesitantly, almost unwillingly. Turning round, I raise my eyebrows enquiringly.

'I was wondering whether you'd like to go out for lunch on Saturday.' His voice is uncertain and I stare at him for a couple of seconds, wondering if I've heard him correctly. 'With me,' he finishes lamely and to my utter amazement his face actually suffuses with colour as he speaks the last two words.

Wondering just when I fell down the rabbit hole, my answer is equally hesitant as a corresponding blush stains my cheeks. 'Err, yes, thank you, that would be nice.' Then I stand awkwardly, not knowing how to continue. Bloody hell, anyone would think I'd never been asked to lunch before.

'I thought perhaps if the weather's good enough we could take one of the College motor whalers and go up to the Ferryboat Inn at Dittisham – if that works for you.' His voice is back to its usual brusqueness, and it's almost as if I imagined his earlier awkwardness.

Swallowing, I nod my head. 'What time?'

'I'll pick you up at the boat float at noon. I'll bring a life jacket for you.' How can he make an arrangement also sound like a dismissal? In answer, I simply bob my head again, and this time I find myself incongruously fighting the impulse to curtsy.

Sighing inwardly, I hurry through the door, shutting it firmly behind me as I go. There's no sign of Dave as I let myself out and start down the hill towards the main gates.

Well what do you know, I've got a date with the knob – wait until I tell Tory...

~*~

Jason Buchannan leaned back against the sofa with a sigh. What the bloody hell had possessed him to actually go ahead and ask Kit out for lunch? Despite his earlier desire to have her get to know him, he knew in his heart that getting close to her would simply complicate matters. Especially since the chance meeting yesterday with Laura.

He sat forward again to pour himself another coffee, glancing over at the drinks cabinet with a small grimace. God, he could murder a shot of brandy now. He recalled that moment in the taxi queue, when the voice that had haunted him for years called his name.

Laura Williamson, the woman he'd met and fallen in love with while under officer training here at Dartmouth, and the person he thought he'd spend the rest of his life with – until he walked in on her making love with one of the lecturers.

He'd walked out of the room that day, and out of Laura's life after they passed out two days later, filled with the firm conviction that if someone he believed to be his soul mate was capable of such deceit, then women in general were not to be trusted. He'd been vaguely aware when she left the navy, stifled the hurt at the knowledge she was to be married, but he'd never uttered another word to her – until yesterday.

He still wasn't sure how he felt. When he'd first heard her voice calling his name in Paddington Station, his primary feeling was one of surprise. She hadn't changed much at all. Still tall, willowy, and impossibly lovely. Her chestnut hair cascaded around her shoulders, unlike her navy days when she'd wear it in a severe bun.

Her delight at seeing him was evident as she walked towards him, her face illuminated by the warm smile he remembered so clearly. Undeterred by his non committal stance, she stepped into his personal space and hugged him close, murmuring how good it was to see him again. Then she asked him if he had time for a coffee. His meeting wasn't for another hour, so against his better judgement, he found himself nodding his head and following her back into the station.

'So how are you Jase? God it's been so long.' Her voice said it had been too long, and as she reached over the table to take his hand, he found himself completely on the back foot – something that hadn't happened in a very long time.

'I'm good,' he finally responded, giving her fingers a quick squeeze before gently relinquishing them. 'How are things with you?' His voice was polite, reserved and he registered her brief frown at his lack of warmth.

'I'm working for the MOD now,' she shrugged, giving an indication that she regarded it as a job, nothing more. 'David and I spent a few years in Italy, but when we split up, I came back to the UK.'

Jason raised his eyebrows at the revelation of her marriage break up. 'I'm sorry,' he murmured, not really knowing what else to say, drawing an answering brittle laugh from her.

'I'm sure you are Jase, but enough about me. I hear on the grapevine that your career is on the up and up – I think the powers that be could have you earmarked for First Sea Lord.'

Jason gave a small shrug of his own. 'You know the RN,' he said caustically, 'One fuck up and you can be relegated to stacking files for the rest of your career. So far, I've simply avoided making any fuck ups.' He looked at his watch. 'Which reminds me, I have a meeting to attend in Main Building.'

He stood up, looking down at the woman he'd loved with all his heart. She still made his pulse race, but beyond that, he couldn't say. With slight surprise, he noted unshed tears shimmering in her eyes as she rose gracefully from her chair and took hold of his hand again, closing her eyes for a second, as though gathering courage. Her next words re-enforced it, and he felt his heart slam into his ribs as she spoke, her voice low and intense.

'Jason, I've so wanted to get in touch. You have no idea how many times I've nearly written to you. I made a mistake, all those years ago.' Her words were hurried as though she'd rehearsed them countless times, but perhaps she had.

'Please Jase, can we see each other again? I know I'm asking a lot, but I've never stopped thinking about you, and… and, I'm not asking you to give me another chance, I understand it's far too late for that. But maybe, just maybe, we could spend some time getting to know each other again, now we're both older and wiser?'

Jason Buchannan was not often lost for words, but as he stared at Laura's anguished face, he had no idea what to say. In the early years, he'd conjured up so many scenarios in which she'd said exactly those words. But now? Unexpectedly his thoughts travelled to Kit and the uncharacteristic feelings she provoked in him.

Shaking his head, he sighed. 'I don't know Laura,' he finally answered truthfully, his words coming out more harshly than he intended. 'I wasn't expecting to see you, and I've got no time now to start examining something I thought dead long ago.'

'Can we at least talk again then?' Laura held onto his hand as he tried to step back. Her voice was anxious, almost desperate, recognizing that he was about to walk out of her life – again.

Jason stopped and closed his eyes briefly. When he opened them again, he freed his hand, and reaching into his brief case, he pulled out his card. 'This has my mobile number on it. If you want to, you can give me a call.' His offer was less than gracious as were his next words. 'Now, if you'll excuse me, I have to go.'

Then he strode away without looking back, his business like pace completely concealing the turmoil inside.

David's discreet cough brought Jason back to the present. 'Admiral Thorpe is on the telephone Sir, shall I put the call through to your office?'

Frowning slightly, Jason dragged his mind back to the matters at hand. As he nodded his head and downed the rest of his now cold coffee, he reflected that his policy on women over the last decade had most definitely stood him in good stead, and, no matter what the temptation, he had no intention getting back involved the machinations of the fairer sex.

~*~

Admiral Shackleford glanced down at his watch as he sat himself at the bar. Damn, he was early. He knew that Jimmy was unlikely to turn up even a second earlier than their arranged time – the bloody dragon would see to that. Maybe a few chips wouldn't go a miss while he was waiting. He resolutely turned his mind away from Mabel's insistence that he cut down on his carbohydrates, reasoning that he could share half the chips with Pickles, so they really didn't count.

It wasn't like him to be adrift for an appointment, but the truth was that he couldn't sit still a moment longer. Mabel likened his fidgeting to a hamster on steroids and finally shooed him out of the kitchen, telling him to go for a walk or something. He didn't actually tell her his walk would take him to the Ship – she complained that the beer was another thing adding to his waistline.

He sighed. Why did bloody women have to nag so. Of course Mabel had no idea of the stress he was under currently, but the problem was, he couldn't share the whole sorry story – not even with Jimmy. He took a long sip of his pint and followed it up with a well salted chip, liberally dipped in mayonnaise. What Mabel would no doubt describe as coronary fodder. Piously throwing the next chip down to Pickles sitting eagerly at his feet, the Admiral thought back to his clandestine meeting with Boris.

He'd been hoping that he'd be able to dissuade the doddering reprobate from insisting he take the ceremony, but no such luck. It might take the old codger three times as long to finish a bloody sentence, but he'd definitely still got all his marbles. And his bowel issues.

The Admiral cringed as he thought back to the glares coming from the tables surrounding them. Boris was completely oblivious – his nose had long since given up the ghost. His enthusiasm for what he repeatedly called, 'the most important role of my life,' was bloody ridiculous; the Admiral doubted the God walloper had even heard of Noah Westbrook before he read about Victory's relationship in the newspapers.

In fact the old bugger probably hadn't even officiated at a wedding for years – he'd been "unofficially" retired since the incident at Greenwich. The Admiral groaned inside. What the buggering hell was he going to do?

Pickles sudden excited barking brought his panicked thoughts to an end, and looking up, he was relieved to see Jimmy coming through the door. His small friend frowned as he climbed up onto the stool next the Admiral.

'Are you supposed to be eating those Sir?' he asked, nodding towards the half eaten portion of chips, 'I thought you said Mabel had put you on a diet.' The Admiral sighed and pushed the rest of the chips away. His appetite had completely gone anyway. He didn't even flinch as Jimmy helped himself.

'Are you okay Sir?' Jimmy asked after they'd been sitting in silence for five minutes. 'Is there, err... something you'd like to get off your chest, so to speak?'

The Admiral looked over at the smaller man with a slight scowl. 'Can't a man have a quiet drink with his oppo without being bloody interrogated?'

Jimmy raised his eyebrows, but didn't apologize, and at length, Charles Shackleford exhaled noisily. 'Truth is Jimmy lad that I'm in a bit of a tight corner,' he muttered.

Jimmy didn't respond, just sat silently, waiting for the Admiral to continue. As he waited, he couldn't help but sigh inwardly. Being the confidante of a man who got himself involved in more tight spots than bloody Houdini was not for the faint hearted.

Finally the Admiral spoke. 'You remember when I got together with Celia – Victory's mother?' Jimmy nodded, wondering where all this was going.

'We met and married within a couple of months – a proper whirlwind courtship. I'd never met anyone like her before. She took my breath away Jimmy. I'd have done anything for her. We had the ceremony up in London – a quiet affair with just a few close friends. You can't imagine my relief when she said she didn't want a big bash. You see Jimmy lad, the problem was, I was already married.'

'Who to?' Jimmy's voice was a whisper of disbelief.

'To Florence Davies. Kit's aunt.'

Chapter Nine

Saturday is cold and sunny and I don't know whether to be glad or sorry. I haven't actually gotten around to telling either Tory or Freddy about my lunch date with Jason. I'm not sure why – maybe because I don't want any negative feedback that might make me change my mind about going. Jason Buchannan may be a difficult person to get to know, but it has to be said he's the first man I've been attracted to in far too long.

After lacing up my deck shoes, I glance at the clock. Eleven fifty. That gives me plenty of time to get to the boat float which is only a few yards away from my flat. Shrugging a wax jacket on, I give my hair a quick flick and I'm good to go. As I lock up, I wonder if I should have made a bit more of an effort. But then, if I did that, it would mean that I care. And I don't. Really I don't...

A few minutes later I'm sitting on the wall overlooking the river. The fine day has brought out all the yachties, and the water is teeming with boats of all sizes. Snuggling down into my jacket, I idly watch the Dartmouth Queen take a few late autumn tourists on a trip up the river to Totnes.

I can't help but wonder if I'm making a mistake. From the first time I saw him in Bloodstone Tower, Jason Buchannan has got under my skin. Obnoxious he might be the majority of the time, but I can't remember the last time a man made me feel so alive.

I think back to the last relationship I had, nearly five years ago now. He was an auctioneer in London. We met on one of my many buying trips, and the whole long distance things worked for me, but ultimately not for him. He really was a sweet guy

- wanted us to move in together. The problem was it would've meant me leaving Dartmouth for the bright lights of the city, and I guess I'm a country girl at heart – or maybe I just didn't love him enough.

Deep in reverie, it takes a couple of seconds before I hear my name being called, and looking down, I spot Jason in one of the college motor whalers at the bottom of the steps. My heart starts beating faster as I jump off the wall and climb down to the waiting boat. Like me he's wearing a warm wax jacket and jeans, complete with a life jacket over the top.

As I step on board, he quickly unties the rope and manoeuvres away from the side, heading towards the middle of the river. Without speaking he points towards another life jacket and indicates I should put it on. So much for small talk.

I struggle into the jacket and sit down, taking the opportunity to surreptitiously watch this enigmatic man while his attention is elsewhere. His profile is as attractive as the rest of him. Hard, uncompromising, his hair tousled as though he'd just got out of bed. I shiver, wondering what it must be like to wake up next to him. I find myself speculating whether he's ever been married. There must be women in his life surely – anyone as gorgeous as Jason Buchannan has to be fighting them off – even if his personality is less than sparkling. Suddenly he turns towards me and I colour up as though somehow he can read my thoughts.

'Have you ever been to the Ferryboat?' he asks after a short silence. I shake my head,

'We usually go to the Anchorstone café in the summer.'

He nods his agreement. 'The pub really only comes into its own in the cold winter months.'

'Do you go often?' I ask quickly when it looks as though he's going to subside into silence again.

'I used to when I was here as a cadet,' he responds after a couple of seconds. 'I've been a couple of times since coming back, but my job keeps me pretty busy.' Back to silence. Maybe he really doesn't do small talk. Hard to imagine how the hell he got to where he is though – every naval officer I've ever met can generally talk for England.

I decide to give up trying to make conversation for now, choosing instead to relax into the quiet as we leave Dartmouth behind. It's actually strangely comfortable. The only sounds I can hear are the occasional seagull, together with the low rumble of the engine, and the soft music of the waves lapping up against the side of the dinghy. Flashes of pulsing light dance along the water as we cut through, and with a small sigh, I close my eyes, revelling in the warmth of the sun on my face.

In what must have been about half an hour, but seems like only a few minutes, my reverie is interrupted as Jason says abruptly, 'We're here.'

Opening my eyes, I spy the small pontoon that services Dittisham, a small idyllic village situated on the edge of the Dart - affectionately known as Ditsum by the locals.

We're approaching the pontoon before Jason speaks again.

'Do you have any experience sailing?' he asks shortly. I'm beginning to wonder why he actually invited me out to lunch today. He certainly doesn't appear to be enjoying himself.

'Some,' I answer cagily, 'I've crewed a few times over past regattas.'

'Are you capable of tying up?' he responds, staring ahead at the area set aside for visitors' mooring.

Thoroughly tired now of his rude (not to mention patronizing) attitude, I answer, 'Quite capable,' in lofty condescending tones, equal to his. He glances over at me in surprise. Could it be he has no idea how bloody charmless he actually is?

Hurriedly I step towards the forward end of the motor whaler and he tells me to throw the fenders over the side. To be fair he has moderated his tone slightly. Then he hands me the rope.

'I'll ease slowly past the mooring as you jump out onto the jetty and tie the rope onto the cleat.' (what's a cleat?)

'Once you've got a few turns on it, I'll put the whaler in neutral so you can pull us in.'

I nod my head dismissively as though I've done this a thousand times. In reality – never. My friend Ben Sheppherd usually takes me on to crew for him more out of sympathy than anything useful I can provide. I'm usually relegated to chief (and only) coffee maker.

I look over at Jason's arrogant features. I'll be buggered if I'm going to give him the satisfaction of backing down now. I'm sure the cleat must be that metal thing you tie the rope round.

Mind you, as we approach the pontoon at what currently feels pretty bloody fast, I have to admit to feeling a little nervous. There are at least five yachty types standing idly watching as we come in. But come on, how difficult can it be? I've seen my crewmates do something similar a thousand times.

As he eases alongside, he shouts, 'Now,' and, clutching the rope, I leap onto the pontoon. Or at least part of me does. Unfortunately, as I jump, my left foot slips awkwardly and only one foot makes it to dry land. 'F**k, stop,' I shout frantically as I slowly start to do the splits.

Glancing round, Jason swears and immediately puts the whaler in reverse, and just as my nether regions are about to be intimately acquainted with a river full of freezing cold water, the gap slowly begins to close, and a warm gnarled hand grabs mine, hauling me up onto the jetty. The same hand deftly takes the rope from me and wraps it expertly around the cleat, pulling the motor whaler into the correct position. As Jason turns off the engine, the hand finishes off securing the rope, throwing the remainder back to my stony faced sailing companion.

Hugely embarrassed, I look up, stammering, 'Thank you,' to my knight errant, who actually turns out to be an elderly lady. Bugger. Everyone watching has identical grins on their faces, and as Jason climbs onto the pontoon, I daren't even look at him.

'Are you hurt?' His voice sounds surprisingly gentle as he takes my arm. Feeling tears of mortification prick behind my eyelids, I wonder if I should pretend an injury. In the end, sniffing slightly, I look sideways at him murmuring, 'Just my pride.'

At my words, he relaxes and now he knows I'm okay, I get the expected lecture as we walk up the floating bridge towards the shore. I ignore most of his words, basking slightly in the knowledge of his concern. Maybe he's not such a knob after all.

Five minutes later we're cosily ensconced on a window seat in the small bar of the Ferryboat Inn which is only a few steps away from the water's edge. Apparently the pub's known locally as the FBI, and looking round, I can't believe I've never been here before. As Jason heads over to get us a drink, I examine the menu, suddenly famished – it must be all the hard work and sea air.

By the time Jason gets back to the table, I've narrowed it down to two - beer battered haddock or seafood linguini, both sound equally delicious. As he seats himself next to me, I take a grateful sip of my red wine - just what I need after my close brush with death (or at the very least a dunking).

Taking a sip of his beer, Jason asks me again if I'm okay. His concerned tone is completely at odds with his earlier surliness and I'm beginning to realize there really are two sides to Jason Buchannan.

Talking about sides, the insides of my thighs are definitely sore, and I think it's very likely I'll be walking like John Wayne by tomorrow morning, but other than that, I've escaped relatively unscathed. I smile back at him and nod my head.

'I'm fine thank you. Sorry I gave you such a scare. I might have neglected to mention that my previous sailing experience has been pretty much restricted to making hot drinks for more experienced crew members.' I smile again, this time ruefully.

'Well, if you're interested, maybe we can look at giving you a few lessons in the spring,' he responds with an answering grin. I feel a bubble of excitement at the thought that he still expects us to be friends in five months. 'That'd be great,' I reply enthusiastically, 'I hope you're a patient teacher.'

'Patient's my middle name,' he responds wryly, then raising his glass, he smiles, saying, 'Here's to our future sailing adventures. Now, what are you having to eat?'

The next two hours fly by. Contrary to my earlier misgivings, Jason turns out to be an entertaining and affable companion –

he obviously knows how to turn on the charm when he wants to. He regales me with stories of his many naval exploits, some funny, others more serious, making me feel on every occasion as if I'd been there. I'm finally beginning to understand just how and why he's risen in the naval ranks as quickly as he has.

'So how about you?' he asks at length as we finish up our fish and chips. 'I didn't realize you were in the event management business, I thought you ran an art gallery.'

'I did, up until approximately six weeks ago. However, the building housing my gallery was sold, resulting in a sudden unavoidable change in career.'

I don't elaborate on the fact that it was my parents who effectively sold me out, and I think he senses my reluctance to go into more detail, because he doesn't pursue the subject.

'Are you married? he asks out of the blue instead, and I almost choke on my last chip. Eyes watering, I take a large sip of wine and shake my head.

'Why on earth would I be here if I was married?' I question, realizing too late that I'm effectively admitting that I think our lunch is a date. Colouring up, I look hurriedly down at my plate.

'Have you ever been tempted?' he presses, his voice so serious that I look back up in surprise.

'Not really,' I respond, equally seriously 'I don't think I've never met the right man.' Let him make of that what he will.

'How about you?' I ask, neatly turning the tables. He stares at me for a second without answering, then just as he opens his mouth, the waitress comes bustling up to our table.

'Was everything okay with your meal?' she gushes, looking coquettishly at Jason.

'It was lovely thank you,' Jason responds with a polite smile, and she giggles, leaning forward to take his empty plate. As her ample bosom brushes against his arm, I feel a sudden unaccountable urge to slap her, telling myself it's because she's acting very unprofessionally and not because just one of her assets is bigger than both of mine.

'Would you like a dessert?' Jason asks after she reluctantly departs with our finished dishes. 'I can vouch for the treacle tart – it was amazing the last time I had it.'

I look over at him, glad I've managed not to show my peevishness about the waitress. Nodding my head, I smile. 'With clotted cream of course,'

'Naturally,' he responds with an answering grin, 'To eat treacle tart with anything else is sacrilege.' As he slides out of the booth and makes his way to the bar, I realize he hasn't answered my question.

It's nearly three thirty before we finally head back to the motor whaler and now the sun has disappeared, the afternoon is turning cold. Shivering, I snuggle down into my wax jacket, wishing I'd brought a scarf. We manage to board the whaler *and* cast off with no unexpected incidents, and as Jason goes back to silent, concentrating on guiding the boat back down the river in the gathering dusk, I hunch down in my seat, going over the events of the afternoon in my head. I've enjoyed it so much more than I thought I would, and sneaking a quick look at Jason's profile, now slightly indistinct in the gloom, I wonder if he's aware of the effect he has on me.

All too soon we arrive back at the boat float. I insist Jason lets me have another go at tying up, and this time I do it without any problems. Tossing the end of the rope back to him, I pose on the bottom step with a triumphant smile before undoing my life jacket. Shrugging the heavy thing off awkwardly, I lean forward to give it back, expecting him to simply untie the rope from the cleat and push off. But, after casually throwing the jacket into the bottom of the whaler, he turns off the engine and jumps out, ostensibly to help me back up the steps.

'Frightened I'll fall in?' I murmur drily over my shoulder as we climb to the top.

He laughs softly, and as I turn round to face him, my heart starts to thud at the look in his silver eyes.

'Did you know your aunt has invited me to her murder mystery evening on Saturday?' he murmurs, gently pushing a piece of hair away from my eyes. I didn't know that, and the realization that I'll be seeing him again so soon infuses my body with a tingling warmth.

'Would you like me to pick you up?' he goes on to ask quietly, seemingly unaware that his thumb is stroking my temple.

Unable to trust my voice, I simply nod and wait, hardly able to breathe, as he continues to watch me, his face unreadable, clearly locked in some kind of silent internal battle. Then, finally, achingly slowly, he bends his head until his lips find mine.

Chapter Ten

'What do you mean you're married to Florence Davies?' Jimmy's tone was appalled and he looked as though he was about to have an apoplectic fit. Not for the first time, Charles Shackleford bemoaned the fact that his closest friend was a bit of a prude.

'I'm not married to her *now* you imbecile,' was the Admiral's irritable though undeniably speedy response. 'We got the bloody thing annulled donkeys years ago.'

Jimmy opened and closed his mouth but nothing came out. 'What has this got to do with Boris?' he finally asked faintly.

The Admiral sighed. 'He was the one who married me and Flo. We were only eighteen, babies really. I'd just joined up and we thought getting hitched would keep us together. Of course we didn't tell anyone. Her father was a right bastard. We thought it was romantic.' He shook his head despondently.

'Boris was the chaplain at Dartmouth when I joined up, but as soon as we'd tied the knot, he was drafted to the Falklands for a bit then buggered off to the bloody wilds of Africa to do a bit of God walloper work - that's where he eventually picked up the problem with his rear end.

'Anyway, by the time he came back, Flo had scarpered off to America with some nutter she met while I was away, I was married to Celia and we had Victory on the way.'

The Admiral paused, taking a sip of his pint and pulling the bowl of chips back towards him. Funny how unburdening tends to help with the appetite. He offered the bowl to Jimmy who shook his head weakly.

'So what happened?' the small man whispered impatiently when it looked as though the Admiral intended to finish the whole bowl before continuing.

'When old Boris found out that I'd not *technically* ended my nuptials with Flo before doing the business with Celia, he was pretty bloody angry at first – at least until I had chance to explain what had happened. He said we had to find Flo pronto and get her to sign the damn divorce papers.'

'Why didn't you tell Celia about Florence before you married her?' Jimmy asked incredulously when the Admiral paused to take another drink.

'Frightened I'd lose her,' Charles Shackleford said bluntly, waving to the barmaid to bring them both another pint. 'It was easier to let sleeping dogs lie I suppose,' he continued more softly, staring morosely into his empty glass.

'Anyway, I did tell her eventually – had to. Boris did all the leg work tracking down Flo - she was living in some bloody hippy commune in South Carolina. He got her to sign the divorce papers and bob's your uncle.

'That's when I came clean to Celia. Thought she'd be done with me when she found out, but instead, she agreed to marry me again. She also wanted Boris to be Victory's godfather, but he refused. Said he wouldn't be around enough to do the right thing.

'Instead he asked if he could be the one to marry her. Joked that he would make sure there were no skeletons in her intended's cupboard like there had been in mine…'

He turned towards Jimmy before saying earnestly, 'That's not the whole story Jimmy lad, but it's the bit that's mine to tell. And it's why I can't let old Boris down. But I can't tell Victory either, because if I do, the rest of it'll come out.

'Truth is, I thought the old bugger had forgotten – and, anyway, Victory showed so little interest in any bloke, I really did think he'd have picked up his one way ticket before she finally got herself hitched.

'I even said he could marry me and Mabel instead.' The

Admiral heaved a sigh and fumbled for a handkerchief in his pocket. For a second, Jimmy wondered if the large man was actually going to cry, and felt like doing the same. In all his nearly seventy years he'd never known another man who attracted as much drama as Charles Shackleford. Calamities seemed to follow him around. In fact it was beginning to look doubtful as to whether he truly knew his friend at all.

Silently Jimmy stared into the amber depths of his pint. He tried to remember when Florence Davies had come back to Dartmouth. It must have been about thirty years ago. He wondered what had made her come back.

Looking back over at the Admiral, he took a deep breath. 'Sir,' he said firmly, 'I don't care what your reasons are for wanting old Boris to do this thing, but at the end of the day, you've got to tell Tory and Noah what they're letting themselves in for. You've got to stop fudging the issue.

'I'm sure you can be a bit sparing with the truth – I know how talented you are at delivering a good sob story,' He ignored the Admiral's frown at his words, determined to get his message across – once and for all.

'But this is the biggest day of your daughter's life and you cannot ruin it to pay off an old debt.'

Charles Shackleford opened his mouth to speak, then nodded his head slowly. 'You're right Jimmy lad,' he muttered eventually, 'But it's a right cake and arse party all the same.' He heaved a big sigh.

'It's my biggest downfall Jimmy. I'm just too bloody kind and sympathetic for my own good...

~*~

Since my lunch date with Jason, I can't deny I've been on cloud nine. I've seen another side to Captain Buchannan, and despite my fear of getting involved with such a complex man, I'm eager for more. The knowledge that Aunt Flo has invited him to her murder mystery bash feels like a warm promise of things to come.

There are going to be ten of us around the dinner table this coming Saturday and we've all received our character outlines, together with instructions for what to wear. The setting is supposed to be Casablanca during the second world war.

My character is a Russian aristocrat fallen on hard times, but I have no idea about anyone else. We've all had instructions to keep the details of our roles under our hats – although I have a pretty good idea about Freddy's persona. He's been doing his starving artist routine for the last week.

Anyway, I've found a spare five minutes to pop to a local charity shop to see if I can pick up some satin and faux fur. It's all very exciting and an opportunity for everyone to step back from the pre-wedding frenzy and chill out. Even Noah, who could be excused for thinking the whole thing a bit lame, is getting into the spirit of things. He's obviously taking the part of a British toff because he keeps going round saying, 'Golly gosh,' and calling everyone, 'Old bean.'

I, on the other hand, have been very sneaky - only practicing my Russian accent in the shower.

I'm just about to head into the shop when my mobile phone rings. Digging it out from the depths of my handbag, I see Tory's name on the screen. Smiling, I swipe to connect. 'Well hello mother of my soon to be godchild, how are things over on the dark side?'

'I'm a bit worried Kitty Kat,' she responds in a serious tone, and, with an internal groan, I wonder what could have gone wrong since our last potential crisis. We're getting on average at least one possible disaster every other day.

'What's happened?' I ask cautiously, knowing that Tory's hormones are currently encouraging her to worry about anything from the colour of the chair ties, to world extinction.

'I think there's something wrong with my father,' she says anxiously. 'He's been far too considerate lately. He even apologized to me yesterday, and Kit, he actually sounded contrite – that's unheard of. He's definitely got something up his sleeve. I know my old man, he's many things, but humble and solicitous is not one of them.'

I can't help but agree with her. The Admiral acting out of character is not good – no matter which way you look at it. I think back to my earlier instincts and his furtive movements outside my flat window. Maybe she has got something to be concerned about.

'Have you said anything to him?' My heart is sinking faster than the Titanic, and my voice comes out a little sharper than I intend. Luckily Tory's so focused on her parental concerns that she doesn't pick up on it.

'I haven't had chance,' she retorts brusquely. 'When he's not being solicitous, he's avoiding me like the plague. I thought at first that maybe he'd guessed about the baby, but after he had a large glass of wine and nibbles waiting for me when I came down to start clearing out my stuff, I realized he couldn't possibly know. And the only time he offers me alcohol is when he's got something nasty to share.' She pauses, sighing loudly.

'When I asked him what the occasion was, he actually *kissed* me on the cheek Kit. I think the last time he did that was just before he broke the news that he'd mistakenly left Dotty in Torquay.

'And then he wanted to know why it was so difficult to understand a father wanting to spoil his only daughter.'

'Bloody hell,' I mutter, not knowing what else to say.

'And *then* he told me how lovely I looked,' she continues, her voice going slightly hysterical. 'Kit, you know what he's like. He *never* pays compliments. I mean, come on, you know my father – he can always be trusted to tell a woman she looks a bloody sight instead of a vision. I'm telling you he's up to something.'

She almost shouts the last bit, and there and then, I reluctantly make the decision to postpone my charity shop rummaging and head over to see my best friend – hopefully to get to the bottom of things, and administer the metaphorical smelling salts. 'Are you at the Admiralty now?' I ask quickly to head off any more histrionics.

'Yes I'm in my old room,' she answers with a slight sniff.

'Okay, I'm on my way,' I say briskly. 'And don't get rid of the glass of wine, you can give it to me. After all, we don't want him to suspect we're on to him...'

It takes me half an hour to get over the river to the Admiralty. Tory's father has apparently gone shopping with Mabel.

'See what I mean?' Tory shouts when she informs me of this little gem. 'When was the last time my father went shopping? You'd normally have to administer a sedative. I think even Mabel's smelling a rat, and Pickles actually growled at him when he kneeled down to give him a fuss. It's like a bloody alien has inhabited his body'

I sit down on her bed and absently stroke Dotty, who's acting like she's not seen me for months. As Tory hands me the glass of wine and plonks the nibbles between us, Dotty's apparent devotion becomes crystal clear.

'Where's Pickles now?' I ask after taking an appreciative sip. It's a very good vintage – the Admiral's guilt is good for one thing at least.

'He's at Mabel's house being spoilt by her son Oscar. I think he's missing Dotty.'

I toss the little dog a cheesy wotsit which she catches with her usual dexterity. 'I don't think it's mutual,' I murmur.

'And there's something else,' Tory continues, popping a peanut into her mouth. 'I was here when he and Mabel received your aunt's invitation. Mabel was thrilled to bits, but you should have seen my dad Kit, he went as white as a ghost. How weird is that? And then I started to think about it. Can you ever remember my father and your aunt being in the same room together? Or even having a telephone conversation?'

I frown, trying to think back. 'Well now you come to mention it, no I can't.'

'Don't you think that's strange? I mean, we've been best friends for absolutely ever, and yet the people who looked after us in our formative years have never even exchanged so much as a phone call.'

She stares at me, her eyebrows raised in question, and I stare back, wanting to dismiss her disquiet, but somehow not able to. Taking another sip of my wine, I try to recall the important events in our lives. Sixteenth, eighteenth and twenty first birthdays, New Years Eve, Easter, Halloween. And finally our last big one a couple of years ago – when we turned thirty and decided to hold a joint party.

Tory's mum had already passed away by then, and of course my parents were half way across the world, but why didn't my Aunt Flo attend. I struggle to think.

'She came down with a sudden bug,' I muse out loud. 'On our thirtieth birthday party,' I continue by way of explanation. 'So why didn't your father come Tory? He didn't come, did he?'

'He had an unexpected reunion dinner in London,' Tory whispers after a short pause, 'Said I didn't want old codgers like him at my party anyway.'

'They haven't come to anything where there's a danger of them bumping into each other,' I clarify. 'The question is, why?'

Chapter Eleven

Try as we might, Tory and I couldn't come up with any kind of explanation as to why our respective parents/guardians have apparently ignored each other for decades. I know I was surprised when my aunt invited Tory's father to her party, but I can't actually believe we've never noticed their complete lack of communication before.

We weren't able to question the Admiral because he decided to stay over at Mabel's. Although the elderly widow spends most of her time at the Admiralty, her son visiting for a few days has meant she's been spending half her time back at her little cottage. Apparently the Admiral is missing her.

Tory's rude snort down the phone when he told her to lock up on her way out, spoke volumes. In the end, we agreed to watch both of them closely at the party to see if we can come up with any answers.

So, Saturday's finally here, and I'm in the process of turning myself into Countess Bogov in preparation for tonight's entertainment. I managed to pick up an old satin bridesmaid dress which I've teamed with some pearls, long gloves and a feather boa. I'm not sure if it's standard Russian Countess attire, but it fits me in all the right places and I don't look (much) like a bag lady. If Jason's going to be there, then that's my main priority.

Anyway I'm finally ready, just putting the finishing touches to my makeup – dark red lipstick in true thirties starlet fashion. I feel a bit Greta Garbo-ish...

I glance down at my watch. Jason is picking me up at seven thirty and it's now seven twenty five. I know military types hate people who are late, so I quickly grab my coat and head out the door.

I still haven't told Tory about our date, so she was understandably surprised when she called to offer me a lift and I had to admit that Jason was taking me. I know it's a discussion waiting to happen though. Her parting words to me were, 'We need to talk.' Freddy's response to my text telling him I'd meet him at my aunt's cottage was a rude one...

I smile as I run down the stairs – an action I seem to be doing a lot lately. I have no doubt my best friend will demand chapter and verse when we're next alone.

Jason is already parked over the road by the time I emerge into the street. This is the first time I've seen him since our kiss, and I suddenly feel panicky. I don't know why – I mean it's not like we're actually dating or anything. Ruthlessly shoving down my sudden anxiety, I hurry across the road, just as Jason gets out of the car. It's too dark to see his expression as he walks round to open the passenger door, but I flash a nervous smile at him as I slip into the seat. I watch him as he walks back to the driver's side looking for any clues to his character, but everything is covered up by a long greatcoat.

Before doing up his seat belt, he looks over at me with a slight smile, saying, 'Hi,' then without waiting for a response, he leans across, and quickly, softly, touches his lips to mine. As he straightens up, I catch my breath slightly, and have to fight the urge to pull his head back to mine for a proper kiss. Instead I blink and shake my head a little as he starts the engine. Get a grip girl, I admonish myself silently, you're not a bloody teenager.

'You'll have to give me directions once we get to Stoke Fleming.' He interrupts my internal monologue as he deftly manoeuvres the car onto the one way system. There's very little traffic and five minutes later we're on the coast road leading to Blackpool Sands and my aunt's cottage.

'How did your trip go,' I ask, remembering that he had to go back up to London the day after our lunch. I can see him shrug in the darkness. 'It's a different world up there,' he answers after a second. 'Unfortunately, having been brought up in a dilapidated old house pretty much in the middle of nowhere, big cities don't really hold much of an attraction for me.'

I think back to our visit to Bloodstone Tower. Dilapidated pretty much sums it up really. 'Do you miss it?' I ask softly, recalling the silent untamed beauty of the loch. He glances over at me in the gloom before giving a small nod.

'When I retire out of the RN, I'll go back to live there, but right now it's a bottomless pit as far as money is concerned. He glances over at me again before finishing dryly, 'As I'm sure you can appreciate.'

I feel another surge of guilt at my wanton, if unintentional, destruction of the curtains in the Great Hall. Okay so they might have been so moth eaten that the material was simply hanging on by a thread, but they were better than nothing. 'I thought Tory was intending to replace the curtains,' I murmur with a wince.

'I informed her that it wasn't necessary.' His voice is polite but abrupt, warning me not to pry, and in the same breath reminding me that, in reality, I know very little about this man. However, just as I'm beginning to wish I'd never brought the subject up, he gives a sigh before continuing in a softer tone. 'It's always been my dream to restore Bloodstone Tower to its former glory. My father's done his best, but the estate has been falling into disrepair for years.

'The death duties when my grandfather died were the final straw, and we've been playing catch up ever since.'

I can't think of an answer, so simply nod my head in understanding and allow the silence to take over.

Ten minutes later we're driving through the village of Stoke Fleming and then down towards Blackpool Sands. The sea on our left is almost invisible in the darkness, with only the moon providing scattered patches of light on its inky surface. As the road begins to rise again, I instruct him to slow down, and point to a driveway almost obscured by rhododendron bushes and palm trees.

'Be careful,' I warn him, 'The driveway runs along the edge of the cliff for the first few yards.'

A couple of minutes later we pull into a large turning area, completely lit up with fairy lights hanging from tree to tree around the edge. I give a small gasp of appreciation. It looks magical.

There are only a couple of cars, indicating that not all the guests have arrived yet. The door to the cottage is open, the hall within lit by warm lamplight and candles, all casting dancing shadows over the entrance.

'Wow,' we both murmur at the same time as he brings the car to a stop.

Hearing the car engine, Aunt Flo appears at the open door, resplendent in velvet and lace. Pepé is tucked under her arm wearing an equally splendid bow tie. 'Dahlings,' she calls with exaggerated affect, 'It's simply too good of you both to come.'

Let the fun begin...

Five minutes later we're walking out onto the terrace overlooking the sea, only the moon and the occasional ship's light piercing the pitch-black. The whole area is lit up in the same way as the drive, complete with heaters and large candles to ward of the chill. Jason has removed his greatcoat to reveal a white dinner jacket and bow tie.

'Very Cary Grant,' I murmur looking him up and down.

'Kirk Ransom the second - American, late thirties. Doomed romantic hero nursing a broken heart and owner of Kirk's African café in downtown Casablanca, at your service ma'am,' he replies with a slight bow and a very credible American accent.

I laugh delightedly and turn to say hello to the three other guests, just as aunt Flo arrives with large tray of drinks and nibbles. Edith Piaf is playing in the background adding to the nineteen thirties atmosphere.

'This is my agent Neil.' She waves her hand to a tall distinguished looking gentleman dressed in a dinner jacket with numerous, very obviously fake, medals decorating the front. 'His alter ego is Hughes Le Grandbutte, Deputy-Mayor of Casablanca, and my husband.'

Neil and I have met many times over the years and I step forward to give him a quick hug.

'Hello Neil,' I smile, 'Good to see you again.' I turn to my companion. 'This is Jason Buchannan. He's the current captain up at the naval college. However, this evening he is apparently a rich American playboy with the enviable name of Kirk Ransom the second.'

Laughing, the two men shake hands and Flo turns to the two other guests still hovering in the background. 'My editor Jacques.' She tucks her arm into that of the small man dressed in a slightly shabby day-suit, before continuing, 'Otherwise known as Seamus O'Hack, dissolute Irish journalist.' She pauses, turning to him with a grin to say, 'Very appropriate.'

We shake hands and I eye him carefully. So this is the man that my aunt has lined up for Freddy. Interesting.

'And this is my good friend and proof-reader Elaine,' Aunt Flo continues, pulling a small lady to the forefront with her free arm. 'Without her, my grammar would be non-existent.' She smiles warmly down at the petite woman who I can now see is dressed in quite a girly manner. The reason why becomes clear as Flo goes on to say, 'Tonight, however, she has the enviable task of playing my eighteen year old daughter Nicole Le Grandbutte.'

'Dear mama, please don't embarrass me,' Elaine murmurs with very convincing bashfulness.

I'm just about to introduce my character when a sudden commotion comes from the hall indicating the arrival of the other guests – en masse if the noise is anything to go by.

'Was this your idea of having a laugh Florence Davies – forcing me to dress up as a bloody Gastapo officer. It's a damn insult.'

I look at Jason and giggle. 'I think he'd even prefer to be a WAFU, and that's saying something.'

'What's a WAFU?' asks Jacques curiously.

'Stands for wet and flipping useless,' Jason grins, 'It's a slightly less than affectionate term used to describe someone in the Royal Navy's Fleet Air Arm.'

We're interrupted as Dotty and Pepé dash through the terrace doors, followed a couple of seconds later by Tory and Noah.

Tory poses dramatically, saying huskily, 'Allo, I am zee famoos sultry, decadent, and exotic French cabaret singer, Cherie Boot. And zees is my companion, Monsieur Oily-Carte who is ze booking agent for Le Moulin Blue nightclub in Paris. He vas educated in England.'

Noah struts in looking every inch a well heeled Brit. He lifts a small monocle to his eye and murmurs, 'How do you do,' with a bored sigh, making it quite clear that he's looking down his nose at the assembled commoners in front of him. Then he grins, saying, 'Hey, good to see you all, I'm Noah.'

I have to say he looks absolutely breathtaking in his full evening dress, and I suddenly remember exactly why he's lusted after by so many of the world's females (not to mention quite a few males).

Mind you, Tory looks pretty damn good too – her curls are piled high on her head, and her curves are shown off to maximum advantage in plum velvet.

'What does a man have to do to get a bloody drink around here? I'm dryer than a popcorn fart.' The Admiral's loud complaint precedes him onto the terrace, and I notice my aunt Flo grimacing slightly before disentangling herself from Jacques and turning to face Tory's father. I watch carefully as they face each other for possibly the first time in... well, I don't really know how many years.

'Hello Charles,' Flo murmurs drily as she steps forward to look him in the eye. 'I see your manners haven't improved any.'

It feels to me as though everything is in slow motion as I watch them stare silently at each other for what seems like ages, but is actually only a few seconds. I glance over at Tory to see her watching them with the same intensity. Then she looks over at me with her eyebrows raised, mouthing, 'What the hell?'

I shake my head slightly and give a small shrug as the spell is broken by the Admiral saying gruffly, 'Hello Florence. You've met my intended Mabel?' The small matron steps forward, luckily completely oblivious to the undercurrents, saying enthusiastically, 'Thank you so much for inviting us Florence, it's very kind of you. I've never been to a murder mystery evening before.' I notice for the first time that she's actually dressed in a very tight fitting, frilly evening dress.

'You look great Mabel, who's your character?' I ask in an effort to get the light hearted party atmosphere back. Surprisingly she chuckles, strikes a pose and fluffs her hair.

'Ingrid Pith, Danish art dealer. I have a special gift for finding the most beautiful paintings from all over occupied Europe,' she murmurs in just the right flirtatious teasing tone, resulting in an impromptu applause. There are so many hidden depths to Mabel Pomfrey.

'And this is Otto von Pinkelwurst, a fanatical, slightly mad officer of the Gestapo.'

She takes the Admiral's arm before continuing, 'You don't understand why you're here in Africa instead of in a senior staff post in Berlin, do you dear?' The last is said with underlying steel as she shakes his arm slightly. The Admiral looks so uncomfortable that I have to take a sip of my drink in an effort to stave off the need to laugh - it's not often you get to see Charles Shackleford so ill at ease.

Mind you, he definitely looks the part, dressed in a long black overcoat, complete with boots and a monocle – although the overcoat does smell a bit strongly of mothballs.

Out of the corner of my eye, I see my aunt Flo relaxing slightly with a small smile. She points to the tray of drinks and nibbles, instructing them to help themselves. Suddenly I realize that someone's missing. 'Where's Freddy? I ask, directing my question to Tory.

'He's gone to the bathroom,' Tory responds, taking a tiny sip of her Champagne and closing her eyes in ecstasy, before thrusting away temptation by putting the glass down hastily. 'He could be anything up to an hour. Said he needed to get into character - apparently he's a starving poet.'

'Well, I hope he doesn't take too long,' I say quietly moving closer to her, 'Aunt Flo's got someone lined up for him to meet.' I nod towards Jacques, now in animated conversation with Noah. 'Jacques is her editor,' I continue as Tory looks over. 'Apparently he came out fairly recently and my aunt thinks they'd hit it off.'

'Well it's about time someone took Dartmouth's answer to Rupert Everett off our hands,' she says lightly after giving the unfortunate agent a thorough once over. 'And talking of wanna be's, who are you supposed to be?'

I suddenly realize that I haven't actually got around to introducing my character. 'Countess Bogov, glamorous, mysterious Russian aristocrat in exile. I am so pleased to make your acquaintance, even if you are a filthy bourgeoisie.'

My Russian accent is nowhere near as good as her French one and she smirks at me, whispering, 'Don't give up the day job,' before turning towards the terrace doors where Freddy is now posing.

Our friend is dressed in a shabby velvet jacket, a plain cloth cap and trousers that looked like their previous owner had been about fifteen stone. He completes the picture by leaning limply on a cane as though he simply can't go on any longer.

'Madam Edith Le Grandbutte,' he breathes as though there's a good chance it will be his last, 'I beg you, hand me a glass of your finest, ere I collapse on the spot for want of alcoholic sustenance.' Laughing, aunt Flo hands him a glass of Champagne which he takes with a sigh, nodding his head weakly.

'Starving writer and poet Pierre Paysanski, of mixed Russian and French parentage, with a bad leg, at your service madam.' Then he limps dramatically onto the terrace. Unfortunately, the effect is slightly marred as Pepé enthusiastically tries to hump the leg he's hobbling on.

Aunt Flo wastes no time in introducing him to her editor Jacques, and I can't help but smile as both the limp and his starving writer affectation instantly disappear. Unobtrusively Tory pours most of her bubbly into my glass with a wink, before wandering over to speak with Noah who's now chatting with Neil and her father. For the moment I'm content simply to people watch.

The Admiral seems to have gotten over his initial discomfort and is busy regaling Flo's agent with his tried and tested story about the Commodore and the parrot. I wonder exactly what is between him and my aunt. There was a definite *something* when he arrived earlier. I have no idea how I'm going to get to the bottom of it, but I'm determined to do so somehow.

'So, you're a Russian countess?' I start as a warm voice sounds in my ear and turn around to see Jason behind me.

'In exile,' I clarify with a dramatic sigh. 'Zese diamonds around my neck are not real. I had to sell ze real ones to escape from Russia.' He grins at me before repeating Tory's advice earlier. It appears that acting is not my forte.

'Good job I'm talented at other things then,' I quip. He raises his eyebrows and smiles slightly, causing my heart to miss a beat.

'Well, I'd certainly be interested in learning where your other talents lie Countess; perhaps you'll consider inviting me up to have a look at your etchings when I take you home.' His voice is light and flippant but his beautiful silver eyes tell a different story as he stares down at me intently. I feel an answering tightening in the pit of my stomach, and I'm embarrassed to say that my response is a little hoarse.

'I'm sure I could dig out a couple of my more interesting efforts.' I briefly wonder if that sounds too forward when Aunt Flo claps her hands, effectively putting an end to what could have been an interesting, though potentially dangerous, conversation.

'Okay everybody, time to get into character.' She takes Neil's arm as she continues, 'I'm Edith Le Grandebutte and this is my husband Hughes. We both bid you a warm welcome to our evening of murder, mystery and mayhem.

'However, before we go in for dinner, I'd like to set the scene for... drum roll...

'A Murder In Casablanca in The Brie, The Bullet and The Black Cat.'

She pauses dramatically, then, putting on her glasses, continues to read from a script.

'The date is October, nineteen forty two. Across Europe and Africa, the war is beginning to turn against Hitler. At Stalingrad, despite suffering months of the most terrible fighting ever seen, Russia is beginning to push the German army back. In North Africa, Montgomery has just launched his assault on Rommel's troops at El Alamein; and in East Africa, British forces have seized control of the strategically vital port of Madagascar. In the words of Winston Churchill: "It is not the end; it is not even the beginning of the end; but it is, perhaps, the end of the beginning."

'Meanwhile France has been divided in two - Paris and the north is occupied by the Germans, whilst the south and the colonies are nominally independent under the puppet government in Vichy.

'Casablanca falls under Vichy control. Despite the presence of German troops, it is still governed by the French civilian authorities. It too has seen fighting, but nothing much worse than the kind of bar-room brawl that helps soldiers of all nations relax when off-duty.

'America has entered the War, but is still officially at peace with Vichy, France. Diplomatic relations between the two governments are tense and will be broken off next month, shortly before US forces land at Casablanca to take the city for the Allies. For now, however, American civilians are safe in Casablanca. The British, on the other hand, are very clearly the enemy.

'You are here this evening at the official residence of the Deputy Mayor of Casablanca, Monsieur Le Grandbutte, for a dinner, where the guest of honour was to have been France's greatest living mime artist, The Black Cat.

'But France's greatest living mime artist is no longer living. He has been murdered. And you are all a suspect...'

The evening has been a resounding success. We didn't actually manage to solve the murder but we had a great time trying. Everyone hammed it up to the nines – even the Admiral threw himself into the role of a fanatical, slightly batty Gestapo Officer, giving the whole “Ve haf vays of making you talk” a completely new slant.

So we're now on coffee and liquors – apart from Jason who's driving – and everyone is feeling mellow and relaxed. Throughout the evening I've been watching the Admiral and my aunt carefully to see whether there has been much interaction between them, and I know Tory's been observing too.

Strangely enough they shared a lot of banter while they were in character, but now we're all back to our boring selves, the chill has returned. I keep wondering if I'm imagining it, and I've spent the last half an hour trying to catch Tory's eye so we can compare notes in the bathroom. Unfortunately, the one time I could do with her feeling sick, she appears disgustingly healthy.

‘So what is your latest book about?’ Mabel asks as we let go of our fictitious personas.

‘I thought you'd never ask,’ Flo retorts with a laugh. ‘This time I've gone for more of a mystery and suspense. Of course there's the usual romance as well as some naughty bits, but I'm hoping this time to broaden my reach a little.’

‘I don't know about your reach, but you're definitely broadening something,’ I pipe up.

My aunt got around to giving me a draft copy, and although I'm only a third of the way through, there already appears to be an inordinate amount of bondage involved…

Aunt Flo laughs again. ‘I always like to challenge my readers.’

‘When did you start writing?’ Freddy questions, clearly fascinated. I'm looking directly at my aunt as he speaks, and notice her glance at Tory's father before responding. The plot thickens…

‘I lived in The States for a while,’ she answers after a short pause, ‘And when I came back, I needed to find a way of supporting myself and…’ She stops with a slight frown, before giving a small shrug and going on, 'I needed to earn some money.'

'Hey, I didn't know you lived in the US,' Noah interjects with obvious interest.

This is news to me too...

'Whereabouts did you live?' he goes on to ask curiously.

I'm still staring at Flo and it's now quite clear to anyone who knows her well that she's uncomfortable with the direction the conversation is going. I had no idea my aunt used to live in The States, and I suddenly realize just how little she talks about her early life.

'I lived in South Carolina for a while, quite near Charleston.'

'I thought you went to Savannah.'

You could have heard a pin drop after the Admiral's interruption, and every eye swivels towards him.

'I mean, that's what the rumour was anyway,' he continues with a visible bluster, 'You know what this bloody town's like, you can never keep anything to yourself.'

All eyes go back to Flo. I think everyone senses that there's much more to this story than meets the eye.

'Savannah's only a few hours away from Charleston,' Neil cuts in smoothly, just as the silence starts to become uncomfortable, 'You were somewhere in between weren't you Flo?'

My aunt bites her bottom lip, giving a quick glare towards the Admiral, before relaxing slightly and nodding her head. 'I lived just over the Georgia border.'

'Why did you go to The States?' I can't stop myself from asking, even though I know full well my aunt would prefer to change the subject. Again, that quick slant towards Tory's father. Anyone who doesn't know aunt Flo well would have missed it. Anyone other than me.

Without realizing it, I'm holding my breath as I wait for her answer. In the end, she gives a small grimace. 'I followed a man I thought I was in love with.' Then she stands quickly. 'Anyone for more coffee?'

I open my mouth, reluctant to let the subject go, but before I get chance to say anything, Tory jumps in with a warning glance towards me. 'I'd love one before we go if that's okay Florence. It's been the most amazing evening, I can't remember the last time I had so much fun.'

'I'm obviously doing something wrong then,' growls Noah in a wounded voice.

His words effectively divert attention from my aunt's past and I'm forced to let it go. For now.

By eleven o'clock we're all beginning to flag, especially Tory who is in danger of giving herself lock jaw if she yawns any wider.

Noah, ever attuned to his fiancée's moods, smiles tenderly at her, saying, 'Honey, I think it's time we got you home. Thanks a bunch for a phenomenal evening Florence.'

Then climbing to his feet, he pushes back his chair. 'I don't know what you guys are doing next Thursday,' he continues as he walks round the table towards Tory, 'But if you're free, I'd love you to come to our Thanksgiving dinner.'

It's clear that Noah is including everyone around the table in his invitation, and I glance quickly at Jason to check out his response, ridiculously pleased as I see him nod his head in smiling acceptance. And I'm not the only one.

Freddy, although feigning disinterest by fiddling with his napkin, is surreptitiously watching Jacques' reaction to the invitation. My heart warms slightly. It really is about time our third wheel had someone special in his life.

In the end, only Elaine is otherwise engaged on Thanksgiving. The Admiral looks as though he wants to make an excuse initially, but Mabel quickly puts paid to that, although her acceptance, while enthusiastic, is definitely a trifle unorthodox. 'I've never been to a Thanksgiving dinner before. Do you have to sacrifice a turkey?'

It's not often I see Noah lost for words...

Chapter Twelve

We spend most of the journey back to Dartmouth in silence, but strangely enough, it doesn't feel particularly awkward. My mind plays back my aunt's revelations about her time in The States.

Although we were the last to leave the cottage, there was no opportunity to get her alone, as Neil, Jacques and Elaine are all spending the night.

Tory and I did get a brief opportunity to chat while she was giving Dotty a last wee before getting into the very posh limousine Noah had hired.

'I had no idea your aunt spent time in America,' Tory murmured putting the little dog on the ground to do her business.

'Me neither,' I answered drily watching Pepé run up to join Dotty in a sniffing extravaganza. 'Somehow I think your father's aware of it though. Did you see the glance they exchanged when the subject first came up?' I could just about see Tory nod her head as we ventured a little way along a small crazy paved path.

'There's definitely some skulduggery afoot,' she agreed in full *Pirates of the Caribbean* mode. 'I intend to find out exactly what dad knows, even if I have to tie him to his study chair. You going to have a word with Flo?'

'I was hoping to speak with her tonight but I think she's avoiding me. I'll try again when she's on her own. I'll find out what I can before Thursday and we can compare notes.' Tory nods her head again before changing the subject.

'Did you see Freddy's reaction when Jacques accepted Noah's

invitation,' she asked in between hissing, 'Wee wee,' to Dotty who was more interested in following Pepé into the bushes.

'Mmm,' I responded softly, just in case the object of our conversation should suddenly pop up like a jack in a box - a regular stunt of our highly strung third wheel. 'I thought for a second he was going to jump up and throw his arms around Noah in excitement. I had no idea he could be so sweet.'

'I hope he doesn't get hurt though,' Tory countered, picking up the little dog after she finally relented and did her business (Dotty that is, Tory generally prefers a toilet...)

I picked up Pepé who was in grave danger of throwing himself off the edge of the cliff in his excited efforts to pee in the same place, then we walked slowly back to where the cars were waiting.

'Do you think Jacques will keep our wedding a secret?' she asked before we rejoined the others. 'There's no way it won't get mentioned over Thanksgiving.'

'I'll get him to sign a non disclosure contract,' I quipped, 'If he violates it, we'll simply lock him up and give the key to Freddy.'

Tory grinned and leaned forward to give me a quick peck on the cheek, murmuring, 'I want to know every last gory detail,' as she did so.

I frowned, feigning incomprehension, but she merely sniffed and tapped the end of my nose. 'I'll call you in the morning. Not too early though...'

I looked over at Jason to check he hadn't heard, then managed to catch hold of my friend's arm as a sudden thought took hold.

'Has your dad given you any idea who this naval chaplain is that he's got to conduct the service? I need to give the security people his name, and to be honest, I thought you'd probably like to get acquainted with him a little seeing as he's going to be officiating on the biggest day of your life.'

Tory dipped her head pensively. 'I keep meaning to ask him, but something always seems to come up. Don't worry, that's another question I'll ask him when he's tied to the chair...'

I'm suddenly brought back to the present as the car stops, and I realize we're not only back in Dartmouth, but Jason has parked the car opposite my flat. The silence seems almost alive as I look over at him, abruptly remembering his earlier request to see my etchings. My nerves are strung like taut wire.

Will he think I want him to stay the night if I ask him up for coffee? Do I want him to stay the night? I raise my eyes to his as he stares at me enquiringly.

After a couple of seconds, he sighs, giving a small quirk of his lips. 'It's late,' he murmurs, clearly offering me a way out.

I drop my eyes, wondering whether I should be playing it cool. Then, all at once I'm tired of playing the game.

I don't want a way out – it's as simple as that. It's time I let myself go and stopped agonizing over what's going to happen tomorrow. Tomorrow isn't here, it doesn't exist yet. There's only tonight.

I raise my eyes back to his and say softly, formally, 'I believe I have some very interesting etchings to show you Captain Buchannan. It would be a shame if you missed them due to the lateness of the hour.'

I can vaguely see his eyes narrow in the darkness, and for a second, I think I've got it horribly wrong, that he really doesn't want to come up with me. Then I discern that the crinkling in his eyes is due to his smile and I relax as he leans forward to kiss me on the lips.

His mouth is soft and warm, tentative. Slowly he lifts his right hand, sliding it gently through my hair to the back of my head. I feel him tremble slightly and recognize he's holding back.

Then he withdraws a fraction - just enough to look at me, to silently ask the question, and I give a small involuntary gasp as I catch sight of his eyes in the shadows, hot and intent.

With a small whimper, I lean into him and press my mouth back against his. He remains still for a second, then groans and pulls me half onto his lap, and with a small surge of triumph, I feel his mouth open hungrily against mine...

I wake up slowly. I know it's early because the morning sun is shining directly in my eyes - I obviously neglected to close the curtains last night. I briefly question how I could have forgotten, when it all comes flooding back.

Turning my head, I stare in wonder at Jason's tousled head lying next to me. He looks surprisingly young and almost vulnerable asleep.

My mind flits back to last night. I can't really remember how we got from the car to my flat, but I do recall that he wasn't really interested in seeing anything except the parts of me that are generally hidden. I feel my face redden and self consciously close my eyes as I remember him tearing off my clothes – the antique lace never stood a chance - then his oh so capable fingers unrelentingly touching, stroking, rubbing, *tasting* every inch of me until I was squirming, gasping under his hands and mouth. Then finally the glorious feel of him, hard and velvety smooth taking me to a place where thoughts have no part and everything is pure, exquisite sensation.

I'm brought suddenly, shockingly back to the present by a warm hand sliding down my body. My eyes fly open to see his silver eyes regarding me in sleepy appreciation.

'Good morning.' His voice is soft, warm honey as his hand continues to explore. Unable to help myself, I writhe under his expert fingers, gasping as he continues to watch me, his eyes heavy lidded with desire. But this time it's my turn, and he catches his breath as I brush the tips of my fingers against the hard contours of his body, my hands dipping lower until they hold the hard smooth length of him, touching and stroking until with a low growl, he pushes me back into the bed and carries us both to oblivion.

An hour later our bedroom intimacy is a distant memory. The embarrassing details of providing a towel, spare toothbrush and the whole "what does he like for breakfast" bit creates an uncomfortable awkwardness between us that I hadn't bargained for. And of course, last night's decision to stop agonizing over tomorrow because it doesn't exist yet was made when I was pretty inebriated. And guess what? It bloody well *exists* now...

Clumsily I hand him a coffee as he comes out of the shower. I should have so planned this better. I should have had freshly ground coffee instead of instant; fresh croissants instead of bread with dots of mould on it.

Note to self: Always plan seductions well in advance.

To my relief he seems perfectly happy with Gold Blend (I do only buy the good stuff), and declines any toast with the excuse that he has a breakfast meeting at eleven (on a Sunday?)

He looks undeniably delicious wearing just his white dress shirt and black slacks, his hair damp and dishevelled from the shower. At least his car's parked outside so he won't have to do the walk of shame.

So instead of agonizing about tomorrow, I'm agonizing about now. Or more precisely, exactly what to say now. The silence is slowly moving from awkward to downright embarrassing. I have no idea what he's thinking – his face is completely inscrutable.

Does he think I bring men back to my flat regularly? I want to laugh. I've had my current bed nearly four years and he's the first person to have slept in it besides me and Tory, and he's definitely the only person to have actually shared it with me.

I think back to the warm passionate man of last night. No resemblance at all to the solemn stranger in front of me. How stupid am I? Did I honestly believe he might want something more from me than a quick bonk? Come on! My experience of Jason Buchannan up to now has clearly told me he's not interested in a serious relationship. How could I have forgotten that so quickly?

I open my mouth, intending to briskly send him on his way before spending the rest of the day wallowing in self pity.

'Would you like to meet for a drink before the Thanksgiving dinner on Thursday?' I stare at him in open mouthed surprise. It's the last thing I expect him to say.

'I could meet you here in town, then we could cross over to

Kingswear on the passenger ferry and have a drink at the Ship before walking up to Noah's house. That's if you don't mind a bit of a hike of course. I just thought it might give us an appetite.'

His voice is actually a little uncertain, almost nervous, and I suddenly wonder again just how much of the real Jason is hidden behind his unreadable face.

'I'd love to,' I stammer at length, before continuing more confidently, 'And the walk back will burn off the calories.' I smile hesitantly at him, and after a second he grins back, his stony expression finally cracking.

'I think it might be better if we get a taxi back,' he responds drily, 'We don't want to overdo it - I might end up carrying you.'

I give an inelegant snort. 'I'll have you know I once completed the Commando Challenge. A mere two mile stroll is nothing to me.'

And just like that, the ice is broken. He puts his empty coffee cup onto the draining board and steps forward, bending his head to kiss me softly. 'Thanks for last night. It... *you,* were amazing.'

'You're very welcome,' I manage to murmur, resisting the urge to ask him to take me back to bed.

He stares intently at me for a second, and my heart starts to thud. I know he can tell exactly what I am thinking. But all he does is stroke over my lips with his thumb before turning away to grab his jacket.

'Shall we meet over at the boat float?' he asks, shrugging his arms into the sleeves.

'Sounds good,' I mutter a little huskily – that thumb stroke was ridiculously the most erotic thing he'd done.

'Dinner's at eight, so shall we say about five thirty? That will give us time to get over to the other side and have a leisurely drink without having to sprint round the headland.'

I simply nod happily, and he steps forward again to give me one last kiss. Then he's gone, and contrary to my earlier intention, I decide that a big fried breakfast at Alf's is the order of the day.

I give Freddy a quick call to see if he fancies meeting me to stock up on some coronary fodder, and, to my surprise, he agrees with very unFreddy like enthusiasm. Not usually a morning person, he actually sounds disgustingly perky, and I'm guessing my aunt's editor may have something to do with his early morning change of personality.

I'm eager to find out more, and hopefully talking about himself (Freddy's favourite pastime) will stop him from ferreting out my business, (his second favourite pastime). After a brief internal debate, I give Tory a quick text on the off chance that she and Noah might like to join us.

As I pull on my coat, I consider whether to give Aunt Flo a call, then decide it's a bit too early for the kind of interrogation I have in mind. She's probably still in bed, especially as Neil stopped over.

She thinks I don't know about their relationship, but I've been aware of it for years. I've never thought about it before, but my aunt is actually quite good at keeping her cards very close to her chest.

Maybe I shouldn't be quite so surprised about any potential skeletons in her cupboard...

Chapter Thirteen

Café Al Fresco, or Alf's as it's more commonly known to the locals, serves in my opinion, the best breakfast in Dartmouth. Situated in an old building with low ceilings papered in newspapers going back years, the interior can best be described as rustic.

The atmosphere is wonderfully relaxed and you can get anything from a full English breakfast to cinnamon toast.

Like nearly everything in Dartmouth town centre, it's only a couple of hundred yards away from my flat, and it's our favourite place to go when it's too early to go to The Cherub…

Walking past the narrow Elizabethan shops along Lower Street, I shiver and tuck my hands into my coat pockets. The weather's unusually cold. Snow is not something we see often in our neck of the woods – the south west of England is more likely to drown than freeze – but glancing up into the iron grey sky, I reflect how lovely it would be if it actually snowed on Tory's wedding day.

Proper snow - not the grey mushy stuff that we usually get. The College would look amazing. A real life *Hogwarts*.

Still, snow or not, I'm relieved when I eventually push open the door to the steamy warmth of Alf's. Blowing on my freezing hands, I pause for a few seconds to let my eyes become accustomed to the gloom.

The place is packed, so I squeeze my way to a spare couple of chairs at the end of a large table. The rest are occupied by a family consisting of two adults, four children and three dogs.

The smallest child is obviously only a couple of years old. She (I think it's a she – the only clue under all the tomato ketchup is a pink bib) is sitting in a high chair with pieces of cut up sausage on the tray in front of her.

Obviously sausage is not her favourite part of a pig as she's busy throwing each piece onto the floor while shouting, 'Bacon,' at the top of her voice.

Fortunately the dogs don't appear to have the same aversion to sausage, and all three are poised ready and waiting to catch each discarded piece as it lands.

There's also a second child in another high chair carefully squeezing scrambled egg through greasy fingers. I have no idea what sex this one is as the bib is covered in baked beans.

Grimacing slightly, I debate whether to join the queue at the counter to grab a coffee while I'm waiting for Freddy, but decide that squeezing my way past the family is probably best done only once. Running the gauntlet past sausage wielding and scrambled egg squeezing infants is not to be taken lightly.

Luckily I'm spared from having to refuse a half eaten piece of sausage held out to me by the bacon lover as Freddy suddenly pops up at my shoulder.

He looks over at the child with a shudder, then glances around desperately in the hope that another table might suddenly become free. By the look on his face I think he's prepared to commit grievous bodily harm to get one.

No such luck however, and after a quick frown, he sits gingerly on the other empty seat right next to the sausage lobber, only to be slobbered over by two of the dogs.

'Pepper likes you,' says the woman with a fond smile towards the larger of the two dogs who is busy trying to climb onto Freddy's knee. I smother a laugh as I watch Freddy trying to push his new best friend down while avoiding a piece of sausage being stuffed up his nose.

In the end, he hastily grabs the offending piece of meat out of the little girl's fingers and throws it under the table muttering, 'Fetch Fido.'

Mercifully the dog disappears to sniff out the booty, leaving Freddy fastidiously wiping his hands on a scrap of tissue dug out of his pocket.

'Have you got any sanitizer?' he mutters, following it with a small whimper as he notices bean juice on his jeans. Taking pity on him, I suggest we swap seats, even offering to undertake the assault course to the counter while he recovers from his ordeal. I really don't think Freddy's cut out to be a father.

He nods his head as I get up, and after giving me his order, plonks himself down on my seat with a small weak smile of apology towards the parents. Both smile back at him cheerily, obviously having developed thick skins regarding their less than salubrious offspring.

'My name's Mary. Why are you wearing a blouse?' pipes up one of the older two children, pointing a grubby finger dangerously close to Freddy's best Dolce and Gabbana shirt.

Cringing, I beat a hasty retreat. To be fair, the kid has a point. Freddy does look like he's wearing something out of *My Fair Lady*.

It takes me nearly fifteen minutes to reach the front of the queue, and all that time I can feel Freddy's eyes boring into the back of my head. Every time I glance over, he glares at me in between fending off grubby fingers and drooling dogs. My mobile phone keeps pinging and the texts are getting increasingly fraught.

Just as I reach the counter, it goes off once more and I glance down at the text before giving our order. YOU'RE PAYING, it says in capital letters. I know better than to argue...

A few minutes later I'm fighting my way back to the table with our drinks, just our table companions are preparing to leave. 'Talk about bloody timing,' mutters Freddy as I set his drink down.

It takes the family another ten minutes to gather everything together, and as they leave with kids and dogs in tow, the table looks like a scene out of world war three.

'Bloody hell, have you guys been eating with your fingers?'

Tory's amazed voice sounds at our elbows a couple of minutes later.

'Not us, it was Dartmouth's answer to The Brady Bunch. You just missed them,' I answer, squeezing forward so she can get past my seat. 'It's good job too, I think it might have put you off kids for life. Where's Dotty?'

I look around, only to spot the little dog vacuuming up the leftovers under the table. Tory bends down to give me a quick hug, then looks over at Freddy, frowning at his uncharacteristic silence. I actually think he could do with something a bit stronger than coffee.

'I think they took a liking to Freddy,' I offer with a grin.

'Oh, nice,' Tory murmurs sitting down, 'That doesn't happen very often.' Freddy refuses to rise to the bait – another sign that he's shell shocked. 'What's that on your shirt,' she asks, pointing to what looks like a large lump of egg yolk decorating his top button. Freddy glances down and gives a small moan before jumping up hastily. With a quick glare at me, he turns and hurries up the narrow winding stairs to the toilet.

'Watch your head on that low beam…' I call, just as I hear a resounding crack, followed by several unrepeatable profanities.

'Ouch, that must have hurt,' Tory says with a wince. She waves over at Noah who's queuing. His disguise of the day is to sport a pair of horn rimmed glasses that look as though they've come from a charity shop.

To be fair, they probably have. One of Noah's favourite hobbies is rummaging for what he calls his props. I hate to break it to him, but I think that most of Dartmouth's residents aren't really fooled. They just like to humour him. After all, it's not every town that can boast a world famous actor as one of their own.

Ten minutes later, Freddy reappears sporting a large wet patch on the front of his shirt, and a shiny red lump on his forehead. To put it bluntly, he's not a happy bunny. The only thing that stops him from flouncing out of the café is the arrival of our breakfasts.

I smile gratefully at the waitress as she clears away the discarded plates, but Freddy simply tosses his head and stiffly begins tucking into his bacon and eggs.

I look over at Tory and pull a face - he's such a prima donna sometimes. She winks at me just as Noah arrives back at the table.

'Wow, you been in a fight with a rampaging water hose buddy?' Noah asks as he sits down.

Tory kicks him under the table and I stifle a giggle. Freddy simply gives a long suffering sigh and continues to eat without answering.

We decide to ignore him. Freddy's best left to come out of a sulk on his own – although that can take anything from seven minutes to seven years…

'I wanted to ask you a favour,' Tory turns to me and tries to pinch a piece of my bacon. I slap her hand away. 'You have no manners,' I retort, giving her a crispy bit speared on my fork. 'What kind of favour?'

'I was wondering if you'd look after Dotty for a couple of nights.' She glances over at Noah with a smile before continuing, 'Noah wants to take me to London tomorrow. He's been asked to switch on the Christmas lights in Oxford Street this year.'

'They asked me months ago,' Noah interrupts with a slight grimace, 'But with everything that's happened since, I totally forgot about it. My agent Matt called me in a panic this morning.'

'Of course I'll look after her for you. Sounds like fun,' I say a trifle enviously.

Tory immediately picks up on my wistful tone, adding hastily, 'If you'd like to come along, I can always ask dad to have her.' I can see Freddy in the corner of my eye, trying very hard not to look interested as I shake my head reluctantly.

'No, that's okay, I have too much going on here. A wedding organizer's work is never done'. I give a theatrical sigh before throwing a quick glance towards our still silent diva.

'I don't know about Freddy though, perhaps he'd like to go along with you.'

'How about it Freddy – you up for a couple of nights in London?' Freddy looks up, eyes shining, his sulk completely forgotten.

'I can't do two nights – the panto this year is full of bloody amateurs who can't tell the difference between Widow Twanky and the Fairy Godmother. 'But I think I could manage to come up on Tuesday for the day.'

'That's settled then,' Tory responds with satisfaction, just as their breakfast arrives.

'So, changing the subject, do either of you have anything you want to tell me?' She's actually staring at me, and unable to help myself, I colour up.

'I knew it,' she exclaims excitedly, 'Tell me everything.'

'There's nothing to tell,' I declare firmly, determined to keep my love life to myself for a little longer. I shut my mouth mulishly (Tory's description), and she knows from old that she's not going to get anywhere pushing the subject. With a small pout, she turns to Freddy.

'So how about you Freddy? Anything new in the wasteland that's been your love life for the last year and a half?'

Freddy gives a pout of his own. 'You know just how traumatized I've been since my fling with the flamenco dancer. I'm determined that any future relationships will be slow burning as opposed to a flash in the pan. No longer will I wear my heart on my sleeve.

'However, since you ask, yes, Jacques and I have exchanged mobile phone numbers. But other than that peeps, my lips are sealed. You can expect an update after the wedding.'

Tory glares at both of us, frustrated by our reluctance to spill the proverbial beans, so I decide another change of subject is in order. 'How's your morning sickness been?'

Tory narrows her eyes at me, telling me she knows exactly what I'm doing, then she slumps slightly in acceptance.

'It's been much better over the last few days actually; I'm hoping I might have kicked it into touch.' She emphasizes her new found cast iron stomach by popping a piece of toast in her mouth.

'That's brilliant. We might not be sending you down the aisle with a bucket after all. So what time do you expect to be back from London?'

'We'll be back by Wednesday lunchtime.' She pauses, taking a quick sip of her coffee, before continuing casually, 'Do you want to come over in the afternoon to help us put up the Christmas decorations ready for Thanksgiving supper?'

I know the way her mind works – she's thinking she can pump me for more information over Christmas carols.

I stick my fork in one of her mushrooms and put it into my mouth in an echo of her earlier action. 'I'd love to,' I say with a knowing grin. 'I'll bring the moose milk.'

Noah pauses with his fork halfway to his mouth. 'Sounds disgusting. I'm assuming it's something alcoholic that doesn't actually come from a real life moose?'

I smile mischievously at him. 'You Hollywood types don't know everything Noah Westbrook. Moose milk is a naval specialty. I pinched the original formula from the Admiral and I think you'll find it to be a highlight in your up to now mundane existence.'

'That's if it doesn't kill you,' mutters Tory moving her plate out of my reach. 'I seem to remember my father losing three days of his life after you had that competition to find out whose recipe was the best.'

'I've perfected mine since then,' I protest half heartedly, 'Made a few tweaks and adjustments so it's not quite so...err...'

'Lethal,' interjects Freddy bluntly.

I look indignantly at him, but before I can come up with a suitable response, my attention is taken by two paws scratching insistently at my knees. Dotty has obviously finished cleaning the floor under the table and is now ready to move on to plated food. Bending forward, I pick her up and put her into my lap.

'You like Aunty Kit's moose milk don't you Dotspot?' I ask softly, rubbing her head against my cheek. Tory nearly chokes on her coffee.

'Don't you dare give her any of that stuff,' she orders, waving her knife at me. 'You know what she's like, the greedy little madam will eat anything.'

'It's a drink, not something to eat. And of course I won't give her any. What kind of aunt do you take me for?' And to emphasize my point, I give Dotty a sizeable piece of bacon fat, which of course is not a health hazard for dogs at all.

Noah leans back with a contented sigh. 'God I love English breakfasts,' he murmurs patting his stomach. Then he looks at me over his coffee cup before saying decisively, 'I would love you to bring some of your infamous moose milk on Wednesday Kit. Whatever it is, it sounds mind-blowing, and if nothing else, we Hollywood types can take our liquor...'

Chapter Fourteen

It's eight o'clock on Monday morning and I'm going over the critical path of the wedding timeline while waiting for Tory to drop Dotty off. Everything appears to be under control and I feel a tiny frisson of pride at what I've achieved. Granted I haven't done it alone, but for a first timer, I do believe I've done okay so far. Hopefully, once the wedding is over and the details come out in the press, I'll be inundated with work. That's the plan anyway.

Maybe Noah can get me my own reality TV show - we could call it *The Wedding Organizer.* I try not to think about the possibility of Jason Buchannan figuring somewhere in my dreams of event management superstardom.

My musings are interrupted as the doorbell rings accompanied by frenzied barking that can only be Dotty. A few seconds later the little dog dashes into the flat and throws herself ecstatically at my feet. Tory arrives at the top of the stairs a couple of minutes later with both arms full. 'Are you sure you don't mind having her?' she asks, dropping the heavy load onto the table.

'Not at all,' I respond, eying the pile of toys, dog food and basket. I really don't know why she bothered with the last two. 'How long did you say you were going for?'

She smiles ruefully, acknowledging that she might have overdone it slightly. I step forward to give her a quick hug, then push her gently back towards the door. 'Go on, have a lovely couple of days, and don't come back without my Christmas present...'

As the door slams shut behind her, I turn back to Dotty who

is already making herself comfortable on my sofa. I bend down to give her a quick fuss, then eye the dull, overcast sky outside. 'Come on Dotspot, let's get the whole walkies thing over with shall we? Then we can curl up and watch movies all day.' The little dog cocks her head to one side and wags her tail. She really is a sweetheart, even if she's spoiled rotten...

Five minutes later we're both wrapped up in fleecy jackets. Looking down at her jaunty little red number, I'm just grateful we don't actually match. The weather outside has continued to get colder, and there's even a slight frost decorating the benches in the Royal Avenue Gardens.

As we walk past the bandstand, I watch them putting up the last of the Christmas lights and decorating the huge tree positioned in the middle of the gardens. I stop to look at a large poster propped up next to the tree. The lights will be officially switched on this Friday. There's going to be a candlelit lantern parade, lots of carol singing and Santa arriving by boat.

'Apparently it's the last leg of his journey from Lapland,' I tell Dotty who seems much more interested in sniffing her way around the bottom of the tree.

It sounds like fun. They haven't gone to quite so much trouble in previous years, although Freddy did mention something about The Flavel Centre being involved in a story telling marathon over the weekend.

I make a mental note to tell Tory and Noah about it. It will be a lovely ending to their Thanksgiving celebrations. And of course Jason might like to tag along too – if he's not involved in the festivities as Captain of BRNC.

Pulling on Dotty's leash, I head out of the gardens and over to the waterfront before turning left towards the Higher Ferry. The river is completely still, a light mist hanging low over the water. The only noise comes from the distant clanking of rigging. There's hardly anyone about and I wonder if everyone is busy with their Christmas shopping. I haven't even started mine. It's going to be a last minute thing this year – after the wedding is over. As always, Aunt Flo has asked me over for Christmas Day, and I can't help but speculate as to what variation on a classic roast turkey dinner she's likely to come up with this year.

Last Christmas she actually created a turkey cake, complete with layers of turkey, sweet potatoes, cranberry sauce, stuffing and mashed potato frosting. Apparently she got the recipe off the internet. I think the less said about it the better really. I smile to myself as I remember Neil's face as she carried it in...

I realize that we're nearly at the higher ferry slip and I debate whether to treat myself to a hot chocolate in the Floating Bridge before walking back. A cosy pub with a log fire would be just the job on a cold day like this.

Decision made, I get ready to cross the road towards the entrance, just as the higher ferry reaches the slip. The queue of vehicles waiting to board starts to move forward in anticipation, and I hurriedly pick Dotty up and step back onto the pavement, deciding to wait until the cars have all embarked rather than risking life and limb by squeezing between them as they wait.

Snuggling the little dog's warm body to me, I idly watch the cars as they file past. Suddenly my heart lurches as I recognize Jason's white Audi begin the move onto the ramp, before pausing to wait for the car in front. I'm just about to step forward and wave, when I realize there's someone else in the car. A woman.

Frowning, I step behind a large bush, unaccountably reluctant for him to see me. She's probably a work colleague. I peer round the leaves to see if she's wearing a uniform, only to see her lean towards Jason laughing. In what feels like slow motion, I watch her raise her hand and stroke his cheek, just as he pulls forward onto the ferry.

Heart thudding, I crane my head in a last ditch effort to see more, but the car is swallowed up. A few minutes later, the ferry pulls away, and I'm left feeling slightly sick, all thoughts of a nice hot chocolate disappearing faster than you can say, 'Cheating bastard.'

I arrive back at my flat in record time. Dotty is more than

happy to be back in the warmth and waits patiently as I strip off her coat with trembling hands. How bloody ridiculous – my hands really are shaking.

My mind persists in replaying the scene in full technicolour, and at the same time I keep telling myself that I'm completely overreacting. She could have been a relative – a distant one. I know he hasn't got any siblings, or cousins. He told me he comes from a long line of only children – on both sides.

Taking a deep breath, I berate myself crossly. A caress on the cheek means *nothing*, I'm simply being overly melodramatic. There could be hundreds of perfectly valid reasons why a strange woman is sitting in his car and stroking his face...

So why do I feel like crying? Why is my heart pounding in my chest as though I've run a bloody marathon? It's not even as if we're dating – I mean, not exclusively anyway.

I pace the floor while Dotty watches me, her ears back in baffled sympathy. Oh God, when did I let him get under my skin? When did he stop being an arrogant knob and become simply Jason?

Groaning, I sink down onto the sofa and lean forward to hug my knees. When did I let myself fall in love?

~*~

Admiral Shackleford was already on his second pint and Jimmy still hadn't arrived. It was too damn much. Charles Shackleford was prepared to accept that his request might have been a little last minute, but Jimmy was only babysitting his bloody carpet crawlers for God's sake. There must be some other mug he could leave them with in an emergency such as this.

Things were rapidly getting out of hand. He'd been about to bring up the subject of old Boris during the murder mystery evening at Flo's place, but then the questions started coming up about the damn woman's stint across the pond, and in the end he had to admit (if only privately) that he'd chickened out. But he'd spotted Victory and Kit glance at each other which had put the fear of God into him.

And then this morning, before she disappeared off to London, Victory had asked The Question - well, one of them anyway – there was getting to be a bloody list now. As much as he hated it, like always, he needed Jimmy's level head.

He glanced down at his watch, and then at Pickles napping at his feet. As if he could feel his master's eyes on him, the elderly spaniel lifted his head and gave a yawn.

'We're getting too bollocking old for all this cloak and dagger stuff old boy,' the Admiral mumbled to the Springer gruffly, 'We both need putting out to bloody pasture.' He bent down to stroke Pickles' head with a sigh. 'Either that or the knackers' yard.'

Abruptly the door opened, bringing in a waft of cold air, but glancing round, Charles Shackleford's relief at seeing his friend was short lived as he noted with disbelief that Jimmy had two of his ankle biters in tow. The Admiral stared wordlessly at the two toddlers as if he'd just seen a couple of aliens.

Jimmy was struggling to hold the door open as he pushed the first one through, while trying to drag number two who was currently kicking and screaming. 'Give me a hand with Abigail will you Sir?' he puffed as he tried in vain to yank his reluctant granddaughter through the rapidly closing gap.

The Admiral remained seated, staring in horror at the scene in front of him. 'Bloody hell, she's got a pair of lungs on her,' he grumbled loudly over the din.

'I NEED YOUR HELP SIR – NOW.' Jimmy's response loud enough to alert the whole of Kingswear – if his granddaughter hadn't already done the job.

The Admiral hesitated another second – obviously reluctant to take orders from a subordinate – then catching sight of Jimmy's irate face, he hurriedly climbed down off his bar stool muttering, 'I know where she bloody gets it from.'

'Please could you refrain from swearing Sir,' Jimmy breathed as he thankfully handed over the first child to the Admiral. Charles Shackleford stared with distaste at the little girl in his arms. There was a definite aroma coming from her nether regions. It reminded him of Boris.

'What the bl... what the hell am I supposed to do with her?' he shouted to Jimmy irritably, completely ignoring the fact that his friend was now busy dragging granddaughter number two through the door by the ankles. The noise was beginning to reach a crescendo, especially when Pickles decided to get in on the act by howling enthusiastically. The Admiral could only be thankful they were the only customers in the pub.

The small girl in his arms continued to watch him solemnly, and thankfully silently, as Jimmy eventually managed to manoeuvre her sister into the pub. After another couple of minutes, the small man finally stood puffing and panting with the reluctant Abigail hanging upside down over his arm.

For a second the Admiral thought he'd gone deaf as she suddenly stopped shrieking, catching sight of Pickles now cowering next to the bar stool. After a couple of seconds blessed silence, the little girl found her voice again, this time yelling, 'Bow wow.' Kicking her legs out in an effort to get down, only Jimmy's quick thinking prevented her foot going straight up his nose.

With incredible patience, he placed his granddaughter back on the ground, this time the right way up. Charles Shackleford privately thought the little bugger was lucky not to have been dropped on her head.

Jimmy bent down beside Abigail to show her how to stroke Pickles gently, and to the Admiral's relief, the child in his arms immediately wriggled to get down too. Pulling a face as the noxious smell wafted up, Charles Shackleford hastily put her down non too gently next to her sister.

'What the bloody hell were you thinking man?' the Admiral demanded when Jimmy finally straightened up.

'Beryl next door is looking after Tommy,' Jimmy answered mildly after taking a welcome swallow of his pint, 'But she couldn't have all three of them. Tommy's only a baby, so while he's asleep, he no trouble. But this pair...' He shook his head, bending down again to stop Beatrice trying to take Pickles a walk by his ears. 'You have to have eyes in the back of your head with

Beatrice and Abigail.'

His voice was full of pride and the Admiral glanced down at the two little girls - one smelling like a pile of manure, and the other with her face streaked with snot and tears. The Admiral shook his head. He prided himself on being a compassionate man, but he was definitely struggling to see the attractions of this pair of ankle snappers. But then, maybe he'd feel differently when Victory finally decided to get off her arse and give him one of his own...

'So what did you want to see me about Sir? Jimmy said distractedly.

The Admiral heaved a sigh. 'I've just got a bad feeling in my gut Jimmy lad,' he said eventually.

'Are you sure it's not an ulcer?' his friend answered glancing towards the Admiral's ample stomach.

'No it's not a boll... a blo.. a damn ulcer,' Charles Shackleford responded irritably. 'You know how intuitive I am.' He ignored Jimmy's derisive snort, putting it down to the small man drinking his pint too quickly – beer could be very gassy.

'I can sense things Jimmy,' he continued earnestly. 'You know, feel when things are about to go tits up, and right now my gut's telling me we've got a bloody tsunami on the way. It's not just Bible Basher Boris. This whole damn business with Flo. I just don't know what to do Jimmy lad.

'It's not often I say this, but I'm worried. Victory's asking questions. If I don't start talking, she's going to add two and two together and come up with five.

'I think I'm going to have to come clean. About everything.'

'No Sir, Jimmy said firmly, looking the Admiral right in the eyes, 'You can't force your daughter to make a decision like that – it's simply not fair. You need to tell Boris that he can't officiate at Victory's wedding, it's as simple as that.

'Tory should not be forced into an impossible situation due to your old cock-ups.' Jimmy paused for breath and the Admiral opened his mouth, intending to object to the word cock-up, but before he could speak, this new confident Jimmy continued, 'As for your... err... first marriage. You need to speak to Florence before you do anything. See if you can both come up with some kind of game plan. Sir'

The Admiral was silent for a moment and Jimmy took the opportunity to stop Abigail from attempting to share the contents of her nose with a more than willing Pickles.

'The thing is Jimmy lad, it's not just the bloody marriage. It's what happened after.'

Jimmy looked up in alarm. The Admiral's voice sounded dead tired – something he hadn't seen in his friend before, even when he was facing a possible stint in the Bangkok Hilton.

'When Florence came back to Dartmouth, she had an ankle biter in tow. A little girl.'

Jimmy felt his heart sink as he stared up at the Admiral in dismay, simply waiting in silence for his friend to continue.

'It was Kit. When she came back from The States, she had Kit with her. I don't know who the girl's parents are, but they're definitely not Flo's brother and his wife.'

~*~

It's six o'clock in the morning when I finally give up all possibility of sleeping and decide to crawl out of bed. Dotty simply lifts her head to look at me incredulously before burrowing back into the duvet. By the time I've thrown on my dressing gown, she's already snoring again.

Shivering, I head into the kitchen to put the kettle on. It's still dark outside and the central heating hasn't kicked in yet.

I've spent the whole night going over an incident that lasted a little less than a minute. Ridiculous right? My imagination has done a sterling job of working overtime - I've jumped to so many conclusions I could write a book, and I still have no idea what to do.

Cradling my tea, I wander back into the living room and perch on the edge of the sofa. It's a good job I never succumbed to the temptation to confide in my friends about my so called *burgeon-*

ing romance. I'd seriously look like an idiot now.

I take a sip of my tea and fight back the tears. But then, I'd so love to have Tory shoulder to cry on right this minute, I don't care if it makes me look pathetic. Damn it, I need something to take my mind off my disastrous love life.

Putting my tea aside, I grab the wedding folder and begin scanning it frantically. The problem is that everything that can be taken care of has been. I can't make any telephone calls at seven in the morning and the one person I really want to speak to could well be cuddling up to the bloody face stroking brunette I'd like to speak to him about.

I glance out at the pre-dawn darkness, now slightly greyer than before. An early morning walk, that will shake off the cobwebs. Then I have a brainwave. I need to talk to aunt Flo. Solving the mystery of her and the Admiral will definitely take my mind off my *possibly* cheating *almost* boyfriend.

AND, I'll walk there. It's only about five miles along the coast. If I get my skates on, I'll be there in time for breakfast. I hurriedly swallow the last of my tea and head into the bathroom for a quick shower. All of a sudden I'm looking forward to a decent bit of exercise. As I shut the bathroom door, I can still hear Dotty's snores. I'm not sure my canine companion is going to be quite so enthusiastic

I think I was actually underestimating Dotty's lack of enthusiasm for an early morning hike. I've been carrying her for the last mile and a half. This is bloody ridiculous. I know she likes her bed, but come on – she's a dog for pities sake. Don't all dogs love to walk any time of the day or night? Okay so it's raining, but it's only a light drizzle, and it's not *that* windy.

Sighing, I tuck her under my other arm, determined that once we get to the top of this hill, she's damn well going to have to walk.

She wasn't too bad during the first part of the walk as we followed the winding coast path through the woods, lots of nice smells obviously. But after Blackstone Point, the landscape is much wilder and emptier, and most definitely not to Dotty's taste at all.

At the top of the hill, I put the little dog back onto the ground and turn inland to follow the path towards the village of Stoke Fleming.

'Come on Dotspot, not too far now.'

Okay, so that might be a slight exaggeration, but we're definitely half way.

I look behind me to see her standing where I'd plonked her, a complete picture of misery. She looks behind her as if trying to decide whether it might be better to go back the way we came, then, obviously deciding that sticking with her mad Aunty Kit is the lesser of two evils, she begins plodding along reluctantly. I can't help but laugh.

My mood has definitely improved since I set out. There's something about physical exercise that puts things into perspective.

As we reach the village, I put Dotty's leash back on and in no time at all we're heading along the narrow footpath leading towards Blackpool Sands.

Glancing down at my watch I note that it's just after eight thirty. I didn't telephone ahead to say I was coming, hoping the unexpectedness of my visit might prompt her to be a little more indiscrete. However, now it occurs to me to wonder that might have been a slight error of judgement. What if she's not actually home? I'm not sure Dotty's up to the hike back without so much as a biscuit. Come to think of it, I'm not sure I am either.

As we emerge onto the access road leading to the beach and the car park, I pick the little dog up and scan the cliffs up to my aunt's cottage, just visible above the early morning mist. There's a steep flight of steps cut into the rock at the other end of the beach which lead up to her garden. God, I hope she's in. I could murder a cup of tea right now.

Ten wheezing minutes later I finally push open the gate into aunt Flo's garden, and figuring that I'm most likely to find her in the kitchen, I make my way round to the terrace.

Dotty has completely regained her enthusiasm, and is now fairly skipping ahead with her usual trademark barking - definitely sensing the possibility of a treat or two (she has no qualms at all about my aunt's cooking). I can hear Pepé's answering yap and I smile ruefully. So much for my surprise arrival.

Dotty's jumping up at the door as I catch her up, but I'm unable to see through the glass as the sun's finally decided to come out and the reflection is actually quite dazzling. Shielding my eyes, I push open the door.

'Hi Flo, sorry I didn't ca...'

Then I stop as my eyes become accustomed to the gloom. My Aunt Flo is sitting at the kitchen table, and opposite her is the Admiral.

Chapter Fifteen

'Oh my God, you don't think they're having an affair do you? I mean, that could be why they've always avoided each other in public. It could have been going on for donkey's years.' Tory sinks down onto the sofa, lengths of tinsel dangling forgotten onto the floor.

'Of course not,' I respond vehemently, perhaps a little too vehemently. Taking the discarded tinsel out of my friend's hands, I place it on the huge Christmas tree in front of me.

'That doesn't fit at all does it? I can't imagine your father ever cheating on your mother – she was a lovely lady, and obviously doted on your dad. I mean come on, who else would have put up with your old man for as long as she did?' I pause, glancing down at Tory, wondering if I've gone a little too far, but she just nods silently.

'Anyway,' I continue, 'If my aunt and your father had been having a long standing thing, why didn't they go public after your mum died? And why on earth would he bother with Mabel?' I shake my head, selecting a bauble out of the box Tory and Noah had brought back from London. 'There's definitely something going on, but the whole affair idea just doesn't fit.'

Tory looks up at me gratefully. 'No, you're right, of course you are. It's just that it's all so strange.' She gets back to her feet and digs into the box, pulling out another exquisite decoration for the tree.

'So what happened when you burst in on their little tête-à-tête?'

'Well, I can't deny they both looked a bit shocked at first, but I have to say they recovered pretty damn quickly. Flo said the Admiral had popped in for a cup of tea on his way to Kingsbridge.'

'Bloody long winded way to get to Kingsbridge.'

'That's exactly what I said, but, quick as a flash, the Admiral replied that he often came this way to avoid the work traffic in Totnes.'

'Did he happen to mention exactly why he was going to Kingsbridge?' Tory's tone indicated that she didn't hold out much hope, but I nodded my head. 'He said he was going to pick up a couple of lobsters from a friend.'

'Well that at least I can check out,' Tory retorts, stepping back from the tree to admire her handy work. 'I really don't know how we're going to get them to come clean Kitty Kat – if indeed there's anything to come clean about.'

'Oh there's something alright,' I answer drily. 'You should have seen their faces before they got their act together. Like two naughty school children caught by the teacher.' I select another length of tinsel before continuing more thoughtfully, 'I can't help but think it has something to do with your wedding.'

Tory glances at me with a slight frown. 'What on earth could my wedding have to do with anything?' I reach for the nagging *something* that's been hovering in the back of my mind, then, when no blinding revelation hits me, I sigh irritably.

'I feel as though somehow I should know. The answer's in my head somewhere – I just can't get at it.'

'Perhaps some of your moose milk will help?' Noah's voice floats down from the top of the ladder where he's decorating the chandelier. I jump slightly. For a moment I'd forgotten he was here.

That's the thing about Noah. He doesn't talk just for the sake of hearing his own voice – unlike most actors I'm told. He generally speaks when he has something valuable to offer.

'That's the best idea I've heard all day.'

'It's only two o'clock in the afternoon,' Tory retorts a little caustically.

'You're just jealous you can't have any,' I respond airily, 'But don't worry, I'll get you some ice cream instead.'

Slightly mollified, Tory shouts, 'Chocolate chip,' at my back as I head into the kitchen.

As I take the bowl of milky liquid out of the fridge, the mellow tones Nat King Cole singing, *Chestnuts roasting on an open fire,* drift from the drawing room, and humming along, I pour two generous glasses, topping each off with a scoop of ice cream, chocolate flakes and a straw. Putting them onto a tray, I scoop out a large helping of chocolate chip ice cream for my expectant best friend, then carry the tray back into the drawing room.

'Come and get it,' I call, putting the tray onto the coffee table. 'I don't mean you little lady,' I add as Dotty forgoes her spot by the fire to investigate. 'You'll have to ask your mum to give you some ice cream.'

'So this is moose milk,' Noah murmurs, holding his glass up to the light. What's in it exactly?' He sits down on the sofa and takes a small sip through the straw. Watching him expectantly, I pause before answering, 'Rum, kahlua, vodka, milk, ice cream and chocolate chips.'

'Wow,' is his response after second, longer sip. 'It's delicious Kit. How come you never made it for me before now?'

'It's kind of a Christmas tradition,' I answer, ridiculously pleased that he likes it. Anybody would think I actually invented the recipe. 'You weren't around last Christmas so...'

'You're gonna have to give me the recipe,' he enthuses, 'Is it okay if I mix the ice cream in?' I grin at him, nodding my head.

This is what makes Noah Westbrook so unique. His boyish enthusiasm for anything new, never ever diminishes. I glance over at Tory who is looking at him with a smile, and the warm love in her eyes takes my breath away.

I've been trying so hard to avoid thinking about Jason, and up to now I've managed to file him away in the "things to think about tomorrow" folder, but seeing the adoration in Tory's eyes as she looks at Noah, brings it all back in a mixture of longing and heartache.

I still haven't said anything to Tory, and she's obviously forgotten her intention to pump me for information in the wake of my earlier revelations, which is the one good thing to come out of the mystery surrounding the Admiral and my aunt.

In fact I haven't even decided if I'm going to say anything to Jason.

I take a large gulp of moose milk. I'm determined not to go down that road today. Today is for fun and friends and solving mysteries that don't include potentially cheating almost boyfriends...

'Hey, why don't we have this for the welcome drink at the wedding?' Noah suggests, looking over at me, then at Tory. 'Come on honey, it'll be great.'

After a second, Tory shakes her head and gives in. 'Why not,' she murmurs wryly, 'I mean vintage Champagne is just so last year...'

Three hours later we've finished decorating. The gloom of the early evening has been pushed back by multitudes of twinkling lights, mistletoe and tinsel, with the piece de resistance being the beautiful fir Christmas tree in the drawing room. As we all stand back to admire our handiwork, it has to be said that Noah and I are distinctly merry.

We all give George Michael a run for his money with a boisterous rendition of *Last Christmas*, then Noah waltzes Tory around to *All I want for Christmas is you*. Of course I have to make do with Dotty, but she doesn't mind – she'll do anything for an ice cream wafer. Then, after finishing the impromptu concert with Bing Crosby's *White Christmas,* we collapse laughing onto the sofa.

'You know, I think we should sit my father and your aunt next to each other tomorrow night,' Tory muses when our laughter's subsided. 'What do you think? It's an ideal opportunity to find out once and for all if there is any funny business going on.'

'I don't want our Thanksgiving dinner turned into an Agatha Christie movie set, thank you very much,' protests Noah. 'We had enough of that at Flo's murder mystery bash.'

Tory pulls a face, then sighs. 'You're right of course sweetheart, it's not the time or the place.' Giving Noah a quick kiss, she pushes herself up off the sofa. 'Who's for some chilli?'

Noah and I both nod hungrily. 'Is there anymore moose milk left?' Noah calls as I follow Tory into the kitchen to give her a hand.

There is – just enough for a small glass each. I'd made sure to bring over a fairly small amount, assuming that Tory wouldn't take kindly to having her husband to be with a hangover on his first Thanksgiving dinner in Dartmouth. I really am such an amazing friend.

We eat our chilli by the fire listening to *Silent Night*. Tory is sitting in Noah's lap and Dotty is sitting in mine...

All in all, a perfect day.

~*~

Of course Thanksgiving is not a traditional holiday in the UK, so everything is carrying on as normal in Dartmouth. Sitting at my coffee table which doubles as a makeshift office, I make a few telephone calls while sipping my first coffee of the day. After finishing the last call, I glance down as my phone pings - it's a text from Tory. Apparently our dresses will be arriving early next week. The smiley face and party poppers at the end of the text echo my feelings exactly. I feel a tremor of excitement inside.

We've only got just over three weeks until the wedding. I know Tory's not really that hard to please, but I so want everything to be perfect. Selfishly, not just for my best friend, but for me too.

Losing the gallery was a blow I'm still privately reeling from, and I really need to prove I can do this. I don't want to keep relying on my friends; it's time I stood on my own two feet.

Resisting the urge to break into the chorus of *I Will Survive,* I turn my thoughts to tonight. It will be the first time I've seen Jason since the face stroking incident, and I still have no idea how to react. But the one thing I do know is, whatever happens, I have to look fabulous.

So now my wedding commitments are over for the day, I can focus on me, and I've decided to go the whole hog and have a facial, a manicure and a pedicure. So what if it means I can't eat for the next few days. At least I'll get a good dinner tonight…

The mud pack on my face is starting to get itchy. There's simply no other word for it. I know it's supposed to be relaxing, but right at this moment it's actually driving me nuts. The background music is sounds of the sea crashing against the shore which is probably supposed to help get rid of tension, but right now it's making me want to go to the toilet.

I'm not sure where the beauty therapist is as my eyes are covered with two cotton wool pads. I wonder if she'll notice if I give my nose a discreet scratch.

Raising my right arm, I cautiously lift the right cotton wool pad. She's not in my line of vision, but unfortunately I'm facing the large picture window and there's a grinning Freddy with his nose pressed up against it. Aren't they supposed to surround customers with a curtain, like in hospital?

It's too much to hope that Freddy will simply go on his merry way. Why would he when he has the perfect opportunity to get me at his mercy. Sighing, I give my nose a quick scratch with the end of my nail and replace the cotton wool pad. Seconds later the door opens and the sea crashing against the shore is drowned out (pardon the pun) by my friend's nasally tones.

'Sweetie, is there a particular reason why you're lying on a bed with your face covered in something that looks like dog poo?' I sense him bending down to give my face an experimental sniff. 'It smells more like moth balls which I suppose is a good thing given the alternative.'

'What do you want Freddy?' I ask bluntly, trying not to crack the mask around my lips.

'Is that any way to greet your second best friend,' is his wounded response, which would normally cause me to raise my eyebrows at his dramatics, but of course, at the moment, I can't. 'Where's the beauty therapist?' I ask instead.

'Nowhere to be seen lovey,' he answers cheerfully, 'She's probably popped out for a sneaky fag, so I've got you all to myself.'

I groan but don't deign to answer. Perhaps if I refuse to rise to the bait, he'll get bored and go away – but needless to say I should've known better.

'Are you going over for Noah's Thanksgiving bash this evening on your own perchance?' is his next question. His voice is deceptively casual which doesn't fool me at all. I have two choices – come clean now and deal with the twenty questions, or save it until later and face the consequences.

But, to be honest, I'm a little tired of keeping everything to myself – although Freddy is not the best person to open ones heart to. I should have told the whole sorry story to Tory when I had the chance.

Sighing, I lift off the eye pads and tell him everything. By the time I've finished, his eyes are like saucers and my face resembles *Thing* out of the *Fantastic Four.* 'Bloody hell, I was only going to ask if you wanted to share a taxi,' is his eventual response.

'Do you think I'm making mountains out of molehills?' I ask quietly.

He's silent for a moment, and his eventual answer is uncharacteristically serious. 'It doesn't matter what I think sweet pie, or anyone else for that matter. It's how you feel about it. Are you in love with the knob?'

'Don't call him that,' I answer wearily, 'And no.. yes... oh I don't know.' The last comes out as a wail and Freddy pats my hand in sympathy.

'Well, all I can tell you is that no relationship can go the distance with fear and uncertainty as its root. You have to speak to him Kitty Kat. You're meeting him early this evening, so that's an ideal opportunity.'

I actually feel physically sick at the thought of questioning Jason. 'But is it any of my business?' I mutter desperately, lifting my head off the pillow.

'Well if it isn't, then you should knock the whole thing on the head right now,' is his matter of fact retort and I sink back with a sigh of acknowledgement. Freddy's right I know he is. I want to cry, but that will finally finish off the face mask.

I lift my head again to see Freddy looking out of the window. 'Is the bloody therapist out there?' I ask irritably, 'Can you see her?'

'I think she must have forgotten about you sweetie,' is his absent response.

'Well what are you looking at then?' I crane my head forward in an effort to see in his line of vision, just in time to see the Admiral loitering on the opposite side of the road.

'That's strange,' Freddy murmurs, getting up, 'Tory said her old man was going over to Torquay this morning - said he had a hospital appointment at ten.'

'Why did you want to know what the Admiral was doing,' I ask, watching Tory's father glance down at his watch then take out his mobile phone.

'I called the Admiralty first but there was no answer, so I gave Tory a ring on the off chance he was there. I just wanted to ask him if he's got an old uniform we can borrow for the panto.'

We're both staring over at the Admiral. 'Is it my imagination, or does he look, sort of, well, furtive to you?' I ask at length. There's a pause, then Freddy nods his head.

'He does a bit. Wonder what he's up to?'

'You have to follow him and find out.' I clutch Freddy's arm as he looks down at me in surprise. 'Whatever for darling?' he asks with a frown.

'Don't ask questions,' I hiss, just as the errant therapist comes through the door, 'Just don't let him see you. Let me know where he goes. I'll fill you in later.'

'Madam, we won't get rid of those horrible dark circles around your eyes if you insist on removing the eye pads.' The beauty therapist pushes me unceremoniously back onto the couch, giving a venomous glance at Freddy.

'Can I help you sir?' she asks primly after slapping the patches back onto my eyes, nearly poking one of them out in the process. Never mind dark circles, I could end up with a black eye. And this is supposed to be therapeutic.

'He's just leaving,' I answer trying to resist the urge to check my eyeball's still in place. 'Go on, get going Freddy,' I whisper urgently, pushing at what I think is his arm. Freddy sighs and a couple of seconds later I hear the door open.

'Keep me posted,' I call, just as the therapist slaps more mud on my face. The door closes and we're back to waves crashing against the shore. Damn it, I really do need the toilet...

~*~

Freddy emerged from Dartmouth Beauty in time to see the Admiral finish on his phone, turn on his heel and disappear. With a small shiver of excitement, he gave a quick glance around, and took a deep breath before closing his eyes briefly to get into character.

Naturally, he needed a disguise, so opening his satchel, he dug around for his Gucci sunglasses and popped them on. Unfortunately, the day being very overcast, they didn't do anything to improve his vision and he nearly got run over as he scurried over the road to peer round the corner.

Undaunted, he slid them down his nose slightly so he could actually see, and nodded to himself in satisfaction as he watched the Admiral hurry up Victoria Street and disappear into the Windjammer Inn. Humming the theme tune to Mission Impossible, Freddy gave chase.

Five minutes later, he pushed open the pub door and a blast of heat hit him from the wood burning stove in the corner, immediately steaming up his sunglasses. He glanced around the room but everything was so dark, he couldn't see a thing. Stepping forward, he tripped over a stool, crashed into a table and went down like he'd been pole axed.

Momentarily stunned, he remained on the floor, expecting the Admiral to clock him at any second and the game to be up. When a few minutes past and nothing happened, he cautiously lifted his sunglasses and looked round. The room was empty. Frowning he climbed to his feet, wincing as he tried to put the weight on his left knee.

This bloody Raymond Chandler malarkey wasn't all it was cracked up to be.

At that moment, the Admiral appeared through a door at the other end of the room - he must have been using the gents. After hurriedly putting his sunglasses back on, Freddy squeezed himself into the nearest booth and picked up a menu, holding it in front of his face. He heard the Admiral speaking to someone, then a loud squeak as the large man sat down in another booth near to the fire.

After five minutes supposedly perusing the menu, Freddy sneaked a quick look. From what he could make out through the bloody sunglasses, the Admiral was nursing a pint of beer and staring pensively at the table. There was another, untouched glass of beer sitting next it. Freddy narrowed his eyes. Kit was right, there was definitely something fishy going on.

Looking over the top of his glasses, Freddy spied the bar maid looking back at him, obviously wondering whether he wanted anything.

Bugger, now what? If he got up, the Admiral would see him, if he didn't, he could tell the bar maid was getting ready to say something. Either way, his cover was about to be blown.

Uncomfortably he felt the sweat begin trickling down his back. He didn't think he was cut out to be a private investigator. To be fair though, it was bloody hot in here.

Just as he was about to throw caution to the winds and climb out of the booth, a welcome blast of cold air accompanied the door opening. Hiding behind his menu, Freddy lifted his glasses and watched as a small elderly man made his way laboriously into the room. The old chap looked well over ninety and for a second, Freddy was afraid he was going to keel over, but after a brief pause, he seemed to gather himself together and tottered over to the Admiral, slowly seating himself opposite.

Freddy covertly watched the two men over the top of his glasses while trying to look as if he was still perusing the menu. There was definitely an art to this.

'Can I get you anything?' The barmaid's strident tones right next to his ear elicited a loud expletive as Freddy nearly jumped out of his skin. He'd been so focused on the Admiral that he hadn't seen or heard her approach.

Leaning back hastily, he stared into the barmaid's suspicious eyes. She was so close, he could see a pimple on the end of her nose and there was a large hairy mole on her top lip.

Freddy stared at the vision in horror, his Crockett impersonation disappearing faster than you could say, 'Miami Vice.' He had absolutely no idea what to say.

Just as he was convinced he was about to be thrown out, the barmaid suddenly lifted her head, sniffing at the air like a bloodhound. Freddy frowned, wondering what on earth she was doing, then, all of a sudden he smelled it, an invisible miasma that coated the inside of his nostrils like a thick layer of Vaseline. The barmaid looked down at him in disgust and Freddy glared back at her indignantly. She couldn't possibly believe that he was capable of producing a smell that bad.

'I'll have a latte,' he said loudly, rediscovering his courage in the face of such a potentially hideous miscarriage of justice. She hesitated briefly, then rushed away with her apron over her nose.

Once she'd disappeared, Freddy gave in and fumbled in his satchel for one of his special lavender scented handkerchiefs. Holding it in front of his face, he glanced back over at the two men who were still sitting in the booth as though nothing had happened.

They were deep in conversation and Freddy couldn't help but note that the Admiral had his nose almost buried in his nearly empty pint glass – a bit like a gas mask. So the smell was obviously coming from his elderly companion.

Leaning forward, Freddy propped the menu up against the saltcellar, bent his head behind it, and unashamedly ear wigged.

'The thing is, I know it's none of my business Boris, but I think the shit's about to hit the fan and I know for a fact that Flo hasn't told Kit that her brother and his wife are not her real parents.'

Shocked, Freddy lifted his head up from the menu and his hankie, forgetting for a second both about the terrible stink, and the fact that he was supposed to be incognito. Despite holding his breath and straining forward, he was unable to hear old Boris's reply.

'Well of course I bloody well know,' the Admiral answered irritably in response. 'You only have to look at her to see it. Can't you just talk some sense into Florence?' Again Boris's answer was indistinguishable and Freddy wondered if he could somehow manage to get closer.

Then another dose of noxious fumes hit the back of his throat and it was all he could do not to gag. It was a few seconds before he could process the Admiral's answer, but when he did, his heart plummeted into his Paul Smith trainers.

'Bollocking hell Boris, you really are going to have to do something with that arse of yours if you're going to officiate at Victory's wedding.'

Chapter Sixteen

How is it that you can spend literally all day getting ready and still be late? The pile of clothes on my bed is testament to my indecision about what to wear, and I only narrowly avoided setting fire to the whole flat in an incident involving my hair straighteners and the nylon carpet.

I've also been trying to contact Freddy on and off all afternoon, but I keep getting his voice mail. That's not like Freddy at all, and now I've run out of time. Still, I'm sure I'll be able to pin him down sometime during the evening's festivities.

Anyway, I think I've scrubbed up pretty well. Standing in front of the mirror I survey myself critically. I've decided on a black crocheted dress which flares from the hips (actually makes me look as though I've got some). The top half is fitted so, after hesitating for a moment, I plump for my good old Wonderbra. It might be like shutting the gate after the horses bolted, but it makes me feel better.

I finish the ensemble with black knee high boots (flat obviously – I don't fancy hobbling a couple of miles up to Noah and Tory's house in heels), and instead of my usual soft approach, my lips are a bold vibrant red. Tonight I'm determined to take control, and ask the questions that need to be asked.

Freddy was totally right (for a change). A relationship based on deceit is no relationship at all.

Quickly grabbing my coat and wrap, I take a last look at the mess that is my flat and reflect ruefully that at least I won't be tempted to bring anyone back.

Jason is already at the boat float when I arrive, and my heart beats faster as he turns and smiles at me. With a wry glance at my statement red lipstick, he bends forward to kiss me on the cheek.

'You look gorgeous,' he murmurs as he straightens up and takes my gloved hand in his. The air is cold and crisp causing our breath to steam as we walk down the slipway towards the passenger ferry.

'Do you think it will snow?' I ask looking up at the first stars of the evening twinkling above us. Helping me onto the waiting ferry, Jason shakes his head.

'Not for the next few days anyway, but who knows, we could be heading for a white Christmas.'

We make our way to the forward deck as the ferry begins to move, and Jason stands behind me, wrapping his arms tightly around me to keep me warm. After a second, I relax back into him, deciding to simply enjoy the warmth of his body and the feel of his heart beating against my back.

The lights of Dartmouth fade away as we reach the middle of the river, slowly replaced by the more subdued ones in Kingswear on the opposite side, and a few minutes later we're walking up the steps to the Ship Inn.

Just as we get to the door, Jason stops and turns towards me, lifting his hand to stroke the side of my face in an almost perfect imitation of the unknown woman's action. My heart thuds uncomfortably as I stare up at his face, virtually lost in the shadow.

His voice, when it comes, is husky and slightly uncertain. 'I think we need to talk.'

~*~

The Admiral glanced down at his watch and felt like crying. It wasn't even six o'clock yet. He still had another hour and a half before they had to be at Noah and Victory's place.

Gloomily he stared down into his pint glass. Mabel was rattling on about some damn film she'd watched with her daughter

– Magic Mick or something. Sounded like some kind of bloody Disney cartoon.

Emily's answer was fortunately drowned out by Jimmy's cough, causing the Admiral to look up across at his friend. 'Ready for another Sir,' Jimmy asked. Charles Shackleford nodded his head, too choked up to speak.

'How about you dear?' The small man pointed towards his wife's tonic water. 'And you Mabel – can I get you another tomato juice?'

A foursome. The Admiral couldn't believe it. Here he was, actually out on a double date with his old Master at Arms and the bloody dragon he lived with. This is what his life had come to – farting vicars and foursomes.

This would never have happened in the old days. He blamed it on the Berlin Wall. Everyone knew where they stood in the Cold War. When the damn wall came down, everything seemed to blur around the edges, and this was the result. An admiral on a foursome with a matelot. Charles Shackleford shook his head sadly.

'Would you like a packet of cheese and onion crisps Sir?'

'Ooh lovely, I'd like a packet of crisps, what about you Emily?'

'Don't mind if I do Mabel, it's a while before we eat. Bring me a packet of Salt and Vinegar Jim.' Emily patted her husband's arm with a smile as he leant over to put down her drink.

The Admiral frowned. He'd never gone for outward displays of affection, but it was beginning to look as if Mabel was turning out to be the touchy feely type. She seemed to be more like Celia every day.

Sometimes it worried him that he'd started mixing them up. He couldn't seem to remember what Victory's mother looked like, and when he tried to imagine her laugh, it sounded like Mabel's.

Troubled, he glanced over at the elderly matron's smiling face as she handed him a packet of crisps, opened in such a way that he could get to the chips inside easily. He felt panic swamp him. Celia used to do exactly the same.

He wanted to dash the bag out of her hand, tell her that no he didn't want a bollocking packet of crisps, and if he did want one, he could bloody well open the bollocking packet himself. Instead, he found himself staring down into the kind warmth of her eyes, and slowly the panic began to subside.

Mumbling his thanks, he took the packet and dipped his hand in. Nothing like a packet of cheese and onion crisps to bring a man back from the edge. Not to mention the touch of a cold nose. The Admiral looked down at Pickles' hopeful face. 'Here you go boy,' he murmured gruffly, handing the spaniel a handful of crisps.

Taking another for himself, he sighed. Times change and it was up to him to change with them. Either that or he might as well top himself now, but Celia wouldn't want that. She'd like Mabel, he knew, and what the hell did it matter if he got them confused every now and then. He took a swallow of his pint as Jimmy sat back down.

'Have you ever been to a Thanksgiving dinner before Sir?' Jimmy enquired after the silence began to stretch between them - they never seemed to have trouble with conversation when it was just the two of them.

The Admiral glanced over at the two gossiping women next to them and coughed. 'Err, well, I seem to remember attending one on a Yank warship when I was a midshipman. You?'

'No Sir, never had the pleasure. I'm really looking forward to this evening though. It was very kind of Tory to invite us.' And bloody stupid, was the Admiral's private opinion.

The uncharacteristic silence descended again as the two men sat and stared helplessly at each other. Suddenly a draft of cold air swept the table as the outside door was pushed open. Grateful for any diversion, both men looked towards the entrance to see Kit Davies and Jason Buchannan walk through the door. The Admiral frowned then looked over at Jimmy eyebrows raised.

Perfectly in tune once more, Jimmy stared back at the Admiral, cocked his head slightly towards the newcomers and shrugged his shoulders.

The next hour and a half might not be so bad after all.

~*~

Without saying anything more, Jason pushes open the door to The Ship, and ever the gentleman, stands aside to let me go through first. The inside of the pub is blessedly warm, and all the tables are empty apart from one. I glance over at the two couples, whose conversation stopped the second we entered, to find four pairs of eyes staring at us, then my heart sinks faster than you can say, 'Bollocking bugger.'

'Oohoo,' Mabel gets in first, punctuating her call with a frantic waving motion just in case we haven't seen her at six feet away.

'Hi Mabel.' My response is definitely luke warm, which of course is water off a duck's back to anyone who sleeps in the same bed as the Admiral. She follows her waving with a rabid patting motion on the bench beside her – there's probably all of six inches between her and the end of the settle. I glance back at Jason who has a very interesting fixed smile on his face – he actually looks as though he needs the toilet.

'Come and join us, do.' Mabel continues with the manic patting. You know Jimmy and Emily don't you?' I nod towards the other couple and step back to introduce them to Jason whose smile now looks as though he's chewing broken glass. With a broad wink, Jimmy jumps up and hurries to fetch another chair. 'Here you go, looks like we're all going to the same place.'

'What a lovely opportunity to get to know one another before the festivities start,' trills Emily.

'Oh we don't want to intrude,' I say desperately.

'Nonsense,' Mabel pipes up, 'You're not intruding at all. We'd love you to join us, wouldn't we Charles?' I turn my attention to the Admiral's face, hoping against hope for a last ditch reprieve, but Tory's father has that look on his face. The meddlesome one that's got him into so much trouble in the past.

'Sit your arse down Kit,' he bellows, pointing to the six inches next to Mabel. 'Jason, park yourself next to Jimmy.'

I can see out of the corner of my eye that Jason is about to be rude – clearly intending to go in to knob mode – so I hastily grip his arm and stare up at him anxiously. 'That'll be lovely won't it Jason?'

The last thing I want is to cause offence to Tory's father, even if the devious old reprobate is only being bloody nosy. Jason looks down at me and raises his eyebrows before accepting the inevitable. 'What would you like to drink?' he asks resignedly.

'Red wine, large one,' I whisper, conveying my thanks by squeezing his arm. As he heads over to the bar, I smile brightly at the two couples and squeeze myself into the miniscule space next to Mabel, only to be immediately accosted by Pickles who seems to think he can sit on my knee.

'So, what are you and old Captain Buchannan doing here together?' The Admiral booms, wasting no time getting to the nitty gritty.

'Err, we just thought it would be a good opportunity to, err, well, that is, to err, chat about the wedding.' I spit out the last part of the sentence in a rush and all four look at me in varying degrees of pity, obviously not impressed by my lying skills.

'How nice,' says Emily politely. 'Would you like a crisp?'

'He's very handsome isn't he?' confides Mabel in a whisper loud enough for the whole room to hear. I smile at the elderly widow whose face is mere inches from mine. There is an overwhelming aroma of cheese and onion crisps as she speaks.

'Err, yes he is,' I answer softly, my face reddening at the thought that Jason might hear my response.

'I once had a handsome fellow like Captain Buchannan on my arm,' Mabel continues with complete disregard to the feelings of her current beau. 'Tall, dark and handsome he was. Looked just like Kernu Reeves.'

'Keanu,' I insert automatically.

Mabel frowns, 'Can I what?' she continues, confused.

I open my mouth to respond, but the Admiral gets there first. 'Bloody hell Mabel, give it a rest, you could talk a glass eye to sleep.'

Luckily at the moment Jason arrives back with our drinks and I take a long grateful swig of wine. Gingerly he seats himself on the chair next to Jimmy who beams at him.

'Chief Petty Officer Noon, at your service Sir,' the small man says with obvious pride.

Jason blinks for a second, then relaxes and gives his first proper smile since entering the pub. 'Very pleased to make your acquaintance CPO Noon, and that of your lovely wife of course.'

Emily blushes and simpers, then, shoving her husband unceremoniously out of the way, leans across him to say, 'Charmed I'm sure.'

Catching Jason's eye, I suppress a sudden hysterical desire to giggle. I feel like I'm in a Noel Coward farce.

'So how long have you been up at the College Sir,' Jimmy asks respectfully.

'Only a few weeks,' Jason replies, 'I'm still finding my feet I'm afraid. Were you ever stationed at BRNC Mr Noon?'

'Call me Jimmy if you please Sir, and yes, I had my last draft up at the College. Looked after the cadets in Hawk Division. Think it might have been before your time Sir.'

'Course it bloody was Jimmy,' the Admiral interjects irritably, 'Don't forget Jason here's old Hugo's boy.'

'Are you married?' Emily cuts in, all but sitting in her husband's lap in her eagerness to speak.

'Err, no I'm not,' Jason responds, taken aback slightly by the sudden change in the conversation.

'So, divorced?' I have to hand it to Jimmy's wife, she's nothing if not dogged.

'No, I haven't yet had the pleasure.' Jason's smile has definitely slipped a bit. Emily narrows her eyes and nods slowly as though trying to gauge if he's telling the truth.

'Captain Buchannan's family home is in Scotland,' Mabel throws in sagely, as if that has something to do with his marital state.

'Unusual for a man to get to your age without having at least one wife.'

'Not even a small one,' Jason responds with an admirably straight face.

'But of course, that must be why you and Kit get on so well.'

'Why, because she hasn't had a small one either?' I can tell he's beginning to lose his temper and I lean forward to intervene.

'It's quite usual nowadays for people to get into their mid thirties without having married.'

'Absolutely dear, we didn't mean to imply otherwise did we Mabel.'

'Of course not Emily. Why I have lots of friends left on the mantelpiece. I think they call them coyotes now.'

There's a small silence, then the Admiral sighs. 'I swear to God Mabel, sometimes I think when you open your mouth, it's only to exchange whichever foot was already in there.'

'Anyone for another drink?' Jimmy offers brightly. I look down at my glass, it's already empty. 'A Shiraz for me please,' I say equally cheerfully. Jason's expression looks as though he's been chewing a wasp.

'I'm sure Captain Buchannan's ready for a top up, aren't you dear?' Emily pats his hand. 'That's not a tonic water is it?' she continues pointing at his empty glass. 'I wouldn't have taken you for a tonic water kind of man.'

Jason takes a deep breath. 'I'll have a *gin* and tonic please Jimmy – a double if that's okay.?'

'Certainly Sir,' Jimmy responds undaunted.

'Does he look like the kind of nancy who drinks tonic water?' the Admiral offers in his usual dulcet tones. 'He's a bloody naval officer. We have gin in our veins instead of blood - what do you say Scotty?' I can see a slight tick start up in Jason's jaw as the Admiral uses his father's old nickname, and I stare hurriedly down at my lap to stop myself from laughing.

'Any naval man worth his salt can drink a half a pint of whisky before breakfast,' the Admiral goes on, as if that's actually something to be proud of.

'I'm afraid I've never tried,' Jason responds in clipped, even tones, 'I'm more of a coffee man myself.'

Looking at Jason's thunderous features, I decide a change of subject is in order. 'So, are you looking forward to the wedding Mabel?' I ask loudly.

'Oh yes, I can't wait,' the elderly matron responds, clapping her hands enthusiastically. 'Charles is taking me in to Torquay to buy a new frock next week, aren't you dear?' The Admiral's expression clearly indicates that this wasn't his idea.

'Don't know what's wrong with the shops on this side of the bloody river,' he grouches, taking a sip of his pint. Mabel tut tuts and actually chucks him under the chin. We all watch fascinated.

'Don't be such a grumpy grouchy old man dear,' she goes on, 'You know you want me to look nice.'

All eyes swing to the Admiral. You could have heard a pin drop.

'I'm wearing puce,' announces Emily with satisfaction.

'Oh Emily,' frowns Mabel, turning back to her friend. 'Is that wise? I mean I'm really not sure you'd look your best in a dress the colour of vomit.'

'It's time we were off,' Jason nearly yells in a strangled voice, hastily getting to his feet, 'It's going to take us a good half an hour to walk.'

'Walk? What on earth are you doing walking up there in the dark?' All four look at us as though we've sprouted two heads.

'You could end up in France if you fall off the cliff.'

'I should think ending up in France would be the least of our worries,' Jason retorts drily.

'We'll give you a lift up,' Jimmy offers, 'I'm sure we can fit you in.'

'You've got a bloody Mini you dipstick, how do you propose to do that?' The Admiral's voice is scornful, but before the argument has a chance to escalate, I prise myself out of my seat, saying, 'Please don't worry, we want to walk, really – it will do us good.'

The Admiral stares at us for a second, his opinion of what's good for us clearly doesn't include a two mile hike round a headland in the dark. For a second I think he's going to protest again, but then he narrows his eyes calculatingly and says, 'I don't suppose you fancy taking Pickles along do you? He enjoys a good walk...'

Contrary to the Admiral's assertion, Pickles does not in fact appear to enjoy a good walk, the evidence of which is his constant refusal to move, accompanied by longing glances back the way we've come. 'It's going to take us all night at this rate,' I puff, dragging the reluctant spaniel.

Jason's face is thunderous. He takes the leash out of my hand and marches up the road hauling the unwilling Pickles, all the while muttering about, 'Bloody people taking bloody responsibility for their bloody dogs.' I hurry after him stifling a slightly hysterical desire to laugh. This is so not the romantic walk either of us had envisaged, and it's definitely not the time for a heart to heart.

He's about fifty yards away when he finally stops to wait for me. 'Sorry,' he murmurs contritely when I finally catch him up, puffing and panting. Too winded to speak, I wave away his apology and stand still in an effort to get my breath back. Looking up, the moon is almost full and the sky is crystal clear and full of stars – an absolutely perfect setting for romance.

'I'm just happy to be here with you,' I say softly after a couple of minutes.

At my words, Jason relaxes and starts to step towards me. When he comes to the end of the leash, he gives a hard tug to get Pickles moving, only to look behind him and see the Springer busy having a large dump.

'Oh my God, did you bring any poo bags?' I ask in a panic.

'No,' Jason ground out, all amorous thoughts disappearing along with the aroma of eau de dog doo. 'Because I haven't got a bloody dog.'

'I think you're overacting a little,' I say a little crossly, rummaging around my handbag to see if I've got a stray bag from Dotty's sleep over - nothing.

'Go and find a stick,' I instruct looking up.

'Are you always this bossy?' he snaps, his expression now back to stony.

'Only when faced with cantankerous people,' I retort, 'Anyone would think you've never been out in the field and had to improvise before.'

'I don't usually do that in a shirt and tie,' he replies angrily, stomping off to the side of the verge to look for a stick.

'Careful you don't fall over the cliff, I might have to send Pickles to look for you.' I shout after him sarcastically.

Five minutes later he reappears with a stick the size of a small tree. I step back slightly, wondering for a second exactly what he's going to do with it. Then I hear a noise. 'Hurry up, there's a car coming,' I mutter, 'We'll get run over at this rate.'

'Nag, nag, nag,' he mumbles, searching for the lump of dog doo in the dark. After a couple of seconds, he locates it and lifts the stick back, almost over his shoulder like a golf club. I'm assuming he has it in mind to get it as far down the cliff as possible.

'Get on with it,' I grumble, now thoroughly chilled and completely pissed off, 'You're not bloody Tiger Woods.'

'Why don't you just SHUT UP.' He shouts the last bit at the same time as swinging the stick, which connects with the lump of poo with a loud smack. The offending pile sails through the air like a missile and lands splat, straight on the windscreen of the oncoming car.

Chapter Seventeen

'Oh my God, stop, please, I can't breathe.' My best friend doesn't seem quite as sympathetic as I feel the situation warrants.

'The only good thing,' I continue caustically, 'Was the fact that the oncoming car had your father in it. That's karma.'

'Apart from the fact that the car is Jimmy's of course.'

I acknowledge her point with a small sigh, then break into a reluctant grin. 'You should have seen the Admiral's face. The poo hit the windscreen exactly where he was sitting. I'm sure he thought he'd been shot.' We both burst into gales of laughter.

'Come on, give me a hand with these drinks,' she murmurs once our hilarity finally dies down. 'I think Jason definitely needs one.'

'Humph,' is my only comment about the bad tempered Captain.

We head back into the drawing room, leaving the outside caterers to finish up in the kitchen. 'The dinner smells heavenly,' I murmur appreciatively as we set the drinks down.

'Much better than it would if I were cooking it,' Tory responds with a wry grin.

'I'm just grateful it's not my aunt,' I return with a slight grimace, 'I'm not sure I could stomach two of her festive dinners in one season.'

I glance round the room. Everyone has arrived. Pickles seems to be undaunted by his impromptu moonlit stroll, and is busy chasing Dotty and Pepé in and out of the hall. Stopping to avoid falling over them, I can't help but note that the Admiral and Flo are closeted in the corner, talking in low tones – and whatever they're talking about, it looks as though they don't agree at all.

I look back at Tory to see if she's noticed, but she's busy handing out drinks to Jacques and Neil. Frowning, I look round for Freddy – I'd expected him to be cemented to the editor's side, but when I finally locate him, he's standing on his own by the Christmas tree, staring at my aunt and the Admiral with a haunted look on his face.

Sudden alarm bells start ringing in my head. Something must have happened earlier when I sent him off to spy on Tory's father – that's why he wasn't answering his phone.

Filled with foreboding, I make my way towards him, only to be unexpectedly intercepted by Jason. I look up at his unsmiling face with surprise. I was expecting him to ignore me for the rest of the evening.

'Would you like a drink?' I say politely holding up a glass of Champagne.

'Would it be rude to take two?' he questions back with a rueful grin. I stare up at him for a second, then laugh softly. 'Be careful, I might pour one of them over your head,' I murmur, unwilling to completely forgive his boorish behaviour just yet.

'That would be a waste of good Champagne,' he smiles, 'You might be better to simply dunk my dim-witted head in Dotty's dog bowl.'

'Don't tempt me,' I retort, only half joking as I hand him a full glass.

He takes a large appreciative sip. 'God, that's good,' he whispers, closing his eyes briefly in pleasure and I'm suddenly filled with an image of his head in other places...

'Have you spoken to Freddy yet this evening?' I ask a little breathlessly, trying to look over his shoulder. He opens his eyes and frowns at the sudden change of subject.

'Only to say hello. Why?'

'Oh nothing really, he seems a little quiet that's all.'

'Well he looks in fine form to me.' I follow Jason's outstretched arm to where Freddy is now in animated conversation with Jacques, and sag with relief at the sight. Whatever is bothering Freddy, it can't be that bad can it?

A half an hour later, we're all sitting down for dinner. There are twelve of us all together, with Noah presiding at one end of the large dining table and Tory at the other. Then there's the Admiral, Mabel, me, Jason, Freddy, Flo, Neil, Jacques, Jimmy and Emily.

The flickering candlelight casts a warm intimate glow over the room, and, as I look at the people around me, most of whom I've known all my life, I feel a comfortable sense of belonging, and wonder how it can get any better than this.

Before we begin dinner, Noah leads the table in giving thanks to God for all his blessings and mercies towards us throughout the year. His words are simple but poignant and unexpectedly I feel tears pricking my eyelids.

Then it's down to the nitty gritty. The food is amazing. Turkey with cranberry sauce and all the traditional trimmings along with some not so usual festive ingredients – to us Brits anyway - sweet potatoes, corn on the cob and to follow, a pumpkin pie.

'Is this how you spend Thanksgiving when you're home in The States?' Jimmy asks with obvious approval.

'Well, every household's different,' Noah responds, picking up his wine. 'But it usually tends to last the whole day rather than just the evening. Some people decorate their houses for Christmas, some wait until after Thanksgiving weekend.

'When I was small, my sister and I would come down on Thanksgiving morning and mom had decorated the house from top to bottom while we were asleep. We used to play silly games, sometimes watched the football, and always, always ate far too much.' His voice is wistful and I suddenly realize how far away from his native land Noah really is. There might only be a stretch of water between us – albeit a large one - but American traditions and customs are actually quite different from ours.

'Do you regret making your home in England?' I ask softly.

For a moment I don't think he's going to answer, but then, 'Yeah, I miss my sister and her family, but it's a long time since I had anywhere I could really call home – until now. I can't remember the last time I was so happy.' He raises his glass to Tory and she blows him a kiss, tears evident in her eyes.

'Bloody hell, I'll be watering my pumpkin in a minute,' says Freddy, dabbing his own eyes.

His words shatter the emotional atmosphere, but as everyone laughs, I look over at my gay friend surreptitiously. Despite his flippant words, he's definitely not at his usual sharp-witted best, and he's studiously avoided meeting my eyes throughout dinner. I make a silent vow to corner him just as soon as we leave the table.

It's almost ten o'clock and we're finishing our coffee, when Noah suddenly stands. 'Admiral Shackleford, I have a surprise for you,' he announces formally, before ruining it with an excited grin and disappearing into the kitchen.

Five minutes later he reappears with a tray of twelve port glasses and a large crystal decanter. Placing the tray on the table carefully, he holds up the decanter to the light. The liquid within glows with an almost otherworldly light and the Admiral stares at it reverently. 'Is that...?'

'It's name is Scion,' Noah interrupts, looking towards Tory's father in delight. 'A one hundred and fifty five year old Port from the Douro Valley in Portugal.'

He walks round to the Admiral's chair. 'Would you like to pass the Port Sir?' he asks softly.

As the decanter is passed around the table, Noah goes on to tell the history of this particular batch. It seems it was a relic discovered by chance a few years ago. I daren't ask him how much it cost.

Once everyone has a glass, he asks the Admiral to break with Thanksgiving tradition and propose a toast to Her Majesty, the Queen. 'After all, this is my home now,' he smiles. After the toast, I take a large sip and grimace. It might have cost a small fortune, but personally I can't see the attraction.

'So, Admiral, are you going to finally put us out of our misery and reveal the identity of the naval chaplain who's going to be marrying Tory and Noah?' Freddy's voice is shrill, and immediately drowns out the small talk, causing everyone to look over at him in surprise. As I look at his flushed, slightly mutinous face, I feel my heart drop in an echo of my earlier apprehension. There is complete silence round the table as each person looks over at the Admiral.

'What's wrong dad,' Tory asks lightly, 'You've not picked a Father Jack to marry me have you?' Everyone laughs, envisioning the elderly, decrepit, foul-mouthed, alcoholic priest from the sitcom Father Ted.

When I say everyone, I actually mean everyone except the Admiral, Jimmy, Freddy and my aunt Flo. What the f**k is going on? I'm suddenly feeling very sick. All eyes are now on the Admiral who looks as though he's just swallowed something nasty.

He coughs self consciously, and now the alarm bells in my head are ringing a bloody symphony. I look over at Tory and her face is identical to how I imagine mine must look.

My friend looks round the table. 'What's going on dad?' she whispers when the Admiral still doesn't speak.

'The thing is Victory,' her father blusters after another excruciating few seconds, 'This padre, he's an old friend of mine, we were very close once upon a time. He did your mother and I a real service when were young.

'At the time, your mum wanted him to be your godfather, but being the fine upstanding man that he was – and is – he refused, saying he couldn't be around often enough to do right by you. He was spending most of his time in doing God walloping work in war zones at the time. So instead, he asked if he could be the one to officiate at your wedding – whenever that was.'

He pauses, then, 'To be honest, I thought he'd have popped his clogs long before you finally managed to get a man to make an honest woman of you Victory – he's at least ninety.'

Tory frowns. 'Well that's a lovely story, and of course I'm happy for your old friend to marry us. Why haven't you told me before now?'

'You haven't seen him,' Freddy cuts in, glaring at the Admiral.

'Is there something wrong with the guy?' Noah asks mildly.

'What's his name,' questions Jason, 'If he's a naval padre, I might well have heard of him.'

'Oh you'll have heard of him alright,' Jimmy throws in unexpectedly. 'Come on Sir, it's time to come clean.'

The Admiral glowers at his friend, then closes his eyes, muttering, 'What a bloody cake and arse party.' His face looks waxy pale in the candlelight. This is so unlike Tory's father, the whole scene looks and feels totally surreal.

'His name's Boris, he...'

'Oh my God, not Bible Basher Boris?' Jason interrupts in disbelief.

'So you've heard of him?' I ask Jason, 'Who is he?'

'He's a legend in the RN,' Jason states matter of factly, 'Mainly due to the fact that he has problems with.. er..., breaking wind.'

'Well that's not exactly uncommon,' the Admiral says defensively, I mean let's be honest, everybody farts.'

'How many people's wind problems are so bad they clear out a room full of over two hundred people Sir?' Jimmy's voice is determined.

'And it really, really is bad, I can vouch for that,' Freddy butts in with a shudder. 'I didn't think I was going to get out of The Windjammer alive.'

So that's what was wrong with Freddy.

'Okay, so what are you saying here people?' Noah asks calmly, 'That we have an elderly guy who dearly wants to officiate at Tory's wedding, but has a major flatulence problem that could potentially evacuate a building full of two hundred people?'

There's a pause. 'That about sums it up,' mutters the Admiral at length.

'Doesn't he realize how bad his, err, problem is? questions Tory, 'I mean have you mentioned it to him?'

'I think he lost all sense of smell years ago.' The Admiral sighs defeated, 'You don't understand, the man is nearest thing to a saint I've ever come across - he doesn't have a vindictive bone in his body. 'How the bloody hell can I tell him he can't fulfil his lifelong dream of marrying my daughter because of his trouser trumpets?

'I mean, he's practically pushing up the daisies, a shock like that would finish him off for sure.'

'Well I just hope that when he gets to the Pearly Gates, St. Peter's stocked up on air freshener,' mumbles Freddy.

'What exactly was the good turn he did for you and Celia?' Mabel asks curiously.

There's another, longer silence and I sense with a sharp stab of fear that whatever that favour was, it's actually the whole crux of the matter. I glance over at Tory and know she feels it as well, then I look over at Freddy's anguished face. It's obvious he's aware of what's coming.

'Dad?' Tory's voice is loud and commanding.

'I think it's time I took part in this story.' Flo's voice is quiet, and she looks over at me as she speaks.

'What are you talking about?' I whisper, fear turning to a sick dread.

Florence glances up at the Admiral. 'Charlie, you're right, it's time we put this whole damn business to bed.' Uncharacteristically the Admiral reaches out his hand and pats her on the shoulder – Tory had kept her promise to sit them together...

'Lies and secrets, Flo,' he says heavily, 'They weigh a body down after a while.'

'As you should bloody well know,' Tory mutters looking daggers at her old man. The Admiral ignores his daughter's comment, still looking at the woman seated beside him. 'Are you going to do the honours, or shall I?'

'I think this is more my story, Charlie,' she responds, pausing before adding wryly, 'But feel free to add your two pennies worth whenever you feel the need.' The Admiral nods his head, oblivious to her slight sarcasm.

'The thing is,' Flo begins, turning back to cast her anxious eyes over the whole table, 'I mean, it was a long time ago, and we were young and very foolish, but you see... I mean what happened was... that is...'

'Get to the bloody point Florence,' the Admiral butts in, obviously deciding he's going to actually get his two pennies worth, 'The thing is, Flo and I got married – when we were both eighteen.'

I don't know what I was expecting, but it definitely wasn't that. The silence is absolute. To be honest I don't think any of us knows what to say.

'Are you still married now?' asks Noah, getting straight to the nitty gritty in his usual relaxed manner.

'No, no, of course we're not married now, but that's where old Boris first came in.' I've never seen the Admiral look so uncomfortable. 'Go on Flo, you tell it from here,' he continues gruffly.

My aunt takes a deep breath, then says simply, 'Charlie and I had a bit of a fling when we were young and stupid. We decided to tie the knot on impulse – more to get back at my father than anything else. He was a tyrant until the day he died, and I think Charlie felt sorry for me.

'Boris was the naval chaplain at BRNC. For some bizarre reason, he and Charlie were close.' She glances up at the Admiral as she speaks, and I can see him visibly forcing himself not to interrupt.

'Anyway, we persuaded Boris to do the honours, but as soon as we'd said, 'I do,' Charlie was deployed east of Suez for twelve months and Boris went off to the Falklands.

'Charlie and I kept in touch for a while, but I think we both realized we'd made a mistake, even before he sailed. Communication was by snail mail then and I got tired of waiting for the postman. I was still living with my parents, despite Charlie's chivalrous attempt to take me away from all that, and after six months, I was desperate to get away.

That's when I met Luke.' She pauses and knocks back the rest of her Port. 'Is there any more of that?' she asks Noah, a little desperately. Face unreadable, Noah leans over to pour her another glass.

'Luke was a, a, well he was different to anyone I'd ever met.' Her eyes return to me and I stare back at her silently.

'He was an incredibly charismatic man, even then. People would hang on his every word. He used to spout about the rights of the working classes, especially the miners – although he'd never been down a mine in his life. His father was one of the wealthiest men in the South Hams and his mother came from a prominent Dartmouth family. He didn't get on with either of them, and when his moralizing became an embarrassment to them, they decided to ship him off to a distant cousin in The States.' She pauses again, staring back down into her glass.

'I went with him,' she continues simply at length. 'I left a note for Charlie to come back to and just, well…'

'Bloody vanished,' Tory's father inserts belligerently. She nods her head and takes another, deeper breath.

'Of course we were still bloody hitched, the Admiral went on. 'I had no idea where she'd gone at that point – I just knew it was somewhere in the USA.

'And then I met your mother.' He turns looks over at Tory. 'I loved Celia from the moment I set eyes on her,' he says hoarsely. 'I couldn't tell her about Flo – she'd have had nothing to do with me. So I kept it a secret and went ahead and married her anyway.'

'You committed bigamy?' Tory gasps, the disbelief in her tone vocalizing everyone else's.

'Aye, and I'd do it again,' her father responds curtly. 'I could never have risked your mother walking out of my life, never.'

'Quite romantic when you put it that way,' mutters Freddy, completely engrossed like the rest of us. Tory throws a warning glare his way and he subsides with a small shamefaced shrug.

'Anyway, that's when Boris came back from darkest Borneo or wherever the hell the bloody navy had sent him by then. Of course he cottoned on straight away that there was some funny business going on and threatened to tell Celia. I explained what had happened and begged him not to say anything.

He agreed not to blab on me as long as I went ahead and got divorced from Flo. Then he did no more than take a bloody year's sabbatical and went off with the divorce papers to The States to track her down. It took him over six months, but eventually he came back with everything signed and sealed. I did my bit, and before I knew it, we were divorced.'

'But your marriage to mum couldn't have been legal if you were still married to Florence at the time, Tory states, angry tears in her eyes. Her father nods his head wearily.

'And what's more you were on the way by the time Boris got back from the US. I knew I had to tell Celia, it was the right thing to do.' He sighs before going on, 'I'm not sure how long old Boris would have kept schtum anyway – he wasn't a big fan of bigamy.

'So, long story short, I came clean to your mother, she forgave me – God knows why - and we got married again – for real this time. That was when Celia suggested he become your godfather and he had the bright idea of being the one to marry you when you finally tied the knot.'

'Did he already have a problem with his, err, bowels?' Emily asks politely after a few seconds when nobody speaks.

'No, that came later, after he had a stint in Sierra Leone – that was the first time they practically sent the silly sod home in a casket.'

'So how come I've never met this man who is apparently so fond of me, it's his lifelong ambition to watch me tie the knot.' Tory accuses sarcastically.

'You have seen him before love,' the Admiral responds, for once refusing to rise to the bait. 'He came to your mother's funeral, but you were too distraught to take much notice. Apart from that, old Boris has spent his whole life doing his bible basher bit.

'Up until he retired, God, The Royal Navy and your mother were the only ones who knew everywhere he was holed up – I certainly had no idea where the bloody hell he was from one year to the next.

'Celia used to send him photos and snippets about you every month, right from when you were a baby. She always knew wherever he was.' He sighs again heavily, 'But then your mother was like that. Old Boris retired from the RN after a bit of an *incident* involving his arse at the old Naval Chapel in Greenwich. Became a missionary full time after that.

'He only came back to this country when he heard about my, err, slight brush with the Law. Said he wanted to support me – although to be honest I wish he'd never bothered because that's when he found out you'd finally bagged yourself a bloke.'

'He's a bit old to be doing missionary work now isn't he?' Neil asks drily.

'God's work is never done apparently, according to old Boris,' muttered the Admiral, 'But aye, you're right, I think he was actually relieved not to be going to back to wherever it was he'd sprung from.'

'So here we are, in this damn predicament, all because you can't tell the bloody truth about what you had for breakfast,' Tory bursts out, after it becomes clear her father's got no intention of elaborating further.

'Honey, please don't get upset,' Noah intervenes before any argument can escalate, 'I promise we'll sort this.' Then he turns to the Admiral. 'Charles, can you arrange a meeting with Boris as soon as possible?' The Admiral nods his head sheepishly and Noah turns to Jason. 'If Boris really is incapable of conducting the service, can we get a hold of someone else at short notice?'

'I'll see what I can do,' Jason responds briskly. 'It doesn't have to be a naval chaplain who takes the ceremony. Any ordained minister can conduct the service, providing we get security clearance.'

'Right then, that's settled,' Noah states to the whole table, although it's clear he's directing his words to Tory who's still throwing poisoned looks towards her errant father.

'Actually, it isn't quite,' I say quietly but determinedly. I turn back to my aunt Flo. 'So what happened after Boris tracked you down in The States?' I question, determined now to get the full story. I can tell by her face that she was hoping that this part of the tale would get lost in melee. She tenses visibly, then closes her eyes in defeat as everyone's attention turns back to her.

'Luke and I went to Charleston in South Carolina,' she finally responds, her voice tired and stiff. 'Luke had relatives there and they took us both in.' She shakes her head sadly, 'I'm not sure what I expected. Maybe that Luke would settle down and get a job, forget about his need to vent about the establishment and every damn injustice that happened to catch his attention.

'To say he wasn't popular with the Charleston set would be a complete understatement. Pretty soon he became totally unemployable, and his relations, who at the end of the day were only second cousins, made it clear we'd outstayed our welcome.

'They didn't actually throw us out on our ear, with Luke being family, instead they offered to let us use a small clapboard house on their property. It was far away enough from town to minimize their embarrassment and remote enough that they thought Luke would give up his constant need to bash the institution.'

She takes a deep breath and, for a second, looking at her tormented face, I'm tempted to tell her to stop, but before I can open my mouth, she continues wearily. 'They couldn't have been more wrong. They just gave him something to focus his rage on. I've already told you how charismatic he was and within three months he'd set up a commune with ten of Charleston's finest youth in it. By the time the good townsfolk sat up and took notice, that little clapboard house was the centre of South Carolina's newest cult, complete with wire fence and sawn off shotguns.'

She pauses and I take the opportunity to butt in sarcastically, 'Didn't Saint Boris have anything to say about that?'

My aunt looks over at me, her face carefully blank. 'He'd already been and gone by that time. We were still in love and in lust when I gaily signed the divorce papers. His second visit was a different matter.'

'So he came over to see you twice?' It feels as though Flo and I are the only two in this conversation. She nods her head, before continuing, her voice now slightly bitter and self mocking.

'Of course like any good cult, its leader believed himself to be above any kind of moral law, and pretty soon Luke was shagging every young nubile acolyte he could get his hands on. I wanted out, but that was easier said than done. I couldn't recognize the old Luke in the stupid, trumped up fanatic strutting around his little kingdom, but I just kept believing he was in there somewhere. Stupid, stupid, stupid.'

She shakes her head, glancing over at Neil who takes her hand in silent support. 'By the time I realized that the Luke I'd fallen in love with was well and truly gone for good, there were thirty idiots running around to do his bidding, more than happy to undertake a spot of confining and restraining. I think he believed that if I deserted him, it wouldn't look good to his newest recruits.' She laughs bitterly, clutching Neil's hand tightly.

'You don't have to tell us if you don't want to Florence,' Noah interrupts softly, and, unable to help myself, I glare at him. Doesn't he realize that I *need* to know? Aunt Flo shakes her head, smiling at Noah gratefully.

'Thank you, but I think this story has been stifled for far too long. Then she looks back at me, holding my eyes with hers.

'I wasn't completely alone. There was one person there who looked out for me. Her name was Sarah, and she was beautiful, inside and out. She took care of me, and I took care of her. We were like soul mates in so many ways.

'There was only one area we didn't agree – Luke.' She sighs softly. 'Sarah was still besotted, still in love with the man she thought he was. I tried, but she was completely blind where he was concerned. And then she became pregnant.

'Oh, it wasn't the first time he'd knocked up one of his female followers, but this time, for some reason, it was different. He thought this child was special, destined for greatness in some twisted way. As the pregnancy advanced, he seemed to become more and more unbalanced, and when the child was born…' her voice cracks slightly and I can see her gripping Neil's hand so forcefully, her knuckles are like bone in the candlelight.

'Sarah died giving birth. She just bled out, right there on the bed because the bastard wouldn't allow her to go to hospital, or even see a doctor.

'And after that,' she continues, her voice descending to a whisper, 'After that, I couldn't leave, I had to take care of Sarah's child, I had to protect her from the monster her father had become.' The tears are now pouring unchecked down her cheeks and still she stares at me, her features contorted into a mask of pleading anguish.

And suddenly I know. Everything clicks into place.

'It was me wasn't it,' I whisper back to my aunt's tortured face. 'I was that child. Sarah was my mother.'

Chapter Eighteen

Well, as evenings go, last night will definitely go down as one of the most memorable. There's nothing like discovering you're the bastard of a budding Charles Manson to get a person into the Christmas spirit.

To be fair, I suppose my father didn't actually murder anybody before he popped his clogs. Although, finding out that the person I'd always thought of as my favourite aunt was the one to give him a helping hand towards an early meeting with his maker before he actually had the opportunity, was a shock to say the least.

You might think I'm being a trifle flippant and you'd be right. It's either that, or I curl up in bed with my head under the duvet for the next six months. And I have a wedding to organize before I fall apart.

Understandably, my two best friends have been frantically phoning me all morning. Flo's little revelation has sort of put Tory's vicar with a flatulence problem on the back burner, and anyway, it looks as though old Boris really is the nearest thing to a saint. He was the one who rescued us when it looked as though daddy dearest had finally lost his tenuous grip on reality.

Well, him and Tory's mother.

Apparently, just after my second birthday, Flo managed to smuggle out a letter addressed to the Admiral pleading for help. Tory's dad was away at sea so the letter was picked up by Celia.

By a stroke of good luck, Boris was back on one of his rare visits to the UK, so Tory's mum was able to enlist his help. Within couple of weeks the saintly padre was hot footing it over to The States to rescue us.

Unfortunately, my father was of the misguided opinion that I would be better off dead than without him, so Florence had to persuade him otherwise. I think it involved one of the sawn off shotguns.

I don't feel anything about that. As far as I can see, he deserved everything he got, and luckily for Florence, the local Sheriff's office appeared to come to the same conclusion.

I'm sad that I never got to meet my real mother, not to mention actually relieved that the cold insensitive bitch I thought was my mother is actually no relation at all.

No, the one thing I can't understand, the one thing that hurts so f**cking much, is the fact that Flo actually *gave* me to that pair of morons and let me believe they were my parents. Why, if she loved me so much didn't she keep me with her? I mean, by the time I finally went to live with her at fifteen, I was practically a woman.

I have no answer, and my *aunt* has yet to give me one. As you can imagine, I left rather abruptly last night.

The pinging of my phone cuts into the endless merry go round that is my thoughts. Looking down, I see Tory has resorted to texting. 'Freddy and I are coming over. Be in the flat if you value your life.' I can't help but smile. It really is true, we can't choose our relatives, but friends? They're a different matter.

My thoughts drift to Jason. What is he exactly, apart from another strand in the tangled web that's my life? Of course he's called me too – twice to my knowledge, leaving messages both times. I haven't listened to them yet.

I glance down at my watch which reads ten thirty. Is that too early for a drink?

By the time Tory and Freddy arrive forty five minutes later, I'm well into my second glass of wine. In the way of true friends, they don't waste their breath berating me about the dangers of early morning drinking, they simply get two more glasses and pour themselves one. Even Tory has half a glass.

'So what are you going to do?' Freddy asks bluntly when they've both made themselves comfortable. That's what I've always liked about Freddy. He doesn't waste time in useless platitudes, simply gets down to business. I shake my head, mumbling, 'I have no idea,' before hastily taking another drink.

'I don't see there's anything she can do, short of going into a decline, taking to her bed and maybe cutting Flo out of her life completely.' Tory's words are matter of fact, but her hand gripping mine tells a different story.

'The decline's going to have to wait, I'm afraid,' I say squeezing her fingers, 'I have a wedding to organize. Once that's over, don't worry, I'll do a Miss Havisham.' They both laugh, relieved I know. I think they were worried I was going to jump into the river.

'So,' I continue brightly, 'What are you going to do about Bible Basher Boris?'

Tory shakes her head. 'I've absolutely no idea,' she says exasperatedly, 'Sometimes I just despair of my father. I swear to God, he thinks he was bloody James Bond in some previous life. He just has to turn everything into some kind of cloak-and-dagger spy thriller. I feel so sorry for Mabel, I really don't know why she puts up with him. I'd love to have been a fly on the wall when she got him home last night.'

'I think he was trying to protect my aun...Flo, as much as anything,' I murmur.

'Bullshit,' my best friend returns bluntly. 'My father hasn't got a sensitive bone in his body. Like always, he simply got himself into a situation he couldn't get himself out of. Still, at least we know why our respective grownups avoided each other for twenty odd years. There's nothing like an illicit marriage and a spot of bigamy to put an end to polite conversation.' Tory's voice is light but brittle, and I can tell she's hurting, despite her glib words.

'No,' says Freddy unexpectedly, shaking his head decisively. 'Your dad loves you Tory, and he loved your mum. I believe that's what made everything so difficult. He didn't want to let your mum down by reneging on their promise to Boris, but he didn't want to ruin your wedding either. Hell of a choice when you think about it.'

'So, what about Florence, my so called *aunt,*' I say bitterly, 'Was that a hell of a choice too? Can you come up with one good reason why she abandoned me when she got back to Dartmouth?'

My friends look at me and in the face of their sympathy, I can't help myself, I burst into tears. Tory simply folds me into her arms and lets me sob into her ample bosom, while Dotty anxiously licks the salt off my face.

Twenty minutes later I look horrendous, but I have to say, I feel slightly better. Sometimes, there's nothing like a good cry to get rid of pent up negativity. Moving away from Tory's warm embrace, I take a deep breath as Freddy hands me a large tissue. After mopping the snot and tears from my face and her cleavage, I give my nose a good blow before saying resolutely, 'Enough. Flo and I will have that conversation *after* your wedding. For now we concentrate on making you the most beautiful bride ever.'

'And darlings, we all know just how much hard work *that's* going to involve.

A couple of hours later both Freddy and I are a little squiffy. I'm about to open a second bottle, when Freddy looks down at his watch, then jumps up with a small cry.

'Shit,' he moans, 'I'm supposed to be getting the Flavel Centre ready for story time starting at four. Part of this Candlelit Dartmouth business this weekend.' With that, he grabs his coat, muttering about sodding little nose miners ruining his nice clean centre, gives me a quick hug and hurries out of the door.

'Somehow, I don't think he's going to turn out to be a natural as an uncle,' I murmur as Tory makes a move to go. She grins at me ruefully before putting Dotty's leash on. 'We'll just have to train him then,' she says lightly, 'He's a quick learner.

'Are you going to be okay Kitty Kat?' she goes on to say anxiously, shrugging her coat on.

Smiling, I nod my head. 'Don't worry about me Tory, I'll be fine. I hope Noah will forgive us for ruining his first Thanksgiving dinner this side of the Atlantic.'

'Are you kidding,' she responds, picking up a reluctant Dotty who definitely prefers staying in the warmth, 'He's already writing the script. Says it's the best plot for a movie he's ever come across.'

After Tory leaves, I wander round picking up empty glasses, grimacing as I realize that Freddy and I nearly finished off two bottles of wine. The mid afternoon light is fading fast and I switch on a couple of lamps to dispel the gloom. The flat feels sterile and empty and I can't seem to settle.

Glancing down at my phone, I see that Flo has left a couple of messages, both alluding to our need to talk. Sitting back down on the sofa, I stare at the texts.

Despite everything, I know Florence loves me, but I'm not ready yet to get back to playing happy families. I have to know what happened to make her to abandon me when she arrived back in England. There's no doubt in my mind that *something* did – but the woman I thought I knew has turned out to be a different person altogether and I need time to get to know the real Florence Davies.

Quickly I message back, suggesting we leave any heart to hearts until after the wedding. Within seconds she responds with another text, and I have to force myself to quell a rising anxiety at her hurried agreement.

Leaning back, I stare into the gathering darkness outside the French window, wishing I'd taken up Tory's invitation to spend the night at hers. Suddenly I remember Jason's answer phone messages. Should I listen? With everything else that's happened, my relationship with the handsome captain seems to have taken a back seat – but maybe that's a good thing. I've got enough uncertainties in my life at the moment without wondering whether Jason's on the up and up, or whether he's simply another lying toad. Idly, I tap on the answer phone to listen.

'Hey Kit.' His deep voice does funny things to my chest, despite my determination to avoid any further complications. 'I'm sorry we didn't get to talk again last night, I can imagine you're feeling a little stunned right now and maybe you don't want company, but if you do, I'm involved in the Candlelit Dartmouth parade tonight, and I'd love to meet up after my part's finished.

'I should be done around seven thirtyish – after the BRNC volunteer band have done their thing. Meet me at the Bandstand if you feel up to it, I'll hang around until eight.' There's a pause and then he continues softly, 'I so want to give you a hug right now.'

Inexplicably, the tears start forming again at his murmured last words and I swallow convulsively past the sudden lump in my throat. Should I meet up with him? Would I be best to simply end the relationship now, before it goes too far and the possible hurt too deep? God knows I've got enough on my plate right now.

But even as I think it, I know that it's too late. For good or ill, I've fallen in love with Jason Buchannan, and even if the answer casts me into the deepest darkest pit of despair, I have to know once and for all if he loves me back.

Wrapping up warmly, I decide to leave the flat early intending to soak in a little of the festive atmosphere, and hopefully shake off the feeling of impending doom that's been with me since last night.

I wander through the crowds, smiling at the children carrying their lanterns, all of them heading towards the Royal Avenue Gardens. The sky is clear and cold and the procession of flickering lanterns, together with the newly turned on Christmas lights have transformed the old town into a magical place. Slowly I feel the pressure inside me begin to ease.

So what if my real father was a total nutcase. I'm not the first person to have to rise above a shitty start in life, and I certainly won't be the last. At the end of the day, it's how you deal with the shit that counts. I need to take a leaf out of the Admiral's book and simply look at life as he does - one big self adjusting cock up...

Smiling to myself, I turn and head towards the bandstand, wishing that Tory and Noah were here. Entering the Gardens, I look around for Jason and finally spot him over near a stall selling crêpes. As I covertly stare at him in his ceremonial uniform, my shiver has nothing to do with the cold.

He's having a discussion with somebody and hasn't seen me yet, but that's okay because I'm early. I debate whether to join the queue for a chocolate and banana crêpe, just as he steps back and I can see who he's talking to.

It's the same woman. The one from his car.

I stand stock still and stare. Whatever their conversation is about, it's obviously something serious, and I feel my heart lurch sickeningly. She's just as beautiful as I remember and I watch helplessly as she lays her hand on his arm, causing him to look down at her, his shadowed features harsh and intense. The connection between them is so strong, it's almost palpable, and in the face of such obvious passion, my earlier determination seems ridiculous, almost childlike.

Shaking, I take a step forward. I have to end this once and for all. Taking a deep breath, I walk slowly towards the two of them, still so wrapped up in their little world that they barely notice me until I stop a couple of feet away. Jason is the first to spot me and his eyes widen in dismay. Seeing his expression, the mystery woman turns her head to stare at me, her gaze unreadable.

'I'm early,' I whisper at length, more to end the silence than anything else.

Jason visibly gathers himself together and makes the introductions. 'This is Laura,' he pronounces impassively. 'She's ...'

'...An old friend,' Laura interjects smoothly as Jason pauses, uncharacteristically lost for words.

'Hi, I'm Kit,' I respond harshly, 'I'm a new friend.' My voice cracks slightly as my efforts to sound like a hard bitch conflict with my need to sit down and cry. I look back at Jason whose face is now a mask of anguish, and I finally have the answer I was looking for.

He opens his mouth to speak but I beat him to it. 'Well, I'll leave you to it,' I say with false brightness. 'It's clear you're busy. I'll see you on the twentieth Captain Buchannan. Get David to give me a quick call if there's anything else you need with regard to security beforehand.'

Then I turn and walk away.

~*~

Tory's dress is absolutely beautiful and it fits her like a glove. Okay so they sent three, but as soon as we opened the boxes, there was simply no contest.

Made out of vintage lace, the dress dips low at the front, and even lower at the back. It's cut in a mermaid style with long fitted lace sleeves and a skirt that flares dramatically from just above her knees.

Tory's mutter of, 'I don't know how I'm going to bloody walk,' falls on deaf ears as both Freddy and I stand and stare wordlessly. I can't wait for the whole world to see my best friend in this dress. The cruel jibes that Noah Westbrook has settled for second best will be stilled once and for all.

Freddy even has tears in his eyes as he murmurs seriously, almost reverently, 'I've never seen you look so beautiful Victory Shackleford.'

'Gorgeous,' I add with a watery smile. Then we look at each other and laugh.

'Can you remember when you were determined to get me a new dress for Noah's cocktail party?' Tory giggles, 'How I complained that I couldn't breathe? Well this is worse. God help me if I bend down too far when we sit down to sign the register - my boobs are likely to end up on the table.'

'And I'll say now exactly the same as I said then,' I answer with a grin, 'Stop bloody whinging.'

'Anyway, if your assets make an unexpected appearance, it will take everybody's mind off the awful smell.' Freddy's caustic remark effectively puts an end to the light-hearted banter.

'When are you going to meet up with Boris?' I ask, carefully unlacing her dress. Tory breathes deeply with relief as the fabric slides down past her hips.

'Tomorrow,' she responds finally. 'Noah's collecting his sister and her brood from Heathrow tonight but they won't get back here until late.'

'How come he doesn't just have them collected in a limousine?' Freddy asks handing me the dress hanger. Tory looks at him in exasperation.

'I think sometimes he just likes to do normal stuff, you know, like the rest of us?'

Freddy raises his eyebrows and shrugs. 'Normal's definitely overrated in my opinion,' he quips, taking the dress from me and carefully hanging it on the wardrobe door.

We're in Tory's old bedroom at the Admiralty where she'll sleep on the night before her wedding. Freddy and I are going to stay too, along with copious amounts of bubbly and chocolate – both of which the bride will be unfortunately unable to indulge in. However, Freddy has assured her that, being the stalwart friends that we are, the two of us will make up for it. Tory's response is an emotional announcement that she fully intends to have one bollocking glass of Champagne before she ties the knot.

'Are you going to tell him that he can't conduct the ceremony?' I ask, going back to the problem at hand.

'I don't know,' Tory answers with a sigh, sitting down on the bed. 'Noah says we'll assess the situation when we meet him.'

'You have no idea what you're letting yourself in for,' Freddy shudders dramatically, 'I just hope you're intending to stock up on gas masks to issue to the guests as they come in.'

Tory grimaces. 'If it really is that bad Freddy, there's no way we can let him take the wedding, but after everything dad said, I really don't want to upset the poor chap.'

'What is it with everyone not wanting to upset him?' Freddy interrupts heatedly, 'The man's got an arse that could be used as a lethal weapon.'

'Have you got anyone else in mind? I ask hurriedly to prevent an argument. Tory's face is thunderous as she glares at Freddy.

'Yes, Jason's got the local vicar on standby,' she responds, giving our insensitive friend one last scowl, 'But how come you don't know this Kitty Kat – haven't you spoken to Jason?'

My face freezes at the mention of Jason's name. 'We've err, both been busy,' I stammer finally, bending down to pick Dotty up for a cuddle in an effort to deflect any questions. I catch a glimpse of Tory's frown as I bury my head into the little dog's fur, but thankfully she doesn't pursue the subject.

Instead she sits down on the bed, saying, 'Okay, it's your turn now. Come on maid of honour, open the box with the bridesmaids' dresses in.'

More than happy to change the subject, I place Dotty on her lap, and with a welcome tremor of excitement, tear open the box in question. The first dress is obviously Madison's, so I carefully put it aside and reach back into the tissue paper. The red velvet is soft and slightly decadent to the touch, and the white fur looks all too real. 'It's definitely faux, isn't it? I ask, suddenly anxious that I might be inadvertently wearing real fur – something I'd never do in a million years.

'Of course,' Tory responds scornfully, 'You know me better than that. Now, try it on, let's see if it fits.'

Worry abated, I hastily I pull off my jeans and top and step into the dress, pulling it up and sliding my arms into the sleeves. Tory remains on the bed with Dotty on her knee, eying me critically.

'Give me a hand Freddy,' I puff, doing up the cuffs on each sleeve. Stepping behind me, Freddy patiently does up each velvet covered button, stepping away finally to view me analytically through the full length mirror. The dress is completely off the shoulder, with both the neckline and cuffs lined with the white fur. It flares from the hips like something Guinevere might have worn in Camelot. It's totally stunning. And too big.

'You've lost weight,' Tory accuses, staring at me, her eyes narrowed. 'Are you sure you're okay Kitty Kat?'

For a second I can't speak, then taking a deep breath, I pull myself together and give a little laugh, causing both friends to look at me suspiciously.

Bloody hell I've got to do better than this. I can't tell the pregnant bride to be that even the thought of food makes me feel ill. She's got enough on her plate.

'I'm absolutely fine,' I say cheerily after a small cough, 'I've just been so busy with the wedding preparations, I don't seem to have time to eat.'

'Well, I know it's not every day you find out you're an orphan,' Freddy mutters bluntly, 'But if you lose much more weight you'll begin to look like Oliver Twist.'

'Oh stop it Freddy,' you can be so bloody insensitive sometimes,' Tory snaps, putting Dotty on the floor and standing up.

Freddy looks round at her in surprise. 'If you can't trust me to tell you both the truth darling, you can't trust anybody. It's what I'm here for.' He actually sounds a little hurt that he could have been so misunderstood.

Sighing, I put my arm through his. 'I know you're only trying to help Freddy,' I murmur as Tory begins sticking pins in my side. 'I promise I won't lose any more weight.'

'Well if you do, they'll probably be playing tunes on your ribs,' Tory adds, obviously deciding that on this occasion, our less than diplomatic friend might actually have a point.

'Ouch,' I mutter as her pin goes clear through the fabric and sticks viciously into my hip bone. But before I get the chance to respond, her mobile phone rings. Frowning, she puts down the pin cushion and looks at the caller.

'It's dad,' she says softly, reluctantly swiping the screen with her finger to answer.

'I think we've had a reprieve Victory,' her father's deafening voice reverberates around the room. Tory frowns, before looking over at us and giving a perplexed shrug.

'What's happened,' she responds finally and I can tell she's not actually sure she wants to know.

'Old Boris has gone and had a stroke,' the Admiral continues, 'He's in Torbay Hospital as we speak.'

'For God sake dad, you don't have to seem so happy about it', Tory retorts irritably, 'You didn't do anything to him did you?'

'Of course I bloody well didn't. What do you bollocking well take me for?' Tory sighs, obviously not deigning to answer.

'Is Boris going to be okay,' she asks instead.

'Don't know yet. I went over to his flat to tell him you and Noah were coming over to see him tomorrow and I found him still in bed, so I called the ambulance. I'm waiting for the sawbone's verdict now.'

'Oh dear, poor man,' Tory murmurs, 'How awful.'

'He seemed pretty happy to me,' the Admiral disagrees, 'Had a proper smile on his face. And come on, the old bugger's ninety three and we've all got to go sometime.'

Tory shakes her head in despair at her father's insensitivity, but says only, 'Can you find out where Boris is in the hospital and we'll go over to see him as soon as Noah gets back from Heathrow.'

'Will do,' the Admiral booms, 'Keep an eye on Pickles for me.' Then he cuts the call and we sit looking at each other in relieved guilty silence.

'It's true,' Freddy mutters at length, 'God most definitely does work in mysterious ways.'

Chapter Nineteen

It's two days before the wedding and everyone playing a part in the ceremony has finally arrived.

Noah's sister and her family are awesome. Kim looks so like her brother, it's uncanny, and her husband Ben is an easy-going affable man who just seems to smile all the time. They have two kids, and both are amazingly well behaved. Eight year old Madison is a clone of her mum and ten year old Joseph has obviously inherited his father's genes. He is so freaking polite it's actually scary – calling everyone sir and ma'am.

The Admiral's currently teaching him how to salute and stand to attention, which seems to involve quite a few interesting expletives which Joseph is no doubt storing up for later.

Ethan Sullivan, Noah's best man, arrived late last night and is still sleeping off his jet lag in one of the guest bedrooms, while Freddy, dressed in his best Armani jeans and shirt, is bouncing around like an excited three year old, hardly able to contain himself at the thought of being in the same room as the singer. He's trying to explain to Mabel exactly who Ethan Sullivan is by showing her YouTube clips – most of which seem to be pretty x-rated.

The only person missing is Jason and I feel a familiar pang. It feels so wrong not to have him here. I sigh and take a sip of my coffee, at a loss as to how the prickly, difficult man managed to get under my skin so damn quickly. I think back to his tormented face at our last meeting and feel a lump in my throat. Maybe Laura can make him happy.

Determinedly I force my thoughts onto happier things. There'll be more than enough time for tears in three days.

'Did you speak to Boris earlier?' Tory calls to her father.

Yep, it looks as though Saint Boris is going to live to fart another day.

Once the old priest was out of intensive care, Tory and Noah contacted the hospital to ask them if it would be possible to turn the padre's room into a makeshift chapel. Of course the nurses were more than happy to oblige – positively foaming at the mouth at the opportunity to meet and speak with Noah Westbrook, not to mention Ethan Sullivan... Of course, the generous donation that Noah's made to the stroke unit has helped too.

So we're all going off this afternoon en masse to witness Bible Basher Boris giving Tory and Noah a Blessing for their union. Everyone involved has been sworn to secrecy and Freddy has stocked up on scented tissues, commenting darkly that we'll all be thanking him later...

Just as I get to my feet, intending to give Tory a hand with lunch, my phone rings. It's a number I don't recognize, so I send it to the answer phone and make my way through to the kitchen where Tory's busy making hotdogs.

'How's your morning sickness,' I question drily, watching her pop a sausage into her mouth. She grins back at me. 'Gone thank goodness, but you already know that, now I'm back to my normal, endearing, adorable self.'

'You forgot enchanting and delightful,' I quip back, 'Not to mention plump if you keep eating those bloody sausages.'

'I've got to make up for lost time,' she answers lightly, 'And anyway, Noah loves my curves.

I laugh, giving in. 'Well don't overdo it or you won't get into your dress.'

'Talking about getting into things,' she mutters sticking a fork into the pan, here, have a sausage yourself - your bridesmaid dress is still a bit baggy.'

'No it's not,' I retort heatedly, nevertheless taking the sausage from her, 'You're going to have to practically pour me into it at this rate.' My phone starts to ring again, the same unknown number as before.

'Aren't you going to answer that?' Tory asks as I push it back into my pocket.

'Don't know who it is,' I mumble taking a large bite of sausage. 'Bloody hell this is hot.'

'It could be something important,' she insists, just as my answer phone pings to indicate a message. Raising her eyebrows in a told you so manner, she turns back to the fried onions as I grudgingly listen to the message.

'*Kit, this is Laura, Jason's friend. I was wondering if we could meet for a coffee this afternoon. I have something important to say to you before I head back to London this evening.*' I stare in bewildered confusion at the phone, then I listen to the message again. Her voice is melodious and confident and I feel sick at the thought of having to see her again. Why on earth does she want to meet with me? She doesn't seem like the type of woman to gloat.

'Who is it?' Tory asks curiously as I listen to the message for the third time.

I swallow an unwelcome lump in my throat for the second time today. I have no idea what to do. This is just too much to deal with on my own, it's time I damn well confided in my best friend. So I take a deep breath and tell her.

~*~

I'm sitting in the Royal Castle Hotel nursing a large glass of wine. Tory's reaction to my tale of woe was predictable. First of all she called me an imbecile for not confiding in her earlier, then she gave me tight hug while assuring me that everything would be okay.

'What do you think she wants?' I asked weakly.

'Well I can't imagine she wants to compare favourite positions,' was her caustic response. 'Call her back and suggest meeting at the Castle. If I were you, I'd be going for wine, sod the bloody coffee.'

'But what about your Blessing?' I stammered, stalling for time.

'You know we're doing this for Boris,' she responded briskly, finally putting the finished hotdogs together, 'You really don't need to be there Kitty Kat. One less person in a room only ten feet square will be a bonus rather than a tragedy. And anyway, I'm sure one of the nurses will record the whole thing. Whoever does it could earn themselves a packet selling the recording after the wedding.'

'You don't mind?' I questioned carefully.

About what? The fact that you won't be there, or the possibility of someone making a lot of money from my happiness?' I shake my head helplessly as she laughs. 'No I don't mind. Go and sort this out sweetheart.'

So, this is me sorting it out, feeling slightly sick and wondering what the hell I'm doing here.

'Kit?' I look up at the sound of my name to see Laura looking like someone out of Dynasty (I watched the re-runs) She's wearing a full length fur coat and matching hat. I gaze at her mutely and all I can think is, 'Bet that fur's not bloody faux.' She takes my silence as an invitation to sit down and we stare at each other for a few seconds.

'What are you drinking?' she asks at length. I glance down at my glass of wine, slightly surprised to see there's still some in there. 'Dry rose,' I murmur, taking a nervous gulp.

'Sounds good,' is her only response. 'I think I'll have the same.' She stands up and heads over to the bar and for five minutes I sit and rack my brain for something witty and clever to say.

Scratch that. As she sits back down, I'll take anything, just as long as it involves opening my mouth.

'I'm sure you're wondering why I wanted to see you,' she gets in first, and I nod my head like the dog off the *Churchill* advert. She goes on to take a deep breath before continuing (this is working out really well - I'm not actually sure I'm required to say anything).

'Has Jason ever spoken to you about me.' This time I shake my head and take another drink. She looks down at her glass and makes a strange noise. After a second, I realize that she's actually crying, and somehow it makes her so much more human. Frowning I put out my hand and lay it gently over hers.

'Please don't cry,' I murmur, not knowing what else to say. She looks back at me, her lashes spiky with tears. For God's sake, she even bloody cries gorgeously.

'Jason and I were engaged back when we were both cadets at Dartmouth.' She pauses and looks over at me. I've no idea what she expects me to say, so I pat her hand, make soothing noises and wait for her to continue.

'We broke up just before we both graduated. It was my fault – I'd been sleeping with one of the lecturers and I mistook infatuation for love.' She hesitates and takes a large gulp of her wine.

'I saw Jason a few weeks ago. We bumped into one another in Paddington Station. It was the first time we'd spoken in nearly twenty years, and I just couldn't let him walk away without telling him the truth.'

The tears are pouring down her face openly now and I hand her a tissue feeling as though I'm in some kind of weird dream.

'What truth is that?' I finally ask softly.

'That I still love him – I never stopped.'

'Oh,' is all I come up with. She blows her nose and takes another long gulp of her drink, before laughing bitterly.

'He loved me sooo much Kit, and when I ended our engagement, he was completely devastated. I broke his heart.'

Of course, that's why the knob like behaviour - I actually want to slap her.

'Okay I get it,' I snap instead, 'You've got a lot of sucking up to do. What's that got to do with me?'

'I said he *was* in love with me,' she retorts heatedly, 'He isn't anymore. When I finally begged him the other night to give me another chance, he looked at me with pity – *pity*.'

She shakes her head as she spits out the last word, and looks at me with so much loathing, I lean back hastily.

Finishing the last of her drink, she places her empty glass back on the table and gets to her feet. 'You can do what you like with what I've told you,' she says harshly, 'But if you really want him, don't leave it as long as I did.'

Then she turns and walks away.

~*~

'How did it go? We both ask the question at the same time. 'You first,' I say, lying back on the sofa.

There's an exasperated sigh on the other end of the phone, then, 'It was fine. Actually more than fine, it was lovely – apart from a slightly sticky moment when Madison asked whether the man in the bed was dead. I'm not sure if she was referring to the way he looked, or the smell that was permeating the room.

'Bloody hell Kit, I'm so glad Boris's not going to be in the chapel the day after tomorrow – the smell was truly ghastly. At one point, I thought Freddy was going to start charging for his scented tissues – you know how money motivated he is.

'But at the end of the day, Boris was happy and that's what it was all about. He really is a very sweet old man in spite of his, err, issues.'

'How did the hospital staff react when you all walked in? Did anybody faint when faced with not just one but two idols in the flesh?

'No,' she chuckles, 'We kept the members of staff who were allowed in the room to a minimum, and most of them seemed to be about Mabel's age. They all had selfies though - I should think they're negotiating with *Hello* magazine as we speak.'

'Do they know about the wedding?'

'Absolutely not. Everyone kept quiet about that, but I hope the nurses aren't too quick to sell their pics - they'll be worth a lot more after Saturday.

'Anyway, no more fobbing me off. What happened with Laura?'

'It seems as though Jason's blown her out.' My matter of fact tone completely belies the butterflies that are playing havoc with my insides.'

'Did she say why?' Tory's voice is cautious – I know she doesn't want me to get my hopes up.

'No she didn't, she just said that if I was going to make a play for him, I wasn't to wait too long.

'Of course that's all well and good, but at this moment in time, I've no idea whether he finished with her because of me, or because he's simply intending to steer clear of women altogether for the foreseeable future and retire to Tibet.'

There's a pause and I hear laughing in the background. 'I should let you go,' I murmur softly.

'Why don't you come over,' she asks, after shouting at whoever's in the room to be quiet.

'Nah. Thanks for the offer, but I really think I need to be on my own right now. I've got a heck of a busy day tomorrow – did you know I'm planning a wedding?'

She laughs softly. 'Nobody else could have done it better Kitty Kat.'

'Save it,' I respond drily, 'You might not be speaking to me by Sunday.'

Chapter Twenty

So it's finally the morning of my best friend's wedding and I wake up to Dotty licking my face enthusiastically – I'm obviously a bit of a bed partner novelty. Snuggling her to me, I look up at the ceiling and go over everything in my head.

Yesterday was absolutely manic, with last minute – well – everything. I spent a large part of the day up at BRNC supervising the Hogwarts decorations with Richard and Rupert from Planet Gold, and by the time we left, I was half expecting to see Harry appear at any minute shouting, '*Expecto Patronum*.' The whole College looks simply amazing.

I never saw Jason throughout the whole day. In fact I couldn't help but wonder if he was still intending to come to the wedding – he could have gone home for Christmas for all I know. Maybe it would be a good thing if he has. I still have no idea what I'm going to do.

When the bloody hell did I become such a coward?

Sighing, I turn over to look at Tory's peaceful features. 'Come on lazybones, it's your wedding day,' I shout, jumping out of bed. Dotty starts barking excitedly as my best friend mumbles something and turns over.

'I need three cups of strong coffee before I can even think of getting out of this bed.' I'd forgotten about Freddy.

'Of course, the word bed might be a slight exaggeration. I feel as though I've spent the night undertaking some kind of medieval penance,' he groans, lifting his eye mask. 'What time is it?'

'Nearly eight o'clock,' I answer, throwing open the curtains and looking out of the window. 'I don't believe it,' I whisper, pressing my nose against the glass, 'It's snowing.'

'Oh my God,' is Tory's panicked response, as she leaps out of bed, 'I hope the ferry's running. There's no way I'm rowing across the river in my bloody wedding dress.'

The three of us stand and watch the snowflakes drift lazily down, slowly turning the world into a sea of white.

I've been on the phone on and off all morning, making sure that all the last minute details have been taken care of. For most of that time, Tory's bedroom has been the centre of operations, with all and sundry dashing in and out to look for everything from safety pins to nail varnish remover. But now, finally, things have quietened down.

Freddy's gone over to do his ushering duties and I can hear the drone of helicopters bringing in the wealthiest guests. I just hope he manages to hold it together in the face of such Hollywood royalty - but then Kim's there too, and with a bit of luck, she'll keep him on track.

Madison's gone off for a last minute visit to the toilet before we get into the car, so now it's just me, Tory and Dotty.

'Are you okay? I ask softly, 'You look absolutely stunning.' And she does. The dress still fits perfectly, despite the sausages, and she's wearing a simple garland of gypsophila in her hair to match her bouquet.

She smiles at me shyly. 'Thanks for everything you've done Kitty Kat, I really wouldn't be here now if it wasn't for you. You've been the best friend anyone could ever ask for.'

I bend down and pour us both a flute of Champagne. 'Junior won't mind,' I murmur handing her a glass, 'Here's to the future. You and Noah are absolutely perfect for each other and I just know you'll be so happy together.'

'What the bollocking hell are you doing Victory, I could have married and had a couple of carpet crawlers in the time it's taken you to get ready.'

We look at each other and laugh. Time to get this show on the road...

~*~

The limousine drives slowly through the main gate of the College and up the winding drive towards the parade ground, finally coming to a halt at the foot of the steps leading to the main doors.

Throughout the short car journey, the Admiral has been uncharacteristically quiet. He keeps glancing at Tory as though he can't quite believe the vision next to him is his daughter. Luckily Madison's excited chatter has prevented the silence from becoming slightly uncomfortable.

The driver comes round to open the door and both Madison and I exit first. After handing my bouquet to my fellow bridesmaid, I lean back in to grab Dotty, all dressed up with her beautiful red bow, and I can't help but grin as I hear the Admiral say brusquely, 'Well girl, while it's a bit of a surprise, I can't deny you've scrubbed up well. Your mother would be proud.'

The snow has lightly dusted the parade ground, and we make our way carefully up the steps to the main entrance. I tense as the huge doors are opened for us. This is the first time Tory's seen the College decorated for her wedding. Her indrawn breath as she steps into the magically transformed main corridor tells me everything. She pulls me to her in a quick hug, mouthing, 'Thank you, before taking her father's arm. Madison squeals in excitement as she takes hold of my hand and we slowly lead the way towards the Chapel.

My heart is beating like a drum, but not because I'm nervous for Tory on her big day. It's more to do with the fact that Jason Buchannan is standing outside the Chapel doors looking this way.

As we walk towards him, I just have time to notice how gorgeous he looks in his ceremonial uniform before the Admiral approaches and he straightens up, saluting smartly.

'You look beautiful Victory,' he smiles, 'Let me know when you're ready and I'll go in to tell them you've arrived.' Only then does he look over at me. My heart gives a leap, then begins to thump erratically as I register the bitter regret carved into his handsome features.

For one, two seconds, everything around us pales into insignificance, then, 'If you two have done making bloody cow's eyes at each other, perhaps we can get this bollocking cake and arse party over with.'

The Admiral's whisper, which has likely been heard by the whole congregation, brings me back to my senses and I reluctantly tear my gaze away and try to drag some air into my constricted lungs.

Handing Dotty's leash to Madison, I gently pull them both through the doors as Jason takes his place near the front. Then I pause to cast a brief glance back at Tory, just in time to see her wink.

Walking slowly up the aisle, I see some vaguely familiar faces from the large and small screen, as well as those I've known all my life. Aunt Flo is sitting with Neil, and we make brief smiling eye contact as I walk by. It's enough for now.

Jimmy is sitting with his wife Emily, who's obviously decided against puce. Jason's father Hugo is there, sitting next to Jacques, and finally, I arrive at the front, level with a beaming Freddy and Mabel on one side, and Kim, Ben and Joseph on the other.

Flickering candles in sconces and on window sills cast fantastical shadows on the beautiful vaulted ceiling and a huge Christmas tree next to the pulpit completes the festive picture.

As I finally come to a halt, I resist the urge to turn round, and stare instead at Noah standing straight, tall and almost impossibly handsome – his black hair virtually blue in the dancing candlelight.

Then, suddenly, there's a collective gasp, the music swells and I know my best friend is walking up the aisle behind me.

The ceremony is beautiful. In fact there isn't a dry eye in the house, and thank God, it isn't because of the smell. Unfortunately I don't actually I hear that much of it because I spend the whole time thinking about the way Jason looked at me. The aching gentleness in his penetrating silver eyes.

Difficult he might be, volatile certainly, but the real Jason Buchannan was opening his heart to me, leaving himself vulnerable for the first time since he'd had his heart broken all those years ago.

Now it's up to me.

As Tory and Noah finally go to sign the register, I guide Madison towards our seats. Once there, I take a deep breath and lift my eyes to meet his.

I'm currently standing outside the main entrance at the top of the steps. Tory and Noah are posing for photos, along with all the guests who've had the good sense to dress for the weather. The rest are helping themselves to moose milk on the Quarterdeck. Contrary to all predictions, the snow has persisted and the whole scene resembles something out of *The Lion The Witch And The Wardrobe.* It's simply breathtaking – beautiful with an almost otherworldly feel about it.

Suddenly I stiffen as I sense a presence behind me. Then, recognizing the spicy smell of cologne that is uniquely Jason, my body relaxes slightly, even as my heart starts to race.

I hardly recognize his voice when he finally speaks - the raw, aching whisper sends a tremor up my spine.

'Ms Davies, you look unbelievably gorgeous. Have you any idea just how much I love you?'

I close my eyes at the shattering tenderness of his words, and after a brief pause, I take a small step back to lean against him. I feel his hand drop to my waist, then gently slide around in front of me, pulling me nearer and tighter to him, and there I'm content to remain, secure in the warmth of my captain's love.

This is Tory and Noah's day. I smile as I watch their carefree laughter. Laying my fingers over Jason's warm hand, I finally believe that one day soon, it will be ours.

THE END

If you'd like to continue Kit and Jason's story, Chasing Victory: Book Four of The Dartmouth Diaries is available on Amazon. (For an exclusive sneak peek, keep reading until the end...)

Author's Note

As I've said in my previous books, the beautiful yachting haven of Dartmouth in South Devon holds a very special place in my heart – not least because I met my husband there :-)

If you're ever in the area, please do take the time out to visit. The pubs and restaurants I describe are real and I've spent many a happy breakfast/ lunchtime/evening in each of them.

Café Alf Resco serves, in my opinion, the best breakfast in Dartmouth, and is definitely not to be missed. (My favourite is the Cinnamon Toast.) They also have a couple of rooms available for those who fancy staying longer than just for breakfast...

The Anchorstone café and The Ferryboat Inn at Dittisham are also a must for anyone who loves alfresco dining and sea food – although The Anchorstone is only open during the summer months.

If you'd like more information about Dartmouth and the surrounding areas, visit the Tourist Information Centre at the following link.

https://discoverdartmouth.com

For all you budding sleuths out there, you might be interested to know that *The Brie, The Bullet, and the Black Cat* is an actual murder mystery game which you can download from numerous sources on the internet, including Amazon.

Having played the game before, I know just how much fun it is (my family and I had a riotous night hamming it up), and for that reason I chose not to reveal the murderer at the end of Flo's party.

I heartily recommend you give it a go...

Keeping in Touch

Thank you so much for reading All For Victory, I really hope you enjoyed it.

For any of you who'd like to connect, I'd really love to hear from you. Feel free to contact me via my facebook page at https://www.facebook.com/beverleywattsauthor

If you'd like me to let you know as soon as my next book is available, copy and paste the link below into your browser to sign up to my newsletter and I'll keep you updated about all my latest releases.

https://motivated-teacher-3299.ck.page/143a008c18

And lastly, thanks a million for taking the time to read this story. If you've not yet had your fill of the Admiral's meddling in the Dartmouth Diaries, you might be interested to read my series of cosy mysteries involving the Admiral and Jimmy, aptly titled *The Admiral Shackleford Mysteries.*

Book One: *A Murderous Valentine*, Book Two: *A Murderous Marriage* and Book Three*: A Murderous Season* are all available on Amazon.

You might also be interested to learn that the Admiral's Great, Great, Great, Great Grandfather appears in my latest series of lighthearted Regency Romances entitled The Shackleford Sisters.

Book One: *Grace*, Book Two *Temperance* and Book Three: *Faith* are currently available on Amazon with Book Four: *Hope* to follow soon.

Turn the page for a full list of my books available on Amazon and for a sneak peek at *Chasing Victory*: Book Four of *The Dartmouth Diaries*...

Books Available on Amazon

The Dartmouth Diaries:

Book 1 - Claiming Victory
Book 2 - Sweet Victory
Book 3 - All for Victory
Book 4 - Chasing Victory
Book 5 - Late Victory coming soon...

The Admiral Shackleford Mysteries

Book 1 - A Murderous Valentine
Book 2 - A Murderous Marriage
Book 3 - A Murderous Season
Book 4 - A Murderous Paradise coming soon...

The Shackleford Sisters

Book 1 - Grace
Book 2 - Temperance
Book 3 - Faith
Book 4 - Hope coming soon...

Standalone Titles

An Officer and a Gentleman Wanted

Turn the page for an exclusive sneak peek of Chasing

Victory: Book Four of The Dartmouth Diaries...

Chasing Victory

Chapter One

'Those are salad tongs, you are NOT putting any bloody kitchenware in there.'

Victory Westbrook, my best friend since forever, is in labour. Nearly three weeks early. And her husband of six months, the totally gorgeous, more famous than the Queen, Oscar nominated actor Noah Westbrook, is stuck in an airport in Canada. Fog bound. In June. Which means I get to be her birthing partner instead...

Wincing sympathetically, I lean forward to wipe Tory's sweating brow. 'Sweetie, you need some help getting junior out. It's been over ten hours and you're knackered.'

Tory moans in answer, and grabs hold of the gas and air. 'I feel like bloody Darth Vadar,' she mutters, plastering the mouthpiece to her face. After taking a deep breath in, she glares at the doctor before saying in a slightly slurry voice, 'Okay, do your worst. Maybe you can check out my tonsils while you're in there.'

Ten minutes later Isaac Charles Westbrook arrives into the world kicking and screaming, a whopping nine pound four.

'Oh my God Tory he's beautiful,' I murmur as the midwife places the little red bundle onto her chest.

'He is, isn't he,' she responds tearfully, stroking his head gently.

As I stare down at mother and baby, I feel the sudden unfamiliar stirrings of envy. I've never considered myself parent material. I've always been pretty blasé about it – if it happened, it happened, sort of thing. The world is vastly overpopulated anyway. But standing there looking at my best friend - weary, but literally glowing with happiness, I feel my maternal instinct kick in with all the force of a charging rhino.

Swallowing a sudden lump in my throat the size of a golf ball, I lean forward and hug them both, breathing in the scent of new baby, helplessly wondering where Jason stands in regards to siring a couple of little Buchannans in the not too distant future.

Although we've been dating since Tory and Noah's wedding last December, and things have been pretty good, we haven't really gotten around to discussing the important life changing stuff like children. To be fair, Jason's job means that we don't get an awful lot of time together – although I have been wheeled out of the closet as his significant other at various naval functions.

Jason Buchannan is a captain in the Royal Navy, and currently he's the Captain of Britannia Royal Naval College - the RN's premier officer training establishment, situated high on a hill overlooking the picturesque yachting town of Dartmouth in the south west of England. It's all very queen and country with a liberal dose of stiff upper lip. Jason suits it like he was born to it. Me? Not so much. But hey, so far I haven't managed to cause a diplomatic incident...

Forcing my mind back to the matter at hand, I follow the orderlies as they wheel Tory's bed up to the maternity ward. As Noah Westbrook's wife, she could have had specialist treatment in a private clinic, but she insisted on having her baby at the local hospital in Torquay and giving them a donation equal to the cost of private care. No idea why, just one of Tory's quirks.

Once she's settled in, I give both her and Isaac a last kiss before heading out to my car. I have a list of items Tory all of a sudden deems necessary for her stay in hospital – although why she thinks a tin opener is likely to be useful is anybody's guess. But if I do the fetching and carrying, Noah gets to head straight to the hospital when he finally arrives. The last text said he he'd just landed in Heathrow.

It takes me twenty minutes to get from Torquay to the Higher Car Ferry. Dartmouth sits at the mouth of the River Dart, so getting to it from the holiday resort of Torbay necessitates crossing the river. All well and good most of the time, but a hell of a challenge at stupid o'clock in the morning. However, Tory's father lives this side of the river, so I have a small detour to make before I cross over.

Turning into a small road, just before the last few yards to the river's edge, I finally pull up outside a massive fence and gate which would do justice to Buckingham Palace.

Tory's dad is affectionately known locally as the Admiral – for the obvious reason that he was an Admiral in the Royal Navy. I say affectionately. There are those who would just as soon ring his neck given the penchant he has for meddling in affairs that are none of his business. But then, knowing him is never ever dull. Goodness knows how little Isaac will fare, having him as a role model...

Climbing out of the car, I press the buzzer next to the gate and settle back to wait. Both gate and fence came courtesy of *The Bridegroom* – a romantic comedy which was a massive box office success two years ago. Part of the movie was filmed at the Admiral's house - a large Edwardian pile with the rather original name of the Admiralty. Tory was living at home at the time. Noah was the leading man and voila – the rest as they say is history.

'You can tell your bollocking editor that I've got nothing to say apart from take your bloody pen and paper and shove it up your duck run.' The Admiral's voice booms out of the small intercom, and instinctively I glance up and step back. Tory's father obviously thinks I'm some kind of undesirable and he's been known to discourage such unwanted visitors by lobbing something unpleasant over the fence. Although to be fair, that little inclination only surfaced to dissuade the more determined paparazzi camping outside his back door once Tory and Noah became an item.

'Admiral it's me, Kit,' I yell back hastily, concerned he might turn off the intercom and that would be that. I'd have a better chance of getting in to Fort Knox. I can hear Dotty and Pickles barking frenziedly in the background, drawing an answering mutter of, 'What a bloody cake and arse party.' Then without warning he changes volume and his voice blasts directly into the intercom, giving me a mini heart attack.

'PIPE DOWN YOU MISERABLE MUTTS OR YOU'LL BOTH BE RELEGATED TO THE BOLLOCKING SHED FOR THE REST OF YOUR BLOODY NATURAL.'

I take a deep breath, heart still pounding, getting ready to add my own contribution to the din, but luckily before I get chance to join in, the buzzer goes off and the gate clicks open. Murmuring a quick prayer of thanks, I hurry through to give Tory's father the good news.

Half an hour later I'm pulling off the car ferry on the Dartmouth side of the river. I can't help but smile to myself as I remember the Admiral's delight when I told him he had a grandson. He insisted on pouring us both a glass of Port to toast his first carpet crawler. When I showed him a couple of photos I'd taken on my phone, he pronounced with satisfaction that Isaac was definitely Victory's as he had the Shackleford chin. I didn't like to ask who else's he thought the baby could be...

After parking my car in the garage, I make a quick phone call to Freddy to appraise him that he's become an honorary uncle, and his squeal of excitement is in complete contrast to his earlier blasé attitude towards Tory's pregnancy. Our gay friend wastes no time in vowing to ensure that little Isaac doesn't lose touch with his feminine side which I'm not sure is necessarily a good thing, and agreeing to meet me and the Admiral at the hospital as soon as he's finished at work. Cutting the call, I pop quickly up to my flat to have a shower and get changed.

Tory showed the first signs of labour at four o'clock yesterday afternoon, so I dashed over to her house with nothing but the clothes I was standing up in, envisioning myself rushing her to the hospital in a car journey straight out of the movie *Fast and*

Furious. However, I don't think they ever filmed *Fast and Furious* during a seaside town's rush hour - it took us so long to get to the hospital, Tory could have delivered triplets. It was a good job her waters didn't actually break until two in the morning.

This time, determined to avoid a repeat performance of *Slow and Laborious*, I'm back outside the Admiralty by three in the afternoon, before the local schools begin regurgitating their pupils. As Tory's father squeezes himself into my ten year old Fiesta, I briefly mourn the loss of my beloved seven seater, sacrificed nearly a year ago on the altar of unemployment. Although things have definitely been looking up since I organized my best friend's high profile wedding last December, I've nevertheless not quite reached the dizzy heights of corporate cardom.

The Admiral is uncharacteristically silent as we head over to the hospital. It actually feels quite strange being in an enclosed space with Tory's dad, especially after the revelation that he and my Aunt Flo had once been married.

'Is Dotty behaving herself?' I ask finally as the silence becomes a little oppressive

The Admiral frowns at me before offering the word, 'Spoilt,' along with a humph that makes his feelings about the little dog perfectly clear. I can't help but wince a little. Being looked after by the Admiral must be akin to going from a five star hotel to a zero star hostel. Still, at least she's got Pickles.

'You spoken to your aunt yet?' The Admiral's question takes me completely by surprise and I cast him a wary glance while frantically thinking what to say.

'I take it that means no,' he continues gruffly when I take too long. 'You can't ignore it forever Kit Davies, the whole bollocking load of horlicks has been under wraps for far too bloody long. It's time to get it all out in the open.'

I throw another, this time incredulous, glance at the man whose penchant for secrets is pretty much legendary, and he has the grace to look a little embarrassed before determinedly ploughing ahead, his voice at once defiant and sincere. 'The thing is Kit, secrets have a way of catching up with you when you least want them to, and let's be honest, I should bloody well know.'

The truth is, I haven't spoken to my aunt about my less than conventional entrance to this world. Despite my initial determination to know the whole sordid truth, there's a big part of me that enjoys being in cloud cuckoo land about the whole affair. Surely it's enough to know that my father was a complete nutcase and I'm lucky Aunt Flo managed to sneak me away from his corrupt influence and bring me back to the UK - after blowing his brains out of course.

Surely that's enough?

Coughing awkwardly, I concentrate on pulling out of a junction into the heavy oncoming traffic. Jason, Tory and Freddy have been badgering me for months to have The Conversation with my aunt. In fact the only two people on the planet who seem reluctant to have this particular tête-à-tête are me and Aunt Flo. Oh things are okay between us, and if we haven't quite got back to the familiar, easy relationship we had before she dropped her bombshell, well no-one would know it apart from the two of us. I think we're just happy to let sleeping dogs lie. Or maybe I just can't bring myself to ask her why she abandoned me in Dartmouth as a scared two year old because I don't think I'm going to like the answer.

Determinedly I turn my mind back to my driving, promising myself that I'll speak to Aunt Flo – soon...

Six hours later, Freddy and I are wetting little Isaac's head in The Cherub, and it has to be said that all the excitement has definitely gone to our heads – or it might be the two bottles of Prosecco we've just consumed.

'I'm going to be the best uncle since *Uncle Buck*.' Freddy's words are definitely slightly slurred.

'I thought he was supposed to be a totally crap uncle in that movie.'

'Nope. He was awesome. Got on the same level as the kids, totally rocked it. That's gonna be me.'

'You're going to have to put some weight on then if you're going to measure up to John Candy.'

Freddy frowns at my drunken observation, looking down at himself in dismay. 'You're right,' he murmurs, 'Damn, I'd better order some chips.'

'The grease will definitely soak up the alcohol.' Noah's voice is wry, which of course is completely lost on both of us and I jump up with a very unlady like squeal, throwing my arms around my best friend's husband in an enthusiastic rugby tackle. Staggering under my unreserved hug, Noah laughs, holding me briefly before setting me carefully back on my feet.

'I'm not sure you guys are a good influence on my son,' he growls, his grin belying his stern words. 'I think it's gonna take more than a few fries to get you both sober, I'll order a couple of pizzas.

'Is Jason coming over?' Noah's last words throw a dash of cold water over my delightfully alcoholic haze, doing a better job of sobering me up than any amount of fast food.

'I'm not sure, I haven't managed to speak to him since yesterday. We've left each other a couple of messages, but so far we've been playing answer phone ping pong. I think he's been in meetings pretty much all day.' I omit the part where Jason's voice in his last message this afternoon sounded cold and distant, causing my heart to flutter uncomfortably. 'I'm sure he'll make it if he can,' I continue determinedly cheerful in the face of Noah's too perceptive glance. Luckily, he doesn't pursue it any further and heads to the bar.

'That's not like you and Jason. Thought you murmured sweet nothings to each other at least twenty times a day.' Freddy's light words do nothing to alleviate my anxiety and my response is sharper than I intended. 'I think you're referring to you and Jacques. Your phone bill must be the size of a small mortgage since he's been in America.'

'God, that's good.' Noah's arrival back from the bar with his pint effectively puts an end to the conversation and I gratefully turn the subject back to baby talk.

'How are Tory and little Isaac,' I ask, delighting in the look of pride and joy that immediately transforms his face.

'Well, aside from my wife being the most amazing woman on both sides of the Atlantic, and my son obviously the most beautiful baby ever to be born, I'm pleased to report that both are doing fantastic. I should be able to pick them up tomorrow morning after the pediatrician's stopped by.

'I can't thank you enough for being there with her Kit, I was going crazy stuck in Toronto.' The relief in his voice that everything turned out okay is palpable and I put my hand over his with a smile.

'Hey, that's what friends are for. And anyway, it was very enlightening – and not just for whole getting to see a baby born thing, which of course was absolutely awesome – I actually think Tory used her father's entire repertoire of swear words. You should have seen the midwife's face.'

Noah laughs again, effectively ending the gravity of the moment. 'Hopefully I'll get to see it next time.'

Then he looks around the small bar at the cluster of regulars who are trying very hard not to eavesdrop, and stands up with a grin. 'I'm not sure if you guys know it, but I've become a father today. Go grab whatever your poison is, the drinks are on me.' His words prompt a smattering of applause followed by lots of back patting, not to mention parental advice. I have time to wince at an old wives remedy for colic, when my phone rings. Glancing down, my stomach does a slight skip as Jason's name flashes across the screen.

'Hey you, had a busy day?' For some reason my voice comes out hoarse and dry.

'Sorry I didn't get back to you earlier.' His voice is clipped and short, a tone I haven't heard from him in months, and my heart slams against my ribs in an instinctive response.

'What's wrong?' I ask automatically, unable to stem the rising tide of fear in my gut.

He sighs, and for a second I think I've imagined everything, then he continues, 'It's my father Kit. He's had a stroke. I'm on my way up to Scotland now.'

Chapter Two

It's two in the morning and I'm lying in bed unable to sleep. The pizza is sitting in my stomach like it was made of concrete, and my mind is going over and over my last conversation with Jason.

It seems he's been aware of his father's deteriorating health for a couple of weeks, so apparently the stroke didn't come as a complete surprise. Except to me.

I wanted to ask him why he hadn't shared his concerns with me, why after six months he didn't feel he could unburden himself, reveal his worries. But the words stuck in my throat, and instead I responded to his impersonal tone in the same monosyllabic voice, not knowing how to comfort him, or what to say to make things better. In the end, when we finished the call, my first thought was that I'd lost him.

He said he'd call me when he got to Glasgow. I glance at the clock. He won't be there yet, even if he drives well over the speed limit. I think back over the last few weeks. How come I'm only now realizing that Jason has been uncharacteristically withdrawn? Have I been so wrapped up with my burgeoning business and Tory's pregnancy that I haven't noticed? What does that say about our relationship, and more importantly, what does it say about me?

I spend the rest of the night tossing and turning, in between staring at the clock and checking my mobile phone. At five thirty, I give in and get up to make myself a cup of tea. Just as I take the first sip, my phone finally rings.

'Hey babe, you okay? How's your dad?' My voice when I answer is breathless, matching the samba my heart is doing against my ribs. To my relief, his response is much more upbeat than our last conversation. 'He's doing okay. Luckily it was only a minor stroke – more of a warning really. When I left him he was sitting up in bed flirting with one of the nurses.'

'Thank God,' I answer with an enthusiasm I don't have to force. Jason's father Hugo is a sweet man and I've genuinely come to care for him.

'He'll be in hospital for a week or so while they run some tests,' Jason continues, 'Then he'll need some kind of nursing care back at the Tower until he's completely back on his feet. I'm just about to drive back to Dartmouth to attend the dinner tonight, then I'll head back up here this weekend.'

The dinner, the bloody bollocking dinner. I'd forgotten all about it. Shit, shit, shit...

'You haven't forgotten that we're entertaining the new First Sea Lord this evening have you?' His voice is now slightly exasperated. Maybe he knows me better than I think. 'Of course not sweetheart, why would you think that?'

'Why indeed?' is his dry response. 'Can you be up at the house for about eighteen thirty? We'll be having pre-dinner drinks on the terrace at nineteen hundred.'

I promise faithfully to be there, my mind already frantically converting the bloody military timing to the bog standard way the rest of us mortals refer to time, as well as cataloguing everything I have to do today: Two new prospective clients, the final preparations for a wedding on Saturday and a funeral on Monday. And I haven't bought anything to wear yet. Bugger, I'd better get started...

I've had the day from hell. This evening can only be an improvement. There's been a mistake made in the order of service leaflets for Mr Alexander Smeelie's funeral service - there's a lovely picture of the gentleman in question on the front with the words Alexander Smellie.

And the favours ordered for Saturday's wedding are mini penises. I think they've got them confused with a hen party.

By the time I dash into Dartmouth's most up market boutique for a little black number that shouts sexy sophistication, it's already four forty five. I frantically search through the dozen long black dresses (Jason was pretty specific over what I should wear

– maybe he should have bloody well bought me one), and quickly decide on a jersey number that I think fits the bill. No time to try it on, but I'm a pretty standard size ten, so I hand over my credit card with a prayer that there's still enough left on it.

After laying my appallingly expensive purchase on the bed, I grab a quick shower and put on my makeup. Luckily my hair is still doing the short pixie thing so needs very little attention. I glance at my watch – five forty five, just enough time for a fortifying glass of wine before I need to get dressed.

With a sigh of relief, I take a large sip of my Pinot Blush and sit down on my bed, stroking the fabric of my new dress with my free hand. It really was horrendously expensive - I hope Jason bloody well appreciates it. Then I stifle a giggle. As my beloved is sending a car down for me, I can go ahead and wear my killer black heels. And I know for a fact that he appreciates those…

All of a sudden I'm looking forward to the evening. Jason wants me there as his partner and I'm determined to make him proud of me. Swallowing back the rest of the wine, I put the glass on the side and pick up the silky length of material. Trying to figure out the best way to put it on, I finally allow it to pool on the floor and step into the hole. The fabric is smooth and clingy. There's no way I'll be able to wear any underwear. I'm actually getting a little turned on by the thought that Jason will know I'm wearing nothing underneath. Now if that's not sexy sophistication, I don't know what is.

I pull the sleeves over each arm and frown slightly. The dress obviously dips at the back. But that's okay, this is one of those times where having small pert boobs actually works in my favour. The front neckline has a slight cowl in it, so I turn towards the full length mirror on the closet to make sure it's sitting correctly. The dress fits me like a glove, the length perfect.

As I stare in delight, congratulating myself on my superior dress sense, I hear a car horn beep outside the flat window, signalling my lift is here. Grabbing my purse and wrap, I hurry down the steep stairs to the street.

Five minutes later we're in the College grounds, winding our way up the hill to Jason's house. The Naval College is a magnificent red brick building constructed at the turn of the century, and as Captain of said College, Jason gets to live in the imposing mansion tagged on to the side of it. I always have to fight the urge to curtsy to him when I'm in there. Needless to say we haven't done the deed on any of the drawing room sofas...

After thanking the driver, I step out of the car, wincing a little at the draft on my back. Hurriedly I settle the wrap over my ensemble and head to the front door where Dave the butler (apparently he's not a butler, he's a steward, but he definitely looks like a butler to me) is waiting.

'Hi Dave,' I smile, handing him my wrap. 'Is Captain Buchannan in the drawing room?'

'Yes ma'am. He asks that you go right in.' Looking forward to Jason's gasp of admiration, I sweep towards the drawing room door, only faltering slightly as I hear Dave's sudden indrawn breath behind me. Bless, it's good to know that I can still affect members of the opposite sex, even if I'm no longer quite the nubile young thing I was in my twenties.

Reaching the door, I pause for effect and as Jason turns towards me, I shiver at his intense silver gaze. His eyes travel the full length of my body and the heat in them shouts his approval. 'Would you like a drink?' he asks finally, his voice gratifyingly hoarse. I nod my head with a wide smile and sashay towards him, only stopping when there are inches between us and he can smell my perfume and feel the heat of my body. He bends his head to kiss my neck, and I lean my own head to one side to give him better access, holding my breath in anticipation.

But instead of the anticipated feel of his lips, he stiffens and stops completely still. Then, before I can ask if something's wrong, he grasps my shoulders and spins me round. 'Hey,' I squeal in surprise, 'What...?'

'...The hell are you wearing,' he finishes, his voice low and furious. I frown in indignation at his tone, trying to turn back round. What the hell's the matter with the bloody man? Surely he can't object to a simple black dress.

Before I get chance to speak however, he ignores my spluttering and marches me towards a long mirror on the other side of the room. Once in front of the glass, he brusquely turns me to the side, exposing my back. My naked back. My very, very naked back, all the way to my very, very naked bottom...

My protests die as I stare at my reflection in horrified silence.

'What are you trying to do?' he finally grinds out, 'Help get me promoted the old fashioned way?'

'I didn't know,' I protest faintly, 'I...I didn't have time to try the dress on. I had no idea it was... quite so revealing at the back.'

'That's putting it mildly,' is his unrelenting response. Mortified, I glance up at his face, as he runs his hand distractedly through his hair, the gesture showing more than anything what an unforgivable gaff I've made. Stepping forward he propels me towards another door, like a child about to be scolded. Lost in misery, I allow him to pull me into the large old fashioned kitchen where several eyes swivel towards us – away from Dave who had obviously been regaling the entire kitchen staff about the inappropriateness of my attire.

'Mrs. McCaffrey, do you have a sewing kit on hand?'

The elderly cook proves to be a dab hand with a needle and thread and potential disaster is averted. I'm back in the drawing room only a few minutes after the First Sea Lord, aka Admiral Sir Philip James and his entourage arrive, and firmly putting aside the horrifying vision of what might have been, I set out to prove that I really do have the necessary grace and refinement to be a significant asset to Jason's naval career, (and not in the old fashioned way...)

Consequently dinner is a resounding success. Sir Philip is totally enamoured with my witty comebacks and sophisticated banter, and I can see Jason visibly relaxing at the other side of the table. I feel giddy with triumph. This is me at my sparkling, charming best. Who knew I had such hidden talents?

As we finish dessert, Jason suggests that we take coffee and Port back in the drawing room and nodding gracefully, I slide back my chair with poise and confidence. That is until my hem gets caught up under the back leg, and as I try to free it, the neatly sewn back of my dress slowly unravels.

Yanking viciously at the offending fabric, I straighten up quickly, glancing around to see if anyone has noticed, but fortunately my back is to the wall. For a split second I panic, what the hell am I going to do? If Sir Philip gets an eyeful of my bottom, every bit of effort I've put it to this evening will go down the Swannee. I might as well just ask if he's brought any condoms. Gnawing on my bottom lip, I wonder if anyone would notice if I just stayed here.

'Darling, could you come over and pour?' Jason's voice is light and relaxed. I feel sick.

'Coming sweetheart,' I respond after a few seconds, hoping my voice doesn't sound too much like Alvin The Chipmunk. Carefully I walk over to the dining room door, pausing slightly, my eyes scanning the room and its occupants in a move that would have impressed Marta Hari. In a few short seconds I note that nearly everyone is sitting on the sofas and chairs grouped around the coffee table. That is everyone bar one. Captain Whatever his name is, is currently admiring the view from the French Windows.

There's only one route open to me to ensure that nobody cops an intimate view of my nether regions. Adopting a serene smile that would have given Mother Theresa a run for her money, I attempt a nonchalant sideways saunter, swaying slightly like I have an irresistible tune in my head. As I catch a glimpse of myself in the same mirror that revealed my original faux pas, I realize that to anyone catching a glimpse it looks as though I'm bloody line dancing. Luckily everyone is busy helping themselves to Port. I can feel the sweat begin to tickle my back as I weave my way around the room with one eye on the group around the coffee table and the other on Captain What's his name, careful to keep my back hidden to both.

It takes me two excruciating minutes to finally approach the only empty chair, the one with the coffee pot and several cups placed conveniently in front of it. However, the last few yards will leave my behind exposed to Captain What's his face in a view that could well rival the one he's currently admiring.

Jason glances up at me with a smile. He's about to speak, I know he is. The minute he opens his mouth, Captain Who Je Me flip is going to turn round.

I panic. With a gay laugh which unfortunately comes out like a maniacal cackle, I launch myself at the chair as though I'm about to throw a rugby tackle. As I slide into it at top speed, I have to fight the urge to shout, 'Geronimo.' Everyone looks up in surprise. I bounce off the arm of the chair and land on the cushion with a resounding woomph and favour them all with a triumphant stare, just as the arm of my dress slides off one shoulder, completely exposing my right breast.

Chasing Victory is available on Amazon.

About The Author

Beverley Watts

Beverley and her husband live in an apartment overlooking the sea on the beautiful English Riviera.

Between them they have 3 adult children and two gorgeous grandchildren plus a menagerie of animals including 4 dogs - 2 Romanian rescues of indeterminate breed called Florence and Trixie, a neurotic 'Chorkie' named Pepé and a 'Chichon" named Dotty who was the inspiration for Dotty in The Dartmouth Diaries. They also have a cat called Honey.

Beverley spent 8 years teaching English as a Foreign Language to International Military Students in Britannia Royal Naval College which is the premier officer training establishment for the Royal Navy in the UK. She says that in the whole 8 years there was never a dull moment and many of her wonderful experiences at the College were not only memorable but were most definitely 'the stuff of fiction'

An avid reader and writer since childhood, she always determined that on leaving she would write a book. Her debut novel An Officer And A Gentleman Wanted is very loosely based on her adventures at the College.

Beverley has written a series of romantic comedies entitled The

Dartmouth Diaries. Claiming Victory: Book One, Sweet Victory: Book Two, All For Victory: Book Three and Chasing Victory: Book Four, are available on Amazon. Book Five: Late Victory is coming soon...

The first three books of her Admiral Shackleford Cozy Mystery series - A Murderous Valentine, A Murderous Marriage and A Murderous Season - are also available on Amazon. Book Four: A Murderous Paradise is coming soon...

Beverley has now embarked on a new series of Regency Romantic Comedies entitled The Shackleford Sisters. Book One: Grace, Book Two: Temperance and Book Three: Faith are available on Amazon. Book Four: Hope is coming soon...

Printed in Great Britain
by Amazon